I0818591

COASTAL VIEWS TO DIE FOR

Books by Sam Lumley

HOW TO HAVE A KILLER TIME IN D.C.

COASTAL VIEWS TO DIE FOR

Published by Kensington Publishing Corp.

SAM LUMLEY

KENSINGTON PUBLISHING CORP.
kensingtonbooks.com

This book is a work of fiction. Names, characters, businesses, organizations, places, events, and incidents either are the product of the author's imagination or are used fictitiously. Any resemblance to actual persons, living or dead, events, or locales is entirely coincidental.

To the extent that the image or images on the cover of this book depict a person or persons, such person or persons are merely models, and are not intended to portray any character or characters featured in the book.

KENSINGTON BOOKS are published by

Kensington Publishing Corp.
900 Third Avenue
New York, NY 10022

Copyright © 2026 by Sam Lumley

All rights reserved. No part of this book may be reproduced in any form or by any means without the prior written consent of the Publisher, excepting brief quotes used in reviews.

Without limiting the author's and publisher's exclusive rights, any unauthorized use of this publication to train generative artificial intelligence (AI) technologies is expressly prohibited.

All Kensington titles, imprints and distributed lines are available at special quantity discounts for bulk purchases for sales promotion, premiums, fund-raising, educational or institutional use. Special book excerpts or customized printings can also be created to fit specific needs. For details, write or phone the office of the Kensington Special Sales Manager: Kensington Publishing Corp., 900 Third Avenue, New York, NY, 10022. Attn. Special Sales Department. Phone: 1-800-221-2647.

KENSINGTON and the KENSINGTON COZIES teapot logo Reg. US Pat & TM Off.

Library of Congress Control Number: On file

ISBN: 978-1-4967-5358-8

First Kensington Hardcover Edition: June 2026

ISBN: 978-1-4967-5360-1 (ebook)

10 9 8 7 6 5 4 3 2 1

Printed in the United States of America

The authorized representative in the EU for product safety and compliance
is eucomply OU, Parnu mnt 139b-14, Apt 123
Tallinn, Berlin 11317, hello@eucompliancepartner.com

COASTAL VIEWS TO DIE FOR

Chapter 1

I didn't expect it to be a trap.

Lunch dates with my managing editor, Drea, are rare since I generally work from home, but they've been known to happen when I have a need to be at the *Offbeat Traveler* editorial offices in San Francisco. What should have tipped me off, in hindsight, is that I wasn't in the office on this particular day. I had been invited, and gone into the city, specifically for lunch, at a trendy Mexican spot with patio seating that served so-called street food at expense account prices with full service. This was a little more luxe than our usual run down to the sandwich-and-salad joint on the ground floor of our office building. Tip-off number two.

Alarm bells would have really gone off if I'd seen the distinctive, copper-colored car circling on the street, looking for parking, but by that point, Drea had already started to drop her bombshell, so I was distracted.

I was dipping a tortilla chip into some salsa when the campaign against me began. Drea had the nerve to make it sound like she was paying me a compliment, which I would discover was merely a clever cover for her ruse.

"So, Oliver," she began, "you're officially in print as a feature writer! Your piece on DC came out so great. Has your mom sent copies of this month's issue to everyone she knows yet?"

"I might have seen a few extra copies lying around the last time I was up in her place," I said, smiling shyly.

"Oh, yeah, that's right! How's the apartment?"

I had recently moved into the downstairs unit of the old high-water house I had grown up in. My mom still lived upstairs, so as independence went, it wasn't a huge step, but I was enjoying it. "It's great. It's still mostly empty, but it's nice to have all that space just for me."

Her eyes sparkled. "We might be able to help you afford to fill up your apartment a little more. I have another feature assignment for you, and if it goes as well as the last one, you might be in line for a promotion soon—if you're interested, that is."

Oh, boy. That was a loaded question. I was proud of the article I'd been able to put together out of the wreckage of my trip to Washington, DC, in April, but the experience had been stressful and chaotic and strange—all words that my Autistic soul liked to avoid as much as possible. I had been almost immediately thrown off my itinerary, had ended up taking on a second, unplanned assignment, and had witnessed—and solved, I had to modestly remind myself—a murder. I had also left a big chunk of my heart with a guy I had met there, which had left me grappling daily with my biggest pet peeve: *unresolved feelings*.

If that was what becoming a full-fledged travel writer entailed, I was fairly sure my answer was *No, thank you.* But I knew that not all assignments could possibly be like that one. I swallowed my nerves and some more chips and salsa, and said, "What's the assignment this time?"

"It's a little closer to home," Drea said. "We're putting together a package on road trips, and I had you in mind for our Pacific coast piece—specifically, the Oregon coast."

"Road trips? But, Drea, I can't drive."

Her eyes lit up again, though it felt like she was looking past me. "That's no problem. I'm pairing you up again, so you don't have to."

"Pairing me up—?" I was cut off, and my question answered, as a figure came up the sidewalk behind me to the patio railing and swooped in over the rail to plant a peck on Drea's cheek before swiveling in close to aim the most devastating, dimpled smile at me.

"Hi," he said, waggling his thick, mischievous eyebrows.

Ricky Warner. Drea's old college pal, the most beautiful man I had ever met, the freelance photographer who had been my guide to Washington and the devil on my shoulder goading me to follow him into mischief and mayhem. The one I had fallen hard for, but had pulled away from when it was time to go home because I couldn't imagine how to sustain a relationship from opposite coasts. Or maybe I had been terrified of the idea of my first real relationship. Maybe I had been terrified of *him*.

I flushed red to my toes, watching as he rounded the railing to come join us at our table on the patio. Seeing him again filled me with a heady mix of mostly unfamiliar emotions: happiness—no, giddiness, maybe—and excitement and maybe a hint of lust. Sneaking through these, though, were also a few more familiar friends: shame and embarrassment and anxiety. Did he know how strongly I felt about him? Had he felt the same way? Did he still? Was he happy to see me? I knew that I hadn't been as diligent about keeping in touch with him since I'd been home as I should have been, as he'd wanted me to be. There had been a few flirty text exchanges that I'd tried my best to keep up with, but felt inadequate to, and a couple of missed calls—which, if I was being honest, had really been calls that I could have answered, but had been too afraid to.

I could barely bring myself to look at Ricky as he dropped into the chair next to Drea and lazily draped an arm across the back of her chair before reaching in for a tortilla chip. But besides the easy comfort he seemed to feel in any environment, which I deeply envied and had sometimes leveraged to my advantage in DC, his body language and expression betrayed little that I could decipher of what he thought of our reunion. When he finally caught my eye, he grinned and winked—again, a baseline level of flirtiness for him that told me little.

"I'm putting my favorite team back together!" Drea could hardly contain herself. "I wanted to surprise you, Oliver, but you'll be working with Ricky again! And he can drive you guys to Oregon. It'll be perfect. I have a great hook I'd like you to use for the piece, too."

"You can't help yourself, can you," I said to Drea, raising an eyebrow. She had concocted my trip to Washington at least partly in an attempt to set me and Ricky up, and as her new trap snapped closed around me this time, I could see that she wasn't prepared to accept failure. "What's this great hook of yours?"

"You're gonna love this." Ricky grinned. "It's so desperate and obvious." He nudged her back. "Go on, tell him."

"You two are no fun, but you're taking my direction on this, and it *will* work, so help me. The hook for your piece is 'Find romance on the Oregon coast!'" She finished with a flourish of her hand.

I blushed again, and goggled my eyes at her, not daring to look at Ricky.

"I've got you booked into a couple of really sweet B and Bs along the 101, and a couple of spas that offer couples packages, some romantic restaurants. There are some hikes to really beautiful spots in nature—it'll be so pretty and relaxing and fun, you're going to love it. And, you know," she said, lowering her voice to a mumble, her words almost running together, "maybe you'll love each other, too, I dunno."

"Wow," I said.

"Shameless," Ricky said. "But worth a shot, no?" He shot me a mock-seductive look, one eyebrow raised, his dark brown eyes melting a little.

Drea pushed back her chair, forcing Ricky's arm away. "I need to powder my nose before our food gets here," she announced. "And you two have some catching up to do."

We both watched her go, and then Ricky turned back to me. "She's about as subtle as a sledgehammer, isn't she?"

"How long have you been here?" I blurted, still confused by Ricky's sudden reappearance.

His golden cheeks flushed slightly, and for a second his eyes darted away in embarrassment. "Yeah, I'm sorry to surprise you like this. It was Drea's idea, but I should have reached out sooner. I got into town last week."

He'd been here a week and hadn't said anything?

"I wish I'd known," I said, surprising myself with my frankness. "It would have been nice to see you in a . . . less . . . trappy-feeling context, but it looks like we'll be seeing plenty of each other anyway. Did you come out specifically for this job?"

Ricky seemed to be studying me. "No," he said finally, shrugging. "I felt the need for a change of scenery. I left DC about three weeks ago—drove down to see my dad in North Carolina for a couple of days, then headed west and just kind of ended up here."

"So you and Drea cooked this one up together?" I cocked an eyebrow and grinned at him, to let him know it would be okay if the answer was yes.

"Not exactly," he said, smiling a little. "We can give her more or less all of the credit for this little scheme."

At that, Drea returned from the bathroom as a server arrived with our food, and we moved on to eating and talking logistics, and Ricky and me being embarrassed by Drea's obvious delight in her machinations and mildly, curiously uncomfortable to be back in each other's presence.

My anxiety edged steadily upward for the few interminable days between the lunch attack and our planned departure on Sunday morning. It didn't much help that all I heard from

Ricky in that time was a brief text on Saturday to confirm my address and the time he'd be coming to pick me up, meaning that the rest of our communications were all in my head, and kept getting more and more dramatic as they alternated between bitter recriminations about my failure at friendship and desperate attempts at declaring undying love, or at least a healthy case of *like a lot*.

I'd packed my bag on Saturday night, then lay awake for hours, thrashing around my bed in a mixture of dread, hope, excitement, and despair at the prospect of spending the next several days alone with Ricky. Finally, I got up and spent the remainder of the night in an increasingly cold bath, stewing through my second and third winds as I played movies at low volume on my laptop, ignoring them as I tried to figure out what "finding romance" looked like, and what *romance* even meant.

Finally, it was morning, and time to get ready to go. I trudged through the motions, everything taking longer than I'd planned, and I was upstairs in my mom's kitchen, still eating breakfast, when my pocket buzzed. I fumbled the phone out of my pocket and saw to my dismay that Ricky had arrived and was waiting outside.

"Oh, shoot," I said, Cheerios and milk dribbling from my mouth back into the bowl. "I have to go."

"Nonsense," my mom said, springing up from the table in her fuzzy pink robe. "I'll invite him in."

Before I could protest, she had flown from the kitchen, and in a second I heard the front door unlatch and my mom call out, "Yoohoo! Ricky! Come on up!" I halfheartedly considered abandoning my breakfast and trying to make a break for my apartment out the back door, but decided I was too tired.

Soon I heard Ricky making his way up the front steps, and my mom greeted him warmly, ushering him through to the kitchen. "Ricky, it's so nice to meet you! I've heard so much about you. I'm Oliver's mom, Robin. Oliver's still eating breakfast—would you like anything?"

"No, thank you, I'm fine." He smiled as he came through the door, lighting up the kitchen. His shorts and crisp, white, short-sleeve, button-down shirt, the top two buttons left undone to expose a tantalizing suggestion of chest hair, indicated that he had been expecting more of a Southern California June than our customary Bay Area gloom, but I didn't mind the amount of golden brown skin they left on display.

"I heard quite a bit about you, too, when Oliver was in Washington," he continued, a note of deference in his voice clearly intended to charm my mom's socks off. "I'm very glad to have the chance to meet you."

My mother, successfully de-socksed, beamed as she poured herself more coffee, then waggled the carafe at Ricky to be sure he didn't want any. He declined with a graceful wave and sat down next to me at the table.

"So, Ricky," my mom asked, "where have you been staying while you've been in the area?"

"In San Francisco. At Drea's, actually," he said.

"That tiny little place? And aren't she and Josh . . . trying? That seems like it might be a little uncomfortable."

"Trying what?" I wanted to know between bites of cereal.

"Trying to get pregnant," my mother said, an eyebrow raised. She and Drea were Facebook friends, and I didn't really use social media, so there always seemed to be a side of Drea's life that my mom knew more about than me.

"Indeed they are," Ricky said. "I think they think they're being discreet about it, but you're right, their place is very small. We've all been a bit on top of each other—uh, so to speak."

"Will you be staying in the area after you get back from this trip?" my mother asked, a glint in her eye.

"I might stick around for a while," Ricky nodded. "We'll

see. I don't have anything pressing waiting for me back home, and it's a long drive, so I'd like to make the most of my time away."

"Oliver," my mother said, unconvincingly pretending that something had just occurred to her. "When you get back, you should have Ricky stay with you!"

I was trying to finish my orange juice, but choked a little at this pronouncement. Ricky whacked me on the back with a bemused grin, and a bit of juice dripped out my nose.

"What," I managed to choke out.

"Well, I'm sure it would be much more comfortable for him, and you've got the whole downstairs to yourself." She stared at me defiantly.

"I'm sure I wouldn't want to impose," Ricky said, his hand still resting lightly on my back. It was the first time he'd touched me since I'd seen him again, and I was relieved to feel the old familiar thrill of it from the last time we'd been together, rather than my usual recoil from physical contact.

"Well, uh," I said, rising from my chair to put my breakfast dishes into the dishwasher and trying to figure out how to gracefully get out of the corner my mother had backed me into. "We'll have plenty of time to figure that out, I guess. I should go grab my stuff from downstairs."

"I'll meet you at the car," Ricky said as he, too, rose from the table. He extended a hand to my mother. "Robin, it was so lovely to meet you. I promise I'll get Oliver back to you in one piece."

For a second they seemed to share a peculiar look, but then she smiled. "See that you do. You boys have fun—take good care of each other."

As I tried to follow Ricky out of the room, she grabbed my arm and pulled me back, wrapping me into a hug. "I mean it," she whispered into my ear. "I want you back in one piece this time."

* * *

I wondered what my mom had meant by *this time* as I settled into Ricky's car and we headed toward the freeway. Had I been that obvious?

"I can't believe you drove all the way here from DC in this car," I commented, trying to recenter myself by taking in the familiar copper-colored vinyl environs of Ricky's '66 Corvair sport coupe, feeling a little like they were those of an old friend.

He grinned a little, his hand on the shifter as we merged onto the first of several highways we would navigate in short order as we made our way north and across the bay, until we made it to US 101, our route for the rest of the way. "I'll be honest—take this as a warning—it's not the most comfortable car for long distances, but it eats up the miles like a champ. I had no problems at all on the trip out."

Uncomfortable, and reliability was a surprise. This boded well. Now that Ricky mentioned it, I became acutely aware of the lack of a headrest, and of how little support the marshmallow-soft bucket seat afforded my back and rear end. I squirmed a little, realizing with dismay that as the adrenaline of our departure wore off and my wakeful night caught up with me, I was growing steadily sleepier in an environment that was not at all conducive to sleep, other than being quite warm and smelling faintly of gas.

Fighting to keep my eyes open, I gazed absently out the window as the car droned up the high, undulating bridge over the bay from Richmond to San Rafael. My mind was busy rehashing all of the repetitive thoughts that had kept me up the night before, and I realized I'd need to do something proactive to change course. I shifted my gaze to Ricky, and tried to come up with a topic of conversation.

"So, this hook of Drea's," I finally started, then realized I didn't know how I planned to finish.

Ricky sensed my pause. "'Find romance on the Oregon coast,'" he filled in with a soft smile, giving the words about as much ridiculous exaggeration as they deserved.

I fidgeted a little, looking at my hands, then blurted out, "So, do you want to? Or . . . are we . . ." I trailed off again.

He chuckled a little, then furrowed his brow and thought hard for a moment. "I don't know how to answer that," he said softly. "I gotta be honest, Oliver, I'm a little confused about where we stand."

"You are?" I said meekly, then admitted, "So am I."

"Well," he said slowly, staring steadily ahead out the windshield to avoid making eye contact with me, or maybe to relieve me from having to make eye contact with him. "It won't do for us both to be confused. Maybe we should see if we can figure it out. What's confusing you?"

"I—uh—" I hadn't been ready for this, and I definitely wasn't awake enough for this. I swallowed hard, trying not to let myself get overwhelmed. "It doesn't feel the same? And I'm worried that's because I've totally messed it up." Without warning, I burst into tears.

"Oh, jeez," Ricky said in dismay, craning his neck to check behind him as he hustled over to catch a last-minute exit off the freeway. He turned from the off-ramp into a gas station, brought the car to a stop, and pulled me over into his arms.

"Don't cry, Oliver," he said into my hair, sounding worryingly close to tears himself. "What makes you think you messed up?"

I sniffled into his chest. "I didn't know how to do it," I mumbled. "I didn't know how to be your friend or keep the conversation going or keep you interested."

"I kind of got the impression that *you* weren't interested," he said gently after a pause. "You didn't seem to want to talk to me. You never called me back."

"I was scared," I said, sobbing a little. He rubbed my back.

"Why were you scared? We didn't have any problems talking to each other when we were together before."

"Yeah, but we were together. And I thought when we weren't together, you'd think I was less interesting or less fun—I *am* less fun when I'm on my own." I let out a half laugh, half hiccup.

"Hmm," was all he said. He held me for a minute longer, but finally I sat up, wiping my nose on my wrist.

"I'm sorry," I said. "We can keep going."

Ricky looked over to me as he turned the engine back over. "We're back together now. We don't have to commit to finding romance, but I'm willing to be interesting and fun together with you, if you're willing to be interesting and fun together with me."

"Sounds okay to me," I said with an only slightly watery smile. "And, you know, if the other thing happens, that might be . . . okay. Right?"

"I think so," he said with a lopsided half smile. "Now, let me know when you're ready to start being fun," he said, his face turning mock serious, as he pulled onto the on-ramp back to the highway.

Laughing, I gave him a weak shot to the ribs.

As we resumed our northward route through the affluent suburbs of Marin County, I slumped against my door, looking out my window and trying to collect myself. I hadn't totally realized how tired I was, and how thrown I had been by not being ready to go when Ricky arrived. And then my mom had stuck her nose in and made things awkward, and then I'd brought out the ultimate weapon in my arsenal of embarrassing reactions to stress and burst out crying. But Ricky had been nothing but kind, and he had held me, and we had even gotten back a hint of our old banter. So maybe the day could recover.

Ricky had clicked on the AM radio and was fiddling with the dial to see what he could pull in, finally landing on a station playing old big band standards. He adjusted the volume down so that the music settled into a soft background, his fingers occasionally tapping time on the steering wheel. My mind wandered back to the bigger picture of our assignment, and after a while I turned back to Ricky. "What even is *romance*, anyway?" I demanded. "What is it we're supposed to be telling people how to find here?"

He glanced at me, his eyebrows raised. "That's what you've been thinking about over there? What do you mean, what is romance? You know what romance is. Everybody does."

I thought about this. "I know what romance is as, like, a genre of books I don't read or movies I don't watch. But that's fiction. What does romance look like in the real world?"

He screwed his face up for a minute. "Huh. Now that you mention it, it is kind of a vague concept to me, too. I mean, it's mostly a state of mind, right? And that might look different to different people. But I think if you asked most people what made a place, for example, feel romantic, they might also describe it as *intimate*. You're put in close physical proximity, the lighting might be low, music, candles, that kind of stuff."

We drove in silence but for the lush strings of a ballad coming from the radio, the cabin of the car heavy with contemplation. Eventually, Ricky seemed to reach a conclusion. "I guess if you want to find romance with someone, you might find ways to be so close to them that, even if you're not, you feel like you're alone with each other. And you'd find ways to shut out distractions, so you're focused on each other and the things you like about each other and about being together, and you can find ways to treat each other well."

I looked around the cabin of the car. We were definitely in close quarters. Other cars rolled by outside our windows, but they were mere background noise; we were very much alone in our own little vinyl-lined cocoon. There was soft music—romantic music, even—coming from the radio. And as I looked at him, I was once again smacked in the face, as I was at least once a day every time we were together, by how stunningly beautiful Ricky was.

He caught me looking from the corner of his eye. "You look awful, Oliver," he said.

"Gee, thanks." So much for those romantic vibes I had been trying to summon.

"No, I didn't mean that—you look exhausted," he said. Keeping his left hand on the wheel, he reached down behind my seat and came back up with a small pillow. "Here," he said, handing it to me. "I brought this with me in case I had to stay at a motel that seemed too questionable. If you put it between your head and your window, you might be able to get comfortable enough to sleep a bit." He lowered the radio volume even further, until the music was little more than the hint of a lullaby.

I did as he suggested, wriggling a little to get my position just right, then quickly drifting off with a delirious feeling that producing this pillow for me at this moment was perhaps the most romantic thing Ricky could possibly have done.

Chapter 2

I'm embarrassed to admit that I slept almost all the way to Oregon. Lulled by the vibrations of the car humming through the glass and only slightly dampened by the pillow between the window and my head, it was a light but dreamless sleep, punctuated occasionally by hazy wakefulness. In those moments, I'd watch the mystical mountain landscape of coastal Northern California through the windshield, the road ahead bordered on both sides by steeply ascending hills and thick, dark, velvety green forests, peering into the depths to where their infrequent patches of dancing, filtered sunlight seductively lured me back to sleep with the false promise of sparkling, romantic dreams.

As we neared our stop at the end of the first day, not quite to the Oregon border, I was awake long enough to entertain a fantasy that, in her zeal to pair me and Ricky off and under the influence of way too many formulaic TV rom-coms, Drea would have "accidentally" booked us into a single hotel room with a single bed. But she liked her job too much to risk it on a scenario that was as likely to end in a sexual harassment lawsuit as in wedding bells, so we retired to adjacent rooms at a modest motel, where, sleep-logged from the car, I lay awake all night again.

As a result, our second day on the road began much as the

first had gone, with me groggily struggling through some initial pleasantries with Ricky before passing out. When I awoke again a couple of hours later, the landscape had changed; where we had been following the mountainous curves of a four-lane highway, now we were idling at a stoplight in the middle of a town.

I took a bleary look around. "Where are we? Why did we get off the highway?"

"We didn't," Ricky said, his eyes locked on the traffic light. "We've crossed into Oregon, and this is still 101, but it turns into the road through town here."

"*The* 101," I corrected. "I'm a Californian."

"Yeah, well, I'm not, and we're not in California." The corners of his eyes crinkled behind his sunglasses as he stuck his tongue out at me. "Speaking of which, as scintillating as your company has been so far, you might want to stay awake from here on out. The road trip aspect *is* part of our assignment, after all."

I felt guilty. He was right; I had been terrible company, hadn't even tried to help as a navigator or something, and at this point I was putting in an embarrassingly weak showing at my job to boot.

I tried on a weak, contrite smile. "To paraphrase something that someone wise once told me, I can stay awake for the drive home, and it'll be the same trip, only in reverse."

He gave me a sidelong glance, eyebrow cocked. "I seem to recall that you were none too happy with me for telling you that."

"And yet, I've come around. But I will stay awake. Sorry I haven't been a very good passenger." I tossed the pillow into the backseat in a show of goodwill.

"All good," he said, dipping into the accelerator a bit as the town receded behind us and the highway headed into its more familiar woodland terrain. "I think you only have an hour or so to keep me company until we reach the first real stop on our itinerary."

Sure enough, about an hour and a few towns later, we turned left off the highway, down a steep access road through a patch of dense coastal forest to the Rose Beach Inn & Spa, a low, rambling, wood-shingled building perched between massive, wind-gnarled pines at the edge of a bluff overlooking a stunningly rugged little inlet. It was still early enough that we would almost certainly be the first to check in, and the small parking lot was nearly empty as we pulled in.

The lobby was fronted by an elegant desk of reclaimed wood, with an uplit partial living wall behind, its profusion of greenery dividing the lobby from a lounge beyond that ran the depth of the building, its windowed wall opposite us affording lavish views of the water. Behind the desk, a woman, trim and blond, probably in her midforties and outdoorsy-chic in an open-necked, summery white blouse under a light fleece vest, stood transfixed in front of a computer monitor, her brows knit. Behind her, a dark-haired boy of perhaps eighteen or nineteen sat in her office chair, languidly reading a book. They both looked up when we entered, the woman pasting on a professional smile, the boy staring curiously and a bit unnervingly.

"Welcome to the Rose Beach Inn," said the woman. "You must be Mr. Popp and Mr. Warner. I'm Mary Alice Thatcher." She extended a hand.

"Yes, we are," I said, shaking the offered hand. "How did you know?"

She chuckled softly. "You're the only new guests checking in today, so it was a safe guess. I have everything ready for you, and if you'd like, I can give you a little tour and some information about the inn as soon as you're settled in." She shifted her attention back to the computer, tapping us into her system. The boy still held his book, but his gaze hadn't left us, and seemed particularly locked on me. I was starting to feel uncomfortable.

A brief look of consternation flashed across Mary Alice's face. "I do have to apologize," she said. "When your booking was made, you requested our two-bedroom suite, but I'm afraid I may have double-booked that suite with another guest who's already checked in."

I felt the color drain from my face. "And you only have one two-bedroom suite?"

Her eyes darted apologetically from me to Ricky and back. "Unfortunately, yes. The room I have available has a comfortable sofa, or I can send down a rollaway bed if you'd like. I'm so sorry about this."

Ricky and I exchanged a quick glance. I had briefly fantasized about this kind of rom-com scenario the day before, but it had been a lark, not something I had actually thought would happen. I couldn't tell what Ricky was thinking, but he said, almost as if he was reading the part of the guilelessly handsome love interest from a rom-com script, "I'm sure we can figure it out. It'll be fine—no need to apologize."

"I appreciate that," Mary Alice said, reaching for a key card. "I'm sure we can find some way to make it up to you. Perhaps I can send a complimentary bottle of wine to your room later."

I wasn't sure whether or how to respond to this offer that wasn't framed as a question, but there wasn't time anyway, as Mary Alice had already moved on to handing over the room keys.

"I have you in suite 202; that's down one level. The elevator is to your right there. Do you need any help with your bags? I can ask my son—Erik," she said, turning to the boy behind her, "could you please help Mr. Popp and Mr. Warner with their bags?"

"I think we can manage," I said quickly, but Erik, still staring at us, had jumped up.

"I don't mind," he said. "I can show you the way."

He trotted out to the car at our heels, and I obligingly let him take my duffel from the trunk. "This is a cool car," he said to me. "Is it yours? I've never seen a car like this before."

"No, it's not mine, it's his," I said, hoping that Erik would latch on to Ricky instead of me.

He was undeterred, staying focused on me as we passed back through the lobby and waited for the elevator. "So are you really a writer?"

"Yes, I am, and he's a photographer."

"I want to be a writer, too," Erik confided, still ignoring Ricky. "I'm on a gap year, but I'm planning to major in journalism when I go to college. In fact," he continued, shuffling shyly under the weight of my bag, "I want to be a travel writer. That's what you are, isn't it?"

Erik led us out of the elevator down the hall to our room and keyed us in. "Here we are," he said, still mostly only to me. He set my duffel delicately down onto a luggage stand, as if it were full of precious breakables, and crossed the room to open a French door to our balcony. "There's a sign next to the hot tub that says how it works," he said, gesturing toward the balcony. "Let me or my mom know if you need anything."

"Thank you, Erik," Ricky said, palming a tip into his hand. The boy seemed to notice him for the first time. I wandered over to the French doors to take in the view. As Ricky ushered our helper out, I heard Erik ask in a slightly awed tone, "Is he your boyfriend? Wow. You're so lucky, getting to go all those places with him. . . ."

I waited to turn around until I heard the door click shut. Ricky turned, too, leaning his back against the door, his hand still on the knob, fanning himself with his other hand and making exaggerated goo-goo eyes at me in a heightened imitation of Erik. "Ooh, is this *your* car? Is he *your* boyfriend? I want to be exactly like you!"

I slumped onto a sofa, wailing, "What did I do? Why me?"

Ricky came and draped himself over the chair next to me, grinning the whole way. "You didn't do anything. The kid has good taste. On a gap year, though—what would that make him, eighteen or nineteen? I thought you were into older guys." He waggled his thumb toward himself.

I gave him my driest look. "You flatter yourself. But seeing as I already have my hands full with you, I'm hoping I can avoid him the rest of the time we're here."

"Well, then, you'd better hope he didn't go back to the desk, because we have to go back up to get the lowdown from Mary Alice."

We dutifully trooped back upstairs, returning to Mary Alice, who was thankfully alone at the front desk. "Is this an okay time?" I asked.

"It's great," she assured us. "Like I said, you're my only new guests checking in today, so I'm totally free. Let's head into the lounge."

She came out from behind the desk, leading us around the living wall into the space beyond. The large room had a long, weathered driftwood bar along one side, with intimate cocktail tables in the center of the space and clusters of overstuffed armchairs along the wall of windows overlooking the ocean. A baby grand piano sat gleaming in one corner. To my dismay, Erik was busily wiping down the bar and tables, occasionally sneaking unsubtle glances at us—I hoped they were at *us*, anyway, but feared they were mostly at only *me*.

Mary Alice led us to a table near the windows. "So, as you've seen," she started as we sat, "the inn is built onto the bluff here. We're on the top level right now; there's one guest suite on this level—that's our two-bedroom unit—and two more levels of rooms below us. We have seven guest rooms altogether, each with a balcony like yours. Did Erik mention the hot tub to you? Every room has one, out on its balcony. Those are a fairly recent addition—in fact, we were recently able to make quite a few upgrades."

I nodded my appreciation for Erik's adherence to his mother's script. "How long have you been in operation?"

"Well, my parents opened the inn when I was very young. I inherited it when my father passed away four years ago, though of course I'd already been helping him run it for many years before that. The spa is a relatively recent addition, in the last three years. That part of the building used to house a kitchen and dining room and library, but those required a level of staffing I couldn't justify anymore, and there's a very good bistro next door anyway that I couldn't compete with. I don't run the spa; I lease the space to them, with an agreement that my guests have access to spa services."

"Is it only you and Erik running things here?"

She laughed ruefully. "Mostly. I have a housekeeper, though I help with that, too, and a couple of local girls who do shifts on the desk, but that's about it. There isn't a huge workforce out here. And, of course, I'll have a challenge when Erik goes back to school in the fall, but summer is our busiest season anyway."

"You mentioned that we were the only guests checking in today—"

"Yes, well, that's because all of my other rooms were booked starting yesterday through the next few days. We do have a fairly full house. We have a happy hour here in the lounge every evening, which might be a good time to get some pictures in here, although . . ."

Her pause lasted so long that I was beginning to wonder if she would ever resume what she had been saying. An internal debate played out over her face for a second before she continued, "Well, I suppose I should warn you that most of my other guests right now are actually relatives of mine. They're all very nice, that's nothing to worry about, but the conversation might be a little insular. I have an aunt who lives nearby, and all of her children and one of their cousins are in town to celebrate her birthday. So you're more than welcome—everybody has been hanging out in here in the evenings, having a great time—but be warned that they all already know each other."

"Ah, I see," I said. The idea of horning in on a family gathering sounded distinctly unappealing, but we did need some pictures, and a family group might make for better interactions in the photos than a bunch of strangers trying to pretend to have a good time. "As long as you think nobody would mind having their picture taken—we have releases they'd have to sign—we probably will at least stop by for a minute to do that."

"I'm sure everyone would be thrilled," she assured us. "Here, let me show you the spa."

We followed Mary Alice back through the lobby, through a discreet frosted-glass door into a pastel-bathed waiting room, enhanced by the usual soundtrack of a burbling tabletop fountain and softly tinkling New Age music. She introduced us to Letitia, the manager of the spa, a wiry, cheerful woman in her sixties with bleached hair pulled back into a ponytail and her bony frame clad in black Lycra.

"I got you guys on the books for a couples massage tomorrow," she said with apparent surprise. "You know that means you'll be in the same room and everything, right? It's kind of a lovers' package sort of thing. I can change it so you're in separate rooms if you want."

"All part of the assignment," Ricky said smoothly as I felt my face burn scarlet. "I'm sure we'll manage."

"Suit yourself," she said with an affable shrug.

Mary Alice led us through the spa's main entrance out to the parking lot. "I wanted to show you the trail down to the beach," she said, walking beyond the inn toward the bluff. "It's right over here. It's kind of a long way down, and if you're afraid of heights it might not be the best for you, but it's perfectly safe."

The path wound down through the trees in a series of switchbacks for a while before reaching a set of stone stairs carved into the bluff heading down below the lower levels of the inn. Further down, the crystalline blue-green water of the shallow inlet lapped onto a small, rocky, deserted beach.

Mary Alice excused herself, leaving us to take in the view. Ricky leaned into me, whispering, "Are you afraid of heights?"

"No," I whispered back. "Are you?"

"No. It actually looks kind of fun. We should go down there, but tomorrow. Don't we have a reservation at that bistro soon?"

I glanced at my watch. "Yeah, in half an hour. We should get ready."

"Okay, but are you sure you wouldn't rather take Erik than me? Why make him jealous thinking you're going on a date with me, when you could take him instead and assure him that I'm not your boyfriend."

I playfully glared daggers at Ricky. "It's a working dinner, not a date. And if you keep up these cracks, you never *will* be my boyfriend."

He raised his hands in surrender. "I take it back! Don't push me off the cliff! Give me another chance, please. And maybe"—he shot me a shy look I hadn't seen on him before—"maybe it could be kind of, like, *partly* a date?"

I gave him a small smile and a curious look as I turned to head back into the inn. He had started off joking, but had ended sounding oddly genuine, like he was really asking me out.

I wasn't exactly in a romantic frame of mind about our dinner at the bistro up the road from the inn while we were busy talking with the owner and the chef, taking notes about the food, and taking photos. But in between bursts of productivity, when Ricky and I were alone, sitting across a small table from each other, exchanging bites of our desserts and talking in low tones about nothing and everything, I caught a glimpse of a date. And I realized that, if that's what a date was like, it looked a lot like the fun and the conversations and the flirtatious sparring Ricky and I had done when we were working together in the past. Which, in a sense, made it seem like we'd been getting paid to go on free dates with each other, which struck me as a good deal.

As we walked back down the darkened road to the inn in companionable silence, I wondered what to do next. Ricky and I had set off agreeing to have fun together on this trip, and then I'd spent the last couple of days being sleepy and edgy and avoidant. Ricky was being patient, but I was tired of the awkwardness, and irritated with myself for being the cause of it. We were headed back to the room that we were sharing, where we'd be alone together, more or less off the clock. I resolved to put my nerves behind me and keep the momentum from dinner going.

Back to *our room*, I mused. *Alone*. Hadn't Mary Alice said something about sending down a bottle of wine? I didn't drink, but I wasn't above giving Ricky some to keep him mellow and flirtatious. . . .

"So, what do we do next?" Ricky said, reading my mind as we rounded the last bend in the road leading to the inn, coming into view of the small parking lot, which was now full. "Looks like the other guests are back. Maybe we should pop in and see about getting some pictures of that happy hour in the lounge."

"Oh, yeah," I said, with only a mild edge of dismay in my voice. Our room would still be there in twenty minutes, I reminded myself.

There was a low hum of voices and a tinkling tune from the piano drifting out from the lounge when we entered the lobby. I followed Ricky into the lounge, where, rather than being the boisterous family gathering we'd been promised, the party, such as it was, seemed to have broken up into a few low-energy clusters.

A handsome, sandy-haired man of about forty played the piano softly, while an elderly woman sat on the bench next to him, her eyes closed, her face tired and drawn but her body swaying slightly in time with the music. Mary Alice sat with two other women, one slightly older, the other perhaps a decade younger, at a nearby table. The younger woman was fiddling nervously with a straw stuck into a can of Sprite and speaking a little too loudly about something someone had said while she was cutting their hair, while Mary Alice tried to look politely interested. The other woman made no effort to look interested at all, instead staring intently at the door over the rim of her wineglass as Ricky and I came in, and looking annoyed that we weren't someone else. Erik was again stationed behind the bar, talking animatedly to two red-haired teenage girls and failing to conceal the fact that he, too, was keeping us locked in his peripheral vision from the moment we entered.

"Ricky," I hissed out of the corner of my mouth, grabbing his elbow to hang back near the entryway, "this doesn't look like a very happy crowd. Maybe we should try another time."

But I was too late. Mary Alice was waving us over, and Ricky broke free and trotted off toward her table. She stood as we approached, meeting us halfway across the room.

"I'm sorry," she said in a low voice. "Things aren't too lively in here tonight. There was some excitement earlier at my Aunt Cecilia's birthday party at her house in town—that's her, sitting at the piano—and I think everyone's a little tired."

"Excitement!" The older woman who had been sitting next to Mary Alice came up behind her. She was tall, dressed elegantly in a linen-colored sweater and matching slacks, with a sweep of deep auburn hair and a brow that seemed resigned to a life of being disappointed in everyone and everything around her. "It wasn't excitement, it was a fire. Some idiot"—she cast an accusing eye over her shoulder to where the younger woman, now alone at their table, was inspecting her nails—"thought it was a good idea to put eighty-five candles on a cake, dropped it, and burned down Cecilia's dining room. What a bore."

She turned to Mary Alice, clutching her by the arm. "Look, I'm sorry, I think Richard is still going to be working in our room for a while, so I'm going to take the girls to a movie. We need some air. God!" She waved a summons to the two girls, who broke away from talking to Erik at the bar, and the three of them swept out of the room.

"A fire burned down their dining room, and it was a bore? She must lead some life," Ricky said to Mary Alice.

She gave a small smile. "A lot of things bore her. Usually, it just means that she doesn't like something. That was my cousin Richard's wife, Rachel, and their daughters. Playing the piano is my Aunt Cecilia's nephew, Wylie, from her husband's side. Over there"—she indicated the young woman with the fascinating cuticles—"is his wife, Tawny. Aunt Cecilia's daughter, Lis, was around here a minute ago, but I don't see her now—I was actually looking forward to introducing you to her; she would have liked some non-family company. Anyway, like I said, maybe tomorrow would be a better time."

I wasn't going to turn down an out. "That's okay by me if it's okay by you," I said, giving Ricky a look.

He caught my eye and lifted an eyebrow slightly. "Sure. Tomorrow will be fine."

As we turned to go, Tawny got up from her table and tottered after us on alarmingly high leopard-print heels. I was surprised at how quickly she could move in them; she caught up to us near the doorway back to the lobby.

"Hi," she drawled, grabbing Ricky into a handshake in some kind of blindingly fast jujitsu move. "I thought maybe Mary Alice was gonna introduce us, but I guess she forgot. I'm Tawny—what's your name?"

"Oh, uh, hi," Ricky said, the look of shock on his face turning into a *help me* look as it landed on me. "I'm, uh . . ."

"Jeff, honey, come on," I said, grabbing him by his other hand. *Jeff?* I had no idea where I'd come up with that one.

"Yeah, Jeff," he said to Tawny as he broke free from her grasp and hustled me toward the elevator. "Nice to meet you, but we have to go, uh, check on our baby."

"Aww, a baby," she cooed after us. "Well, look, Jeff, I'm gonna go get some air, so if you need some, too, after you're done with your baby and all—" She kept talking at Ricky until the elevator doors slid closed.

I burst into laughter. "I'm sorry, I tried to help, but she did *not* care if you had a gayby with me."

"Yeah, whatever happened to the sanctity of the family?" he laughed. "Thanks for the fake name, by the way, but *Jeff*?"

I shrugged at him with my most enigmatic smile as the elevator released us onto our floor. I keyed us into our room, feeling suddenly adrift as I wandered in. I had wanted to be here, alone with Ricky; now I was, and I didn't know what to do about it. Our upstairs neighbor was loudly playing classical music in the room above us, and I didn't know whether to be annoyed that it was shattering the illusion that we were alone, or grateful.

"Sounds like a party upstairs," Ricky commented as he flopped down on the sofa. He turned a wolfish grin on me, patting the cushion next to him. "Good. We can make as much noise as we want and they won't be bothered."

"What kind of noisy activities did you have in mind? Popping balloons?" I sat daintily on the edge of the offered seat, pushing myself into not pulling away.

Ricky pondered this for a moment. "I guess I don't know what would actually be that noisy," he admitted. He shot a glance toward the balcony. "We could try out the hot tub. We'd be outside, away from the music, and the jets might drown it out if we can still hear it."

My stomach contracted. My mom watched enough reality dating shows for me to know the enticing terrors that could await me in a hot tub with a handsome, mostly naked Ricky. My mind hadn't dared to go to any *mostly naked* places before, but I had wanted to try to move forward with Ricky. *Keep pushing yourself, Oliver,* I reminded myself.

"Um, okay," I finally squeaked.

Ricky's wolfish grin came back as he got up, flicked on the light switch next to the balcony door, and stepped out to turn on the heat and the jets. I sat, pinned to the couch in fear, as he came back in, fished a bathing suit out of his bag, and stepped into the bathroom to change. Then I realized that I wasn't ready to see him when he came out, all bare-chested and bare-legged and—*oof*—so I got up and hunched over my duffel, rooting around and pushing my own swimsuit down to the bottom of the bag so I'd have to dig a while longer to get it out. I heard the bathroom door open, heard his bare feet pad toward the balcony behind me, and bolted for the bathroom to change into my suit.

I leaned over the vanity for a minute once I had my trunks on, trying to take calming breaths but mostly wishing I wasn't so skinny and pale. Over the faint swelling of the music upstairs, I heard Ricky getting into the hot tub with an exuberant splash. Not sure I was feeling quite so pumped myself, I steeled my nerves, draped a towel over my shoulders in an effort to look insouciant while actually covering as much of my upper body as possible, took one more deep breath, and stepped out and headed for the balcony.

Through the door, I could see Ricky's back, his broad shoulders glowing golden in the dim light from the bulb next to the door, tapering down into shadow at the narrow small of his back, his butt—*god,* that *butt*—covered in a gloriously short pair of red shorts. *Wait*—his butt? Hadn't I heard him getting into the hot tub? How was he standing beside it now, perfectly dry?

I realized I had stopped moving toward the door, that I was standing, staring, transfixed. Then I realized that Ricky wasn't moving, either, and seemed transfixed by some novel sight of his own. Slowly, he turned toward the door, his face frighteningly pale.

"Oliver," he called in flatly through the door, not seeming to see me right in front of him.

"I'm here," I said, still stuck to my spot in the middle of the room, now a little frightened for a new reason. The world had gone silent, the music upstairs suddenly gone, the mechanical hum of the hot tub's jets fading as my ears filled with curious dread. "What's wrong?"

"Oliver." His eyes were wild, finally latching onto me.

"*What?*"

"The hot tub."

"What about the hot tub?"

He was starting to go glassy-eyed, blinking slowly and swallowing hard before saying, "Well, it has a dead guy in it."

Chapter 3

Ricky and I had been here once before, crossing paths with a dead body. I tried to remember what I had done the last time, and realized that I'd gone into shutdown mode. I checked in with myself to see if that was going to happen again. I was more than a little unnerved, to be sure, but a hand to my chest confirmed that my breathing was normal. A quick scan behind the eyes confirmed that my brain had no immediate plans to check out. All systems remained in operation, so that probably meant it was time to try to help Ricky.

"What happened?" I edged cautiously toward the door as I tried out this obviously weak opening gambit, both curious to see the scene and not entirely sure that I wanted to.

Ricky was still planted to his spot, his torso twisted toward me, his face a mask of glassy shock. "I was opening the door when this guy fell from . . . somewhere . . . into the hot tub," he said flatly.

I was close enough now to see a leg draped over the edge of the hot tub and an arm bobbing on the surface of the water, both pulsing in time with the jets. The leg was clad in a pair of chinos, a patterned dress sock on the visible foot; the arm was inside a sweater, probably much darker green than usual from being submerged in the water. There didn't seem to be any bubbles coming from the submerged upper body, but to be certain I asked, "Are you sure he's dead? Should we be trying to get him out?"

"He hit the edge of the tub before he went in," Ricky said, turning back toward the body and staring blankly into the water. "There was a nasty crack. His eyes are open, too. I'm pretty sure he died on impact."

I took this in. I wasn't shutting down, but I also wasn't feeling too swift. Finally, I said, "Well, uh . . ."

Ricky nodded, as though this had been a useful contribution to the situation. "Yeah."

Suddenly, something in my brain snapped. "Jeez," I said, as I turned and took a wild look around the room, trying to locate a phone. The first one I found was the room phone, so that's the one I picked up.

I was fumbling with the buttons when Mary Alice's voice came through the handset. "Hello? Mr. Popp? Mr. Warner?"

"Uh, hello," I said breathlessly. "I was trying to call 911."

"Oh, no! What's happened? I can put that call through for you," she said quickly.

I forced myself to listen to my breathing instead of the hum rising between my ears. "Could you? That would be great. A guy fell into our hot tub, maybe from the balcony above ours or something, and we think he's dead."

"Oh my god! I'm calling right now!" She hung up without waiting for a response.

Ricky hadn't moved. I padded to the door. "Mary Alice is calling 911 for us. Could you hear me? Was I coherent?"

"I dunno," he said without moving his gaze from the lifeless limbs coming out of the hot tub.

I reached out, gently grabbing his arm. "Why don't you come inside," I said, pulling him stumblingly through the door and leading him to the couch.

As soon as I had gotten him seated, there was a panicked rap at the door. I let Mary Alice in, then the paramedics a few minutes later, and the sheriff a short time after that, and for a little while it was all Ricky and I could do to sit, still and silent, side by side, as our room went from a scene of disaster to one of total chaos.

Eventually, after fumbling through a few questions from the sheriff, we were allowed to leave the room so that we wouldn't have to watch the body being removed. Mary Alice led us up to the lounge and gave us each a mug of cocoa before bustling off again. We sat silently, warming our hands on the mugs but not drinking, for a long time. Finally, I ventured a look at Ricky. His face had lost the glassy look and settled somewhere in the neighborhood of ashen, and very, very tired.

I pried a hand from my warm mug and reached over, brushing Ricky's hand with a finger. "Are you okay?"

He lifted his eyes to me and searched me for a second, looking for words. "Oliver, I . . ." His voice broke, but he pushed on. "Last time . . . I didn't—I don't think either of us actually *saw* . . . but I *saw* it this time. I saw, and I heard, and . . ." He kept his brown eyes locked on me, still searching, coming up short.

I felt myself coming up short, too. For lack of anything to say, I gently hooked my finger under one of his, sharing the warmth of his mug and the first contact between us that I'd ever really initiated. After a moment, he pulled the rest of my fingers into the rest of his, and we sat like that for a while.

There was a commotion in the lobby as the elevator doors clanged open and a trio of EMTs poured out, the clatter of gurney wheels mingling with their swift footsteps toward the door as we both looked down into our mugs to avoid seeing anything. When we looked up again, Mary Alice was rounding the divider from the lobby into the lounge, coming toward us and slumping into a chair at our table.

"You guys, I'm so sorry about this," she said, apparently too tired for her usual formality. "I'll get you into another room, but is it okay if I sit here for just a sec?"

"Of course," I said. "Thanks for taking charge back there."

"That's my job," she said with a tiny, sad hint of a smile. She leaned forward, setting her elbows on the table and tenting her fingers in front of her mouth, her eyes closed. When she opened them again, she said, "That was my cousin. Richard."

"The man in . . . ?" It felt indelicate to finish the question.

She nodded. "He was staying in the room above yours. With his wife, Rachel, who you met earlier, I think. It looks like he fell off his balcony, which is weird, but maybe he was drunk or something."

"He died on impact," Ricky said dully.

She nodded again. "It looks that way. You guys didn't hear anything going on up in his room beforehand, did you?"

"There was music," said Ricky, his monotone taking on a slightly dreamy quality.

"That's right," I said. "He was playing classical music. Kind of loud. I didn't hear anything else."

"I guess that makes sense," Mary Alice shrugged. "As far as we know, he was alone in there. His wife is at the movies." She shot a look over her shoulder toward the lobby, as if realizing that at any moment Rachel could return and walk unwittingly into devastation.

"I don't want to be insensitive," I said slowly. Mary Alice gave a small nod of encouragement, so I went on. "Could it have been suicide?"

She thought for a second. "It would surprise me if it was, but I suppose you never know. The sheriff is looking through their room right now, so maybe they'll find something, but I really think it had to be an accident."

I thought about this for a moment. It seemed so odd. "I didn't really look at the balcony in our room too much. Are the railings particularly low? Would it be easy to fall over?"

Mary Alice shook her head. "They're a standard height. Not especially easy to go over, but I suppose you wouldn't have to work too hard to do it, either. Richard is—was—fairly tall, I guess."

The elevator dinged again in the lobby, and Mary Alice turned to look as the man who had been playing piano earlier rounded the corner into the lounge, his eyes on the floor and his mouth drawn down. I tried to remember who Mary Alice had said he was—a cousin of her cousins, I thought, on their father's side, and he had been married to that pushy flirt, Tawny.

Mary Alice called out to the man, "Can I get you anything, Wylie?"

He looked up, seemingly confused by seeing us for the first time. "Oh, hi. Yeah. Um, what did I come in here for?"

She rose and started toward the bar, giving Wylie a concerned look. "It sounds like you heard what happened."

"Yeah. A deputy came to our room a minute ago. Some milk. I think I was supposed to get some milk for Tawny. Do you have any?"

Mary Alice bent over behind the bar, emerging with a carton of milk. "You sure this is all you want? She doesn't want anything stronger?"

He shook his head. "No, I suggested that, but she insisted on milk. I don't get it. He was *my* cousin, and we used to be close and all, but Tawny's the one going to pieces. I just feel numb."

"Sounds like shock to me," Mary Alice said, pushing a tall glass of milk across the bar. "Everybody reacts differently. Is Tawny going to be okay?"

Wylie slumped on a bar stool, clutching the milk. "I'm sure she will. I don't think they hardly ever spoke, so I don't get why she's upset, but she's down there shrieking and crying. I guess I should see if she's any better, and take her this milk." He stood up slowly. "Thanks."

On his way out of the lounge, he passed the sheriff's deputy, a small woman with a long blond plait swinging down from underneath her wide-brimmed brown hat. She went directly to the bar. "Any sign of the wife yet, Miz Thatcher?"

"No, not yet," Mary Alice said.

The deputy took a stool, swiveling to angle herself with the lobby doors in view. "Okay if I wait here for her? Sheriff wants me to catch her before she goes to the room."

"Makes sense to me," Mary Alice said.

The elevator dinged yet again, and the deputy tensed a little, only relaxing when a woman I hadn't seen before, a tall woman in her midforties with a flaming red asymmetrical hairdo, came into the lounge. Her eyes were nearly as red as her hair, and her voice trembled a little as she addressed Mary Alice, saying, "I finally got Mother to sleep. She's in my room; I know you'll need to shuffle things around to make room for everybody."

She had stopped near our table, talking to Mary Alice from across the room, and now she turned her attention to Ricky and me, lowering herself into the chair recently vacated by Mary Alice. "You must be Mr. Popp and Mr. Warner. I'm Elisabeth Rose, Richard's sister, but call me Lis. I'm so sorry you've had to go through all of this."

Ricky was still holding my hand, and at some point in the last several minutes his head had sunk onto my shoulder, so I figured it was up to me to take the lead in responding. I only wished I knew what to say. "I'm sorry, too," I tried, feeling sure I was getting the tone and emphasis all wrong. "About your brother, I mean."

She nodded solemnly, but didn't say anything more for a moment, leaving me to wonder whether I'd gotten it right after all, or even more wrong than I'd thought. I decided a little clarification might help. "We had a shock, but you've had a loss. What we've gone through doesn't compare to what your family is going through."

"That's very kind of you to say," she said, finally setting my mind at ease. "But I don't think we should minimize your shock, either. You both look exhausted."

Mary Alice rejoined us at our table. "Perfect timing," said Lis to her cousin. "How can I help with getting everyone situated, especially these two? You're down two rooms, right?"

"That's right," Mary Alice said. "I'm afraid the sheriff has asked that you move out of your room," she told us, "not that you'd probably want to stay there anyway." I nodded my agreement, though I wondered if another room would look any different.

"Okay," said Lis. "Well, Mother is with me, so that frees up her room for Mr. Warner and Mr. Popp. Richard and Rachel had a second room, didn't they, for the girls? Could Rachel move in there?"

"Yes, I think that would work," agreed Mary Alice. She pulled a phone out of her pocket. "I'm asking Erik to give Aunt Cecilia's room a quick once-over," she said as she finished tapping out a message, raising her eyes to me. "We'll get you into your new room in about ten minutes, and then you can both get some sleep, okay?"

When Erik led us to our new room a few minutes later, I was too tired to notice whether he still found me fascinating. The only thing fascinating to me was the idea of crawling into bed.

The room was largely the same as our old one, but as long as I avoided looking in the direction of our balcony, I found that it didn't bother me. Almost reflexively I flopped onto the bed, kicking my shoes off and deciding that that was as much as I needed to change before going to sleep.

Ricky gave me a dull-eyed stare. "I guess I'll take the couch."

"Don't be silly," I murmured, my eyes closing and my brain going into that weird near-sleep state where nothing really gets to me the way it usually does and I say whatever I want without having to think about it, the way I assume everyone else's brains always work. "We can share. I don't care. Neither of us should have to sleep on a couch."

"Thank you, Oliver," Ricky said quietly, and I felt him sit down on the bed somewhere behind me, then felt the shift of his weight as he lay down beside me. I reached an arm behind me in his general direction with a vague idea to give him a welcoming pat on the arm or back, but ended up thumping him a little harder than I expected to in the middle of the chest. I still didn't care. Sleep-me was pure id.

"G'night, Ricky," I drawled into my pillow, and I heard him emit a soft chuckle in response.

At some point in the night, something in the position of my body jolted me awake. I discovered that my unconscious maneuvering had brought me right up to Ricky's back, our legs curved together and one of my arms draped over him. I was, I realized with more than a little surprise, spooning him.

It felt nice, but in my sudden clarity, something terrible occurred to me. Ricky had asked me on a date once before, back when we were in Washington, mere minutes before a body crossed our path for the first time. He had asked me again this afternoon, and again a dead person had crashed our evening. Were we cursed? What disaster was I courting with this fresh new act of apparently deadly intimacy?

Figuring I should beat a retreat, I gingerly began to extract my arm, but with a happy little moan, Ricky's sleeping hand intercepted my wrist and pulled me back into him.

I felt a tiny pang of guilt, but as sleep descended once more and my impulsive side took back over, I decided that this felt good enough to risk it and hope that we didn't wake up to more news of death and mayhem.

By morning, we had drifted apart once more. I wondered if either of us was going to say anything about our somnolent activities; Ricky didn't, so I didn't either.

As I was waiting for Ricky to finish getting showered and dressed in the bathroom, I braved a look toward the French door to the balcony. All looked peaceful, so I crept closer to the door for a better look. After confirming that there was nothing out there that shouldn't be, I was able to relax enough to take in the sweeping view of the ocean, sparkling blue where the rising sun hit it as it left the little inlet directly before the inn and stretched out to the west. Somewhere more directly below was the little beach, but seeing that would require actually going out onto the balcony, a step I wasn't quite ready for.

Ricky came out of the bathroom and joined me in front of the door looking out at the view. He put an arm around me, pulling me into a sort of side hug. "Thanks for stepping up last night," he said.

"Of course," I said, reaching around to give him a little squeeze back. "I'm sorry you had to see that. Are you feeling any better?"

"Much."

"And looking out at the balcony isn't too . . . much?" I turned to study his reaction.

He remained placid. "No, it's okay."

I pulled away from him and went to the sofa. "I'll be honest, it was a little unsettling for me at first this morning." Ricky turned, leaning his back against the glass door to look at me.

"And something else," I continued, then paused. "No, it's silly. It's a coincidence, that's all."

He raised a curious eyebrow and gave me a small smile. "What is?"

"Well . . ." I could feel myself starting to blush. "It's just that . . . you've asked me out twice now. . . ."

His smile broadened. "I have, haven't I. And I don't really recall you saying yes either time. That *should* bother you—it bothers me."

"No, that's not it," I said, starting to feel even more flustered and embarrassed than I already had, which I had thought was quite a bit. "I didn't say yes? Well, I didn't say no, did I? Anyway, no, what I mean is, both times you—I didn't say no, did I?—but, both times somebody . . . um, died."

Ricky's brow knit, and he came to sit next to me on the sofa. "That's a heavy thought," he said slowly. "But, Oliver," he said, taking my hand, "you know it *is* a coincidence, right? There is zero connection between one thing and the other—you know that, right?"

I looked down at my shoes, not seeing them because I was blinded by embarrassment and shame. "Intellectually, yes, I know that," I said in a small voice. "But I'm having a hard time not feeling weird about it."

We sat there a moment, still hand in hand though I couldn't bring myself to look at Ricky. Finally he said, "I mean, I'd be willing to leave a trail of dead bodies in our wake if that's what it took—"

"Ricky!" I was looking at him now, trying to convey horror at his bad taste but mostly trying not to laugh. He was unperturbed either way.

"—But if you feel weird about it, we can drop the subject for now." He started to get up, reaching for the camera bag he had flung on a nearby chair the night before. "Don't we have a hike to do this morning or something? Let's get out of here.

Change the subject. Change the vibes. Get away from this talk about death."

I followed him toward the door, but as he reached it he stopped and turned back, putting a finger to his chin, pretending to have an idea. "You know, there might be a way to break this little curse you're so worried about."

I rolled my eyes and smiled. "What's that?"

"Next time I ask . . . say yes."

Chapter 4

Our itinerary for the day did indeed start with a hike, before our spa appointment in the afternoon for a couples massage. I was grateful to Ricky for pulling us back in the direction of plans and order.

It also occurred to me to be grateful for the natural beauty all around us as we motored north on the highway, the road hugging the coastline, sometimes along the sides of ruggedly forested coastal bluffs, sometimes dipping down to sea level and running along marshy or sandy beaches. There was a peace here that almost allowed me to forget what had happened the evening before.

Ricky seemed to be feeling the mellow vibes, too; his driving, which tended toward the aggressive in crowded urban settings, became more relaxed and smooth—almost sedate, even—in these calming environs. His summer wardrobe, already a little questionable in Northern California's June gloom, had made few concessions to Oregon's even grayer skies; he was still in shorts and sunglasses and a nautical-looking Breton stripe T-shirt, but in a nod to today's activity he had at least traded his sandals for sneakers. As he steered his car through the highway's sweeping curves, he began to whistle softly.

"You really are feeling better, aren't you?" I said.

"Yep," he said cheerfully, then turned a funny smile on me. "I—well, not to make you uncomfortable, or to feel obligated to do it again, since apparently we're a deadly combination—but I'm very responsive to touch. So when you cuddled me last night—"

My face burned red. It seemed we were going there after all. "Would we call it that?"

"Call it what you want," he smirked. "Anyway, it was very helpful, and I appreciate that you did that."

"It's okay," I said stiffly, trying not to let myself get too flustered.

"No, I really am grateful. I'd like to do something for you in return."

I gave him an incredulous look. "You do lots of things for me, all the time. You've done all the driving, for one thing. And you help me talk to people, even though it's not your job, and you . . . you . . . wear those shorts. . . ." I trailed off, staring at his legs more boldly than I ever had before and not catching myself because I was too busy wondering how that last bit had made it all the way out of my mouth. Not that it wasn't something I deeply appreciated, but I was surprised at myself for saying it.

Ricky glanced down at his legs and grinned as he flicked the turn signal to leave the highway and head inland toward our trailhead. "You're welcome for that," he laughed, returning his eyes to the road, which was now a winding two-lane country route following a small river through a narrow green valley. "And for the other things, but you did make me think of something I could do for you."

He pulled the car onto the loose gravel shoulder of the road and turned off the engine. He turned toward me and put his arm across the back of my seat. "Also, I've been thinking about something I'd like to propose."

My stomach did a little flip, and my mouth went dry. I gulped and croaked, "What's that?"

"I've been thinking about our assignment here—Drea's whole 'find romance' thing—and I had an idea about how we could get into the right frame of mind."

I was suddenly flooded with visions of what ideas Ricky might have had, which I realized were actually ideas that, on some subconscious level, *I* was having, all of which were wildly inappropriate and terrifying and thrilling. I forced myself to nod so he'd continue.

"Well," he went on, pushing his sunglasses up onto the top of his head, revealing the mischievous sparkle in his eyes, "when you're just good friends, like we are, being told to go out and 'find romance' feels like a lot of pressure, right? Going on a trip in search of romance is something that people who are already in romantic relationships do. So, what if—only for this trip, for the purposes of this assignment, mind you—*we pretend that we're already in a romantic relationship*?" He finished with a satisfied smile.

"Huh? You lost me," I said.

"You pretend I'm your boyfriend, and I'll pretend you're my boyfriend. That way, seeking out romance will feel more natural. And, since it's only pretend, there's no pressure to *actually* be romantic; but it'll help you think that way."

This seemed like a stretch, but I was starting to see an upside. If Ricky and I were pretend boyfriends, it might provide some cover to get past this whole *will we or won't we* pattern I felt like I kept getting us stuck in and to finally go for it. I wondered if Ricky was thinking along similar lines; something in the faintly wicked arch of his eyebrows told me he might be.

"So, how would this work?" I said slowly. "How do we pretend to be boyfriends?"

"I think it's pretty much all mental," he replied. "You don't have to second-guess me, because you know I'm your boyfriend and I like you, and I can think the same way about you. So we can be more comfortable together, and be more present in the moment to look for the romantic angle for our story, because our relationship is established. We don't have to do anything different physically," he said, his grin turning into another smirk. "We don't have to hold hands or cuddle or get all lovey-dovey or anything. And you don't have to keep pretending to objectify me and my little shorty-shorts. Unless you really want to."

My face was engulfed in flames of embarrassment. "Um, okay, good," I stammered.

"Maybe it would help with your curse, too," he said, twisting the knife even deeper. "What do you think? It's kind of a goofy idea, but maybe it would help?"

It was a deeply silly idea, one that, if I agreed to it, would be as purely a pretense on my side as I hoped it was on his, a shortcut to getting to where I really wanted to be. I tried to summon the same nerve I had the night before when he'd proposed going into the hot tub. "Okay, sure. Let's do it," I finally said.

"Great!" He reached the hand that had been draped over my seat back up and through the hair on the back of my head, half tousling and half massaging. I wondered if he was going to pull me in for a kiss—wondered, hoped, tomato, tomahto—thinking that that would be a very non-pretend way to embark on a pretend relationship, but instead, after a second he pulled his hand away, reaching his arm back over me to his side of the cabin.

"So, for my first official act as your pretend boyfriend, and to repay your kindness last night, I said I had thought of something I could do for you," he said. "It would also kind of be something you did for me, too; you mentioned that I had been doing all the driving. . . ."

I wondered where this was going. "What did you have in mind?"

"Would you like to learn how to drive?"

"What, now?" I hadn't expected this.

"Sure. It's quiet here. We have a little time. Did you ever want to learn?"

I thought about this for a minute, hoping that if I dragged out this answer, I might also be able to postpone responding to Ricky's offer. "Maybe I kind of did, when I was younger," I said. "My dad really wanted to teach me, but then, right before I was old enough, he died."

"Aha," Ricky said. "I could see where that might dampen your enthusiasm."

"I suppose it did, for a while," I agreed. "And then I was in college, and then working, and getting around fine without it. So eventually I kind of forgot about it. It didn't seem necessary."

"I could see that," Ricky said thoughtfully. "But it seems funny that you're a travel writer, but you can't do the simplest, most spontaneous kind of traveling, you know?"

"I hadn't really thought of it that way before," I said.

"I mean, driving around town can be a real pain," he said. "I get why you wouldn't mind not having to do that. But getting out on the open road and going somewhere—I don't know, I like it. And it's always nice on a road trip with your pretend boyfriend when you can share the driving duties." An eyebrow shot up as he smirked at me.

"Sorry," I said, feeling a little guilty again.

"I'm teasing, mostly," he said. "So how about it?"

It was a gray, cool day, but I suddenly felt very sweaty, much more nervous than I had been when Ricky made his proposal, which I had mostly felt intrigued by. I nervously took stock of the metal dashboard of Ricky's car with its flight-deck array of inscrutable gauges and lights, the rudimentary lap belts around our hips, that terrifying ball-on-a-stick shifter sticking up between us. "Is this the best car to learn in?"

"Absolutely. Best way to learn. Manual transmission, no power steering or brakes—if you can learn to drive this car, anything else will be a piece of cake."

"Uh, gee, I don't know. I mean, I don't have a learner's permit or anything."

"I don't think you need one at your age," Ricky deadpanned.

I regarded him suspiciously. "Is that true?"

He grinned and shrugged. "If it isn't, who's going to know?"

I usually like to build myself up to learning new skills. But Ricky wanted to do this for me, and I wanted to make him happy, and there was the hot little Ricky devil on my shoulder once again, now my fake-but-maybe-secretly-not-so-fake boyfriend, even, making me want to do things that previously I'd never have wanted to do, so I said, "Okay, then. Teach me to drive."

"Yes!" Life-size, non-devil Ricky gave the steering wheel a celebratory thump.

My legs were only a little wobbly as Ricky and I each rounded the car to switch places, but upon taking the driver's seat I found my sweaty palms slowly sliding their way down the thin plastic rim of the steering wheel as I goggled in complete incomprehension at the instrument panel and wondered if I should be doing anything with my feet.

"Okay," Ricky said from the simplicity that I hadn't known to cherish of the passenger seat. "Don't look at the instruments for now. Let's start with the feet. There are three pedals, right?" I nodded numbly as I shifted my gaze down. "You can remember them like this: A, B, C. From right to left, you have your accelerator, your brake, and your clutch. You'll use your right foot for the accelerator and the brake, and your left foot for the clutch. The car's off right now; when we go to turn it on—not yet—you'll want your right foot firmly on the brake, and your left depressing the clutch, all the way down."

I practiced putting my feet on the correct pedals. "Jeez, why don't they feel the same? I want them to feel the same. Don't I want them to be in sync or something?"

"No, you don't," he said firmly. "Now, before we turn the car on, but while you have the clutch in, let's practice shifting gears. We have the car in first right now; you can see the shift pattern on the knob there. Keep the clutch in, and see if you can go from first to second, then to third, then fourth." I obediently tried to wrangle the knob through the gears, mostly successfully, I think.

"Now let's find neutral," Ricky said, and he put his hand over mine on the shifter and a shiver ran straight up my arm. He guided my hand gently to the center, wiggling the knob to demonstrate. "See, here you're not in any of the gears. You might go into neutral if, say, you're getting off the freeway and there's a red light at the end of the off-ramp. You're reducing speed very quickly, right? So you could go from fourth into neutral while you brake, without having to go down through third, second, first."

"While we're here," I said coyly, "why don't you guide me through all the gears?"

"There he is," he grinned, onto my ruse, but he humored me and guided my hand through the full shift pattern.

"So, are you ready to drive?" he asked.

"Nope," I said with conviction.

"Good. Put it in first, foot on the brake, clutch in, and turn the key."

Oh, boy. I followed the steps, and the car rumbled to life. The steering wheel vibrated a bit under my grip. Ricky showed me how to release the parking brake.

"Now, the clutch is in, right?" I stared down at my feet and nodded. "Okay, take your foot off the brake. We're not going to give it any gas yet. You're going to slowly lift off the clutch, only until you feel it start to release and the car start to move. Then you're going to hold the pedal in that position and drive with only the clutch for a minute. Does that make sense?"

"Nope," I said cheerfully, knowing it wouldn't matter.

I watched as I gingerly took my right foot off the brake, then craned my neck for a better angle on my left foot as I started to release the clutch. Millimeter by millimeter, my foot raised further from the floor until finally, slowly, the car started to creep forward.

"Okay, good, hold your foot right there," Ricky said calmly. "And, Oliver?"

"Mmm-hmm?"

"Please look out the windshield."

My neck snapped up, my eyes wide in terrified realization, and the car sputtered to a halt as the engine stalled. "Oh no! What did I do?"

"Well, you probably came off the clutch when you looked up. The trick is to work the pedals *without* having to look at them. But the road is very straight here and there's nobody around, so it's okay. Let's try again."

I tried again, and again and again, stalling a couple of times but mostly getting the hang of letting the car creep forward with the clutch partially out, then bringing it to a stop by pushing the pedal back down. Finally, Ricky decreed that I was ready to try giving it a little gas.

"You know where to hold the clutch to start moving, right?" I nodded, a little more confident but still too nervous to speak. "From there on out, as you release the clutch further, you'll start to slowly push down on the accelerator."

This was more working together than my feet were used to doing, but after a couple of tries, I was successfully off the clutch, puttering slowly down the road in first gear, sweat running into my eyes from my forehead.

"Okay, Oliver, you're doing great!" I didn't feel great. "We're looking out the windshield, we're off the clutch, we're moving. Ready for the next step?"

"What's that?" I asked, slightly frantically.

"The next step is to breathe."

"Oh, jeez," I said on a ragged exhale. I brought the car to a stop.

"Are you feeling okay?"

I considered this. My stomach was still knotted in panic, but there was something strangely exhilarating about learning this terrifying new skill. And, I thought with pride, learning the hard way, not only finally being able to drive, but lapping many of my peers by being able to drive a stick shift.

"You know," I said, "I think I am. Thank you for doing this."

Ricky smiled broadly, his dimples appearing as he flashed his perfect teeth, which by itself was almost reward enough to have made the whole stressful exercise worthwhile. "I'm excited for you! And you're really doing well. We can stop soon if you want to, but first I want us to try one more thing—let's see if we can get you out of first gear and into second. You think you can try that?"

Of course I wasn't sure, but I gritted my teeth and nodded through Ricky's explanation of the mechanics of changing gears while on the move. As I started up the car again, I resolved to methodically walk myself through the steps.

Brake on; clutch in. Turn key; release parking brake; foot off the brake; slowly lift off the clutch until you feel it engage; gently start to push the gas. Look out the windshield; breathe. Notice the curve in the road ahead and wonder whether to try shifting before or after getting to it; reach the curve while still debating; feel the car start to buck because it's still in first. Hear a horn honking nearby, getting louder and angrier; try to give it more gas to stop the bucking, which somehow makes it worse; look around frantically for Ricky to give some instruction; catch sight of the rearview mirror for the first time, and notice the flashing headlights on the honking pickup behind you. Start to flap your hands and scream in panic.

Yep, I had hit all the steps. Except for the one about trying to get into second gear. And the screaming and flapping might have been an improvisation.

"Oliver, it's okay, it's okay," Ricky was shouting over my screams, grabbing the steering wheel and giving it a gentle rightward tug toward the shoulder. "Let it stall. Just get off the gas."

I realized as the car juddered to a stop that I hadn't been able to hear any guidance from Ricky over my intense focus on following the steps. The pickup on my tail, which had seemed enormous in the rearview with its lights flashing and horn blaring, turned out to be a little old red Toyota as it zipped past. I labored to catch my breath as Ricky reached over and rubbed between my shoulder blades.

"Sorry," he said. "I threw a lot at you this morning. Becoming fake boyfriends, learning to drive—big day!"

"Dead guy last night, too," I wheezed. "Lots of ups and downs."

"Yeah," he agreed. "Maybe I'd better take back over the driving."

I was a little alarmed to see the red Toyota pickup in the parking area for the trailhead at the end of our drive, but as we began our hike and didn't encounter anyone, the quiet and solitude around us calmed the last of my jangling nerves, and I tried to refocus on taking in the details of our hike for my story.

The narrow trail followed a stream that bubbled and burbled along over rocks, winding its way through a thick, emerald-green forest, occasionally dipping out of sight through a thicket of giant, primordial ferns. Opposite the stream, the trail was hugged by a hillside, with the odd giant boulder shouldering its way out through the verdant vegetation. Rivulets of water trickled down some of these, pooling a little where they met the ground, then getting absorbed under our feet on their way to join the stream.

At one point, the trail passed through the wide, low-hanging canopy of a tree; Ricky parted the leaves, which reached nearly to the ground, and together we entered its private, cool green embrace. The trunk of the tree grew up along the edge of the path, and as we passed through, Ricky stopped, leaned against the trunk, and grabbed my arm, pulling me up next to him. I put my hands behind my back, feeling the rough bark of the tree against my arms, while on the side of my right arm I also felt the cool skin of Ricky's arm next to me.

"See, this," he said at length, "this is a romantic spot."

I took it in some more. It was definitely private. Our closeness within the sweep of the hanging leaves felt almost overwhelmingly intimate, and the dappled light flickering through the branches onto Ricky's face brought out the gleam of his teeth and the sparkle of his eyes and deepened the shadows in his gorgeous dimples and the crinkles at the corners of his eyes as he smiled at me.

I smiled back. "What kind of romantic things does it make you want to do?"

I was angling for him to show me, not tell, and for a second as he seemed to lean further into my arm, I got really excited. "Well, the obvious answer is that this would be an excellent make-out spot," he mused—absolutely the right answer—then, to my eternal frustration, he pulled away. "But I think what I really want to do is to take a picture of you here."

This was disappointing news. I hated having my photo taken. "Are you sure? Sometimes the obvious answer is the right one," I said.

"Yeah, but I feel like that would violate the spirit of our fake relationship, which is that I get to tease you with suggestions like that, not actually act on them. C'mon, I want to take a picture. This is a perfect spot."

I groaned, but let him position me against the tree trunk, trying to follow his instructions and not look too posed.

After he'd snapped off a couple of pictures, I broke the pose. "Why don't you tell me how to take your picture? You'd make a better model than me."

"Been there, done that," he said breezily, slinging his camera back over his shoulder. "Anyway, I got what I need."

We left behind the cocoon of the tree and continued down the trail. As we neared its end, the rushing of the stream grew louder and the hillside grew steeper and the boulders grew more numerous until, rounding a corner, we were greeted by the sight of a magnificent waterfall cascading hundreds of feet down a rocky bluff, splashing over boulders and pooling and churning into a small pond that lapped at our feet at the trail's edge before feeding into the stream.

I stood for a moment, taking in the awe-inspiring scene, made even more magnificent by the sun finally breaking through the morning's cloud cover. I sensed Ricky moving by my side and turned to see him dropping to the ground, where he began to take off his shoes and socks. I grinned and sat down next to him, following his lead, and together we dipped our toes in the freezing cold pond and stepped gingerly from one slippery rock to another in its shallows, laughing and occasionally reaching out to grab each other by the hand or arm to stay upright.

Finally growing too cold, I scrambled up the side of a massive boulder at the water's edge, finding a luscious pool of sun on its top where I could stretch my legs and feel my toes returning to an acceptable temperature. Ricky stayed below for a while, snapping photos, before coming up to join me in my basking. He spread out next to me, our arms again touching. I reached over and began lightly tracing an idle path on the back of his hand with my index finger.

"Now you're teasing me," he purred after a moment, his face still pointed to the sun with his eyes closed behind his sunglasses.

"Two-way street." I grinned.

The sun was getting higher, suggesting that we should think about heading back to the inn for lunch before our couples massage in the afternoon. We climbed down from our perch, put our shoes back on, and began the hike back to the parking area in comfortable silence. As we passed back through the drooping tree, a wicked impulse seized me and I paused for a moment, taking Ricky's hand as he drew up alongside me. I pulled him close and brought my face toward his, as if to kiss him. I hovered there for a beat, teasing him, then in a husky whisper said, "You're right. This would be a great make-out spot."

Then I dropped his hand and ran.

He ran after me, laughing and wheezing out, "You're getting too good at this!"

We had slowed to a trot, still giving each other goofy grins, by the time we emerged from the trail into the clearing, dotted with picnic tables and punctuated to one side by a small copse of trees, between the trailhead and the parking lot. I had my eyes on my target, Ricky's car; the red Toyota pickup was still parked nearby and another car, a gray Mazda hatchback, had parked next to Ricky's.

"Hey," Ricky said in a low voice, grabbing my arm to get my attention. I snapped back out of my focus, noticing for the first time that his wasn't the only voice nearby. My gaze followed his in the direction of the farthest picnic table, almost obscured by the clearing's lone grove of trees, where two figures sat, deep in conversation. Facing us was a woman in her mid- to late forties, with somewhat boxy short brown hair and wearing a somewhat boxy gray windbreaker. The second woman, sitting with her back to us, had vaguely familiar flaming red hair.

Ricky was still looking intently. "Isn't that the sister of the dead guy? Lis? The redhead," he clarified.

Vaguely familiar, indeed. "I think you're right."

"Should we go say hello?" He started toward the trees.

I stayed rooted to my spot. I wasn't sure why we had to go out of our way to talk to this woman we barely knew who hadn't seen us. But Ricky seemed determined. "Ricky, wait," I hissed at his back, then jogged to catch up.

He was deep in the shadows of the trees by the time I caught him, and just as I did, he stopped short. The boxy brunette's voice had risen, and now her words reached us.

". . . Don't you get it?" she said, the exasperated edge growing sharper with every word. "Richard's death is the opportunity we've wanted. Do you know how much is on the line here?"

"Yeah, let's not interrupt them," I whispered to Ricky.

"Shh," he said, furtively looking around to make sure we were still cloaked in shadow and that the women hadn't seen us.

Lis's companion went on. "You've laid the groundwork to get back in her good graces. You need to make sure she changes the will. The time is now."

Lis's head fell into her hands, and her back shuddered as though she was crying. The other woman lowered her voice, reaching across the table and apparently trying to tamp down her own emotions to comfort Lis.

"Okay, come on. Let's go," I whispered to Ricky, uncomfortable with spying any longer. We turned and walked as quickly and as quietly as we could back to the car.

Ricky and I were both silent as he began the drive back down the narrow, winding country road. I was puzzling over what we had overheard, trying to figure out what it could mean. Ricky and I had both stopped in our tracks when we heard the woman mention Richard's death. And the mention of a will, with a great deal on the line, was a tantalizing mystery. Richard's death had looked like a ghastly accident; I wouldn't have called an accident like that an "opportunity," and I didn't think I'd want to know anyone who would. To speak so crassly to his sister, when the wound was so fresh—and she had seemed affected by it. But now I wondered: was it grief . . . or guilt?

CHAPTER 5

"So, that conversation," I said to Ricky as we neared the highway back to the Rose Beach Inn. "That sounded kind of . . . suspicious, didn't it?"

"I was thinking the same thing," he nodded. "It seemed easy to assume that what had happened last night was an accident, but what if it wasn't? Nobody seems to know if he was drunk or otherwise impaired, but if he wasn't, how likely is it that a presumably healthy middle-aged man would simply fall off a balcony?"

I thought about this. "I wonder what the sheriff's deputies found in his room. Are they treating it as an accident?"

We both pondered this for a minute as we motored up the highway, following its curves as it dipped toward and away from the coastline.

My ponderings took a turn. I'd been having a great morning for the most part, other than my terrifying driving lesson, and even that held a certain kind of satisfaction. Most importantly, all of the morning's activities had been largely successful at keeping my mind off last night's horrors. I had a job to do, a promising fake relationship to nurture—into the real thing, if I could figure out how—and some sense of equilibrium and order to maintain. Whatever had happened to Richard Rose, and whatever his sister and her companion had been talking about, seemed like Rose family matters, not something Ricky and I needed to go bumbling into.

I turned to Ricky. "We're not doing this again, are we?"

"Doing what?" He raised his eyebrows in a mock-innocent look.

"Making a mess of our plans by playing detective. It's none of our business. The police are on it. We have work to do. Besides, don't we have more important, more fake-boyfriendy things to be doing?"

"Hmm. When you put it like that," he said, his expression turning from mock-innocent to mock-solemn. "But there's no harm in keeping our eyes and ears open, is there?"

I was incredulous. "Really? After what happened last time, in DC?"

"What happened last time? I had fun," he said. "And we got our work done, too. Our job here is basically to be on vacation. That's not that hard. And there are lots of couples that solve mysteries together. Like Nick and Nora Charles. And Holmes and Watson, and, um, the Curies, solving the mysteries of science."

"Huh." I thought back to my trip to Washington. My sense of the experience had been colored over time by the stress of getting my article ready for print and my feelings of guilt and regret over not keeping in better touch with Ricky. If I put myself back in those moments, though—racing around town in Ricky's car, seeing places and meeting people I otherwise wouldn't have, laughing and joking and bouncing ideas around with Ricky, learning after a lifetime of preferring to work alone that I could do so much more if I had the right person to do it with—*had* I had fun?

Maybe I had.

* * *

We stopped near the turnoff to the village of Rose Beach, down the highway from the inn, at a bakery and deli that Drea had wanted us to include in our piece. We chatted briefly with the owner, Ricky took pictures of their beautiful displays of towering cakes and gem-colored petits fours, and they sent us on our way with two generously layered sandwiches on fresh-baked bread so that we could get back to the inn in time for our massage appointment.

We decided to eat our lunch quickly in the lounge and then go straight to the spa. As we entered the lobby we encountered Mary Alice in deep conversation with her late cousin's widow. Rachel stopped talking at the sound of the door, turning her sharp, perpetually displeased glare toward us. After what she had been through in the last day, I was willing to let her feel however she liked. She was as carefully and tastefully put together as she had been last night, but there was no disguising the dark circles under her eyes.

She reached out a hand to stop us as we passed through to the lounge. "Is one of you Oliver? You're the ones from the magazine, right?"

"Yes, that's right," I said.

She lowered her hand to her hip. "I wonder if I could ask you a big favor. My daughters and I were hoping to get a little rejuvenation at the spa—it has been a trying day, you know."

I nodded, wondering what this had to do with us.

"Well, anyway, they were saying that the soonest they could get us in for a massage was at four o'clock, but they mentioned that you had an appointment at one, and I was wondering if you'd mind taking the later time so we could go sooner?"

Aha. I didn't even bother to think about whether the change would affect any plans we had for the afternoon. "Of course we can do that. No problem."

"That's wonderful, thank you," she said. "I'll let Letitia know, so you just come at four." She waved us on and turned back to Mary Alice, and we continued into the lounge.

Rachel either didn't know or didn't care that there was no privacy between the lobby and the lounge; as we arranged our lunch on one of the round tables in the center of the room, she resumed what she had been saying to Mary Alice, at full volume. "Anyway," she said, "I simply want to be sure that you understand. Richard's death doesn't wipe the slate clean. The money came out of my trust fund, for God's sake! He shouldn't have even loaned it to you."

"I do understand," we heard Mary Alice murmur in return. "I'll do my best to keep to the repayment agreement I had with Richard. You know how grateful I am for the improvements we've been able to make to the inn."

"Improvements!" Rachel snorted audibly. "If he had never made you that loan, there would have been no hot tub for him to fall into. What a stupid way to die!"

Ricky and I stared across our sandwiches at each other, eyebrows raised, but it seemed the conversation was over. A few seconds later, we heard the ding of the elevator doors, and the light tapping of Mary Alice's computer keyboard resume in the lobby.

"It was okay to take the later appointment at the spa," I said to Ricky, "right? I don't think we have anything else this afternoon that we can't work around."

"Yeah, it was fine," he said. "It was the right thing to do. Those ladies need the break."

"What do you want to do instead after lunch?"

As Ricky was thinking, a short, round-faced man with close-cropped salt-and-pepper hair rounded through the doorway from the lobby into the lounge, headed directly for our table. He was wearing brown suit pants, his shirtsleeves rolled up and his tie slightly loosened. His gold watch and brown leather shoes looked moderately expensive—more than I'd be able to afford, anyway.

"Excuse me, sorry to interrupt," the man said. "You're Mr. Popp and Mr. Warner, correct? Mary Alice said I'd find you here. May I join you for a second?"

I invited him to take the empty chair across from us, and he sat down. "What can we do for you?"

He pulled a business card from his shirt pocket, passing it across to me. It read, BRADLEY P. BENSON, ATTORNEY AT LAW. "I'm the personal attorney to Mrs. Cecilia Rose," he began. "As I think you know, her son Richard died unexpectedly last night. Mrs. Rose asked me down here today to help her draft a new will as quickly as possible. A will in Oregon has to be attested by two witnesses, and it's best if they have no potential interest in the estate. Mrs. Rose called her personal secretary in, but we need a second witness. Since you two are the only guests here who are not related to Mrs. Rose, I was hoping I might impose on one of you to be that second witness? Perhaps you, Mr. Popp?"

Ricky and I exchanged a quick glance. His eyes were dancing—keeping our eyes and ears open, indeed! After the conversation we'd overheard earlier about this very will, to have this opportunity drop into our laps was catnip to him. I had to admit to myself that I was probably almost as curious. We nodded at each other.

"I'd be happy to help," I said. "You tell me when and where."

"If you're not busy now," Mr. Benson said. "As soon as you finish your lunch, that is."

He remained at the table with us while we finished off the last bites of our sandwiches, then I got up and followed him to the elevator, down two floors, then up the hall to Mrs. Rose's room. He let us in with a key card, rapping lightly on the door as he opened it.

Mrs. Rose was sitting on the couch near the door to the balcony, her hands limp in her lap, staring straight ahead at nothing. I had only seen her briefly in the lounge the evening before, but she gave the impression today of being noticeably smaller than before. She wore a simple black dress, against which her pale face and red-rimmed eyes stood in stark contrast. Only when we had made it all the way across the room to stand before her did she seem to notice us.

"Cecilia, this is Mr. Popp," the lawyer said, and I stepped forward to offer my hand. Mrs. Rose made no attempt to rise, but weakly shook my hand. Sitting in the armchair next to her was a birdlike woman in her late sixties, with long dark hair and wearing a floral print dress, her hands working deftly at knitting a small brown hat. "And this is Mrs. Rose's personal secretary, Miss Trixie Moon," Mr. Benson said.

"Well, I'm retired now, actually, but always happy to help when Cecilia calls," Miss Trixie said to her knitting, ignoring my offered hand. "I was with her for over forty years, so there's not much I haven't done for her already."

Mr. Benson invited me to be seated, and as I sank down into the armchair next to Miss Trixie's, I sensed Mrs. Rose regarding me more intently.

Finally, she addressed her lawyer. "Is this one old enough?" I blushed as I realized she was pointing at me. "He has to be over eighteen to be a witness, right?"

"I'm, uh, twenty-four," I stammered. "I'll be twenty-five in two months."

"Oh?" Her voice was weak, but her tone carried a note of amusement. "Well, I suppose you'll be old enough then to witness a will *and* rent a car. Brad," she said, turning to the lawyer, who had sat down next to her on the sofa, "do we really need strangers for this? Couldn't you do it, or your secretary? Or someone from the family?"

"No, Cecilia," he chuckled. "I can't draw up the will as your lawyer *and* witness it. And neither can my secretary, and besides, he's not here. It's best to have witnesses who would have no expectation of inheriting."

"Gee, thanks," Miss Trixie mumbled to her clacking needles. "It was only forty years, after all."

Mrs. Rose ignored her. "Well, then, get that Tawny tart to do it. She should know not to expect anything from me, and she might as well know that, thanks to her, Wiley shouldn't, either. She and Trixie can do it, and we don't have to bother Junior here."

"We have two people here now," Brad said firmly, "and I don't think bringing your feelings about Tawny into it would be especially useful. Can we proceed? All we need Mr. Popp and Miss Moon to do is to watch you sign, and then they sign to attest that they saw you do it. It's not complicated."

"Yes, well, that's as may be," she said, again regarding me sharply. "But maybe let's not be strangers anymore, then, eh? Get to know each other first. What about you and your friend, the Black fella? You're here together?"

"Yes, ma'am, that's right," I said, taken aback by her blunt description. "His name is Ricky Warner. We're working together on an article for a travel magazine."

"But you're sleeping together, too, right?"

"Cecilia!" Brad flashed me an apologetic look. I blanched, wondering if Ricky and I were fake boyfriends to the public, too, or only with each other, but Mrs. Rose was unperturbed.

"What? I'm old. I'm allowed to stop pretending I have a filter at my age. You two are fancy boys, right? What word do you like these days? Gay? Queer? My daughter used to say that one was a bad word, but now she uses it, so who knows anymore."

"I suppose you could use either of those words, as long as you say them with respect," I said, as gently and with as much sympathy as I could muster for this grieving, if apparently bigoted, old woman. "But yes, we have a personal relationship as well as a professional one." I guess that decided that.

"Well, I don't mind telling you I've never quite understood all that," Mrs. Rose said. "But I'll tell you why I asked. I don't think you should sign something if you don't know what's in it, and that includes my will. Just don't go blabbing about it to my family, you got that?"

"Certainly," I nodded, wondering where this was going.

"See, my daughter, Elisabeth, she's like you and your friend," she continued. "And I'm trying not to have a problem with it anymore. I still don't understand it, but I suppose I can admit I don't see what's so harmful in it, either. Especially now that . . ." She choked a little on a rising sob, looking down to her lap and reaching one of her wiry hands to her attorney, who took it and patted it reassuringly.

She composed herself and returned her slightly bleary eyes to me. "You see, my children, Richard and Elisabeth—and my husband's brother's son, Wiley, he was like a second son to me. They were all so close. And when Elisabeth told me that she was . . . that way . . . well, I didn't understand, and we quarreled terribly, and then for years we didn't speak to one another. So I took Elisabeth out of my will, and put Wiley in as a secondary heir; if Richard went before me, Wiley would get everything. But over the last couple of years, I've been thinking about it. Against my expressly stated wishes, Wiley married that *woman*, that Tawny character. And Elisabeth has been very patient and kind with this old woman who gave her nothing but grief for the last twenty-five years. And now my Richard is gone. . . ."

Her voice warbled as her tears rose again, but she continued, her words wavering unsteadily. "I simply have to do right by my child. Elisabeth is my child. I did so much for Wiley, who isn't even my own son, and he took from me when he wanted to and rejected me when he wanted to. Elisabeth never asked anything from me but love and understanding, and she still loved me when I couldn't give her those things. I was such a fool."

Miss Trixie, her knitting still in one hand, had been digging in a large tote bag at her feet with the other, and now produced a large blue handkerchief, which she passed to Mrs. Rose. Mrs. Rose dabbed daintily at the corners of her eyes.

"Well," she said, clearing her throat again. "Now you know what you're signing. I'm making sure that Elisabeth is my sole heir. It's a lot of money. What is it these days, Brad, over a hundred million?"

"It's not quite a billion," he said, "but it's several hundred million now."

"You see, my late husband's family . . ." Mrs. Rose continued, unfazed by the vastness of her fortune. "Well, Rose Beach is named after the Rose family, obviously. We were big in timber around this area back until the eighties. But I came from a more modest background, and I wanted my children to know how to take care of themselves, so once they were done with their educations, they were set loose. No trust funds or anything like that, though then Richard married Rachel with her big fat trust fund. And Wiley can keep fending for himself, too; he's a grown man, and if he wants his independence with little Tawny, let them have it. Tell me, are you close with your mother and father?"

"With my mother, yes," I replied. "My father passed away."

"And she knows? She knows you're sleeping with a—"

I nodded, again trying to summon compassion, and hoping to curtail her line of inquiry.

Her voice dropped to a whisper. "—With a *Black* man?"

I was running really low on compassion. "Yes, she knows," I said through gritted teeth.

"Cecilia, I think we've harassed Mr. Popp enough," Brad said. "Can we get on with the signing?"

"My first husband was Black," Miss Trixie piped up from her knitting.

"Paul was your husband?" Mrs. Rose regarded her with a mixture of shock and curiosity. "I thought you were shacking up with him, that's all. I never thought you'd marry him."

"Cece, we were married before I even met you. I probably should have stayed married to him." Miss Trixie finally looked up, only to stare dreamily into space in front of her, as if gazing into the past. Then she turned to me. "They're such wonderful lovers, aren't they?"

No wonder the marriage hadn't lasted. I'd had enough. "Ladies, this is all getting very offensive," I said, indignation momentarily overcoming my usual dislike of confrontation. I knew I'd feel terrible later, and they probably wouldn't, and I hated that outcome for all of us, because it all seemed totally backward. "If you want me to help you, let's get on with it and stop making these generalizations and, and . . . comments, and . . ."

Brad jumped in smoothly as my nerve petered out. "That's a great idea. Cecilia, here's a pen," he said, pulling the small stack of documents on the coffee table toward her. She harrumphed a little as she signed the final page of the will, and then Miss Trixie and I each signed in turn as her witnesses.

"Well, thank you, Junior," Mrs. Rose said as I rose, extending her hand to me. "I am glad you have it easier with your mother than Elisabeth did with me. And enjoy your friend. He is a looker, isn't he?"

Brad walked me to the door. "Sorry about all that, and I do appreciate your help," he said, stepping halfway out into the hallway with me as I left. “And please do keep what she told you in confidence. About the will, that is—you can talk to your therapist or something about the other stuff if you need to.” He laughed nervously at his attempted joke. I didn’t know what to say, so I turned and headed toward the elevator to go find Ricky.

Chapter 6

Ricky wasn't in our room, so I returned to the lounge and found him sitting at the far end of the bar. He had a book open in front of him, but he was staring out the massive picture window toward the infinite westward expanse of the Pacific, his chin resting in his hand. At the other end of the bar, the two redheaded girls we had seen the night before, Richard and Rachel Rose's daughters, were slumped together, talking listlessly with Erik behind the bar.

I slid onto the stool next to Ricky, saying in a low voice, "Well, that was interesting."

He turned, smiling at me. I had been feeling confused and unsettled after my conversation with Cecilia Rose, but Ricky seemed genuinely happy to see me, which both recentered me and, in a whole new way, threw me off my guard. "You're back! What did you find out? Do you know who's in the will? Tell me everything!"

I was still dazzled by his shining eyes for a second, but as I gathered myself, the one solid thought about the meeting that settled in my mind was that I had been sworn to confidentiality. "I can't tell you everything. Mrs. Rose is very rich, and also kind of a racist homophobe. I think that's all I'm allowed to tell you."

He knit his brows. "What do you mean, you can't tell me?"

"I mean, they asked me not to say anything. About the will, anyway—I was given permission to talk about the racism and homophobia."

"I like gossip as much as the next person, but I thought we were going to get some intel—and by 'we,' I mean *we*, not just you." Ricky poked my arm accusingly.

My stomach knotted a little. Didn't Ricky understand confidentiality? "But I promised," I protested. "I said I wouldn't say, and that means I won't say."

Ricky looked a little hurt. I felt awful. "Okay, I understand," he said. Then he brightened again. "How about I take a guess. You don't have to say anything, except whether I've guessed right."

I considered this. I felt like looking for loopholes was not really in keeping with a confidentiality agreement, either, but I had hated that hurt look on Ricky's face. The knot in my stomach twisted. "I don't know. Maybe."

Ricky stroked his chin in a pantomime of deep thought. "Richard and Lis are her only kids, right? Can you tell me that?"

I nodded. That was fair, I figured.

"So, logically, if Richard is dead, that means Lis is now the sole heir, right?"

I shrugged as my stomach did a couple of somersaults.

"That's it? A shrug? How about you blink twice for yes, once for no."

I kept my gaze steady on Ricky, not blinking. He gave me a strange half smirk.

Finally, he shrugged, too. "Okay, I get it. You're not going to tell me."

"It's just, I promised I wouldn't," I squeaked.

His face softened, and so did the pit in my gut. "I won't

push. I'm sorry." He stuck a bookmark into his book, closing it, then looked back at me out of the corner of his eye. "But Lis is now the sole heir, right?"

I tried to summon an enigmatic smile, and blinked three times. Let him figure that out.

"Anyway," he said, rolling his eyes and turning fully back toward me, "I've been thinking. About what we overheard, and about this will you won't tell me about, and how they might be related. Lis and that other woman were concerned that Cecilia should change her will as soon as possible—and now, here she is, changing her will. That's an odd coincidence. And it also seems odd, immediately after the death of a brother, for the sister to only be concerned about how it affects her standing in a will. Which makes me wonder whether she wasn't concerned about this will *before* Richard died, and maybe did something to help him die to allay those concerns. Can you tell me what you think about that?"

I considered this. The whole way that the Rose family related to one another, with every family tie wrapped up in financial considerations, seemed odd to me, and the conversation Lis had been having had seemed callous at best, if not outright suspicious.

"I think," I said carefully, "that you're right that there is something strange about this family. Maybe being super rich does that to you—makes all your relationships about money."

"Which," Ricky said, "is awfully dehumanizing, and might make it easier to do something to someone who's standing between you and even more money. To Lis, maybe Richard only represented the difference between half a fortune and a whole fortune."

"That's possible," I said, with some relief that Ricky had landed more or less on the truth about Mrs. Rose's will without my having to tell him anything.

Ricky continued, "What do we know about the circumstances of Richard's death? We know he was in his room upstairs, supposedly alone. His wife and daughters had gone somewhere, right?"

"To a movie," I said. "Rachel said he was working in their room."

"That's right. When we came back to our room, we could hear that he was playing music. Then the music stopped, and he fell off the balcony. Or, it was made to look like he fell, I should say."

Ricky's last words were lost to me as I got caught up in a strange sense memory. I snapped back into focus. "Ricky," I said, "are you sure the music stopped *before* he fell?"

He went still for a moment, thinking hard. "I don't know," he said slowly. "Logically, I assumed that he had to have turned it off before he fell. But I don't actually know."

"And if the music went off *after* he fell . . ." I said.

Ricky completed the thought. ". . . Then that means he wasn't alone."

We both thought in silence for another minute. *What had come first, the music stopping or the fall?* I couldn't remember.

Ricky cast his eyes down to the bar. "I'm sorry, all I can think of when I try to remember the sequence of events is the body falling. I don't have any idea whether the music was on or off at that point."

I felt bad for forcing him to revisit that moment. I wished I could remember, but all I kept coming back to was how strangely still Ricky had gone, and how much it had terrified me. "Don't think about it," I said, rubbing his arm lightly. "I'm sorry. I'll try to remember, don't you worry about it anymore."

He shuddered. "Yeah. Didn't need to go back there. But it makes me wonder what the cops found in his room. Like, was anything amiss there? Nobody's talking about suicide, so I assume they didn't find a note or anything. But was there any clue to what he was doing before he fell? Or any sign of another person in the room?"

I looked at Ricky curiously. For someone who didn't want to revisit his memory of seeing Richard fall to his death, Ricky seemed awfully willing to dwell on every other aspect of the situation. "Are you sure you want to be asking all of these questions?"

He looked pensively away from me for a minute, out the big windows again, then turned to stare across the bar and shrugged. "It's hard to explain. I don't want to picture that moment, but I guess it feels like if I understand what happened, maybe I'll be able to face it. Does that make sense?"

I considered this. The Rose family's drama had felt like a big distraction, none of our business, but we kept getting dragged into it, and I had to admit that my curiosity was bubbling up. And, on the one hand, I wanted to be sensitive to what Ricky had witnessed and not upset him, and maybe try to focus on working on our article, but on the other, he seemed to think that getting involved would help, not hurt. What was a good fake boyfriend to do in this situation?

Oh, who was I fooling? My anxiety, my fear of failure, my impostor syndrome always made me feel like Ricky's excitement for these extracurricular shenanigans was a distraction, from doing my work and achieving my professional goals. But on some level I knew that all he was doing was giving me permission to do what I really wanted to do—to color outside the lines a little, try something risky for once, and dig into something and find some answers purely because we wanted to, not because someone else wanted us to. He was the little devil on my shoulder, but the little devil is always voicing your own true impulses and desires, isn't he? All a good fake boyfriend had to do in this situation was smile and go along with it.

So I smiled. "Sure, I think that makes sense. So how do we answer those questions?"

"Maybe this will help," Ricky said, looking past me down the bar.

I followed his glance and caught the backs of the two girls leaving the lounge, and Erik ambling toward us, giving me a little wave and a bashful smile.

"Hi, Mr. Popp," Erik said shyly, ignoring Ricky as was his custom. "It's Erik, remember me?"

I groaned inwardly, but tried to keep my outward expression neutral. "Of course I remember you," I said, as patiently as I could.

Erik was chewing a little at the corner of his mouth and seemed to be trying to make his eyes as big and brown as he could. It sobered me to realize that he and I were closer in age than Ricky and I were, and under other circumstances he might come across as appealing, even cute, but right now his act seemed a bit much.

"So, um," he was saying, "remember how I said I want to be a travel writer, too? I hope you're not embarrassed or anything—I Googled you, to see what you've written."

I hoped that this exercise had taken away some of my shine for him; there would not have been a very impressive number of results. But instead, he leaned over the bar with a conspiratorial smile, suddenly seeming far less coquettish and far more confident. His voice became husky with excitement. "Did you really get to solve a murder in Washington, DC?"

I hadn't thought of it as a job perk at the time, but I was realizing now that I could be as proud, if not more so, of that fact as I was about the article I had written about the trip. "Yes, *we*"—I indicated Ricky, who gave Erik a wave—"we did figure out what had happened, I guess."

"God!" Erik seemed positively thrilled. "I love to travel,

you know, but what I really want is adventure. I can't believe your job is even better than I was hoping!"

I knew we wanted Erik to help us, but I didn't want to lead him on too much. I had some sense of professional ethics to consider. "Um, you know that's not a normal part of this job, right? I don't think you should expect anything like that to happen if you become a travel writer."

Erik's enthusiasm was undiminished, which was perhaps a good sign of his potential usefulness to us in the present circumstances. "And now you're here and there's been another death! Do you think this one was murder, too? Are you going to solve another case?"

Ricky leaned in. "Maybe it was. What do you think?"

Erik became solemn. "It was definitely weird. Who falls off a balcony? Maybe he was pushed. Or maybe he was already dead, and his body was thrown off the balcony!"

Ricky and I exchanged a glance. There was a look in Ricky's eyes that I had seen before, one that used to make me nervous. It was a look that usually preceded some impulsive action, and it was the look of a man who I was powerless to stop—that had been my lie to myself, anyway. Now I knew that it was the look of a man who was going to take me somewhere I wanted to go but was afraid to enter on my own.

He turned back to Erik. "So have you heard anything? Did you hear about anything the cops found in his room?"

"I was there," he said, his chest swelling a little with pride. "I let them into the room, and was there while they searched."

I didn't stop myself from being almost as shameless as Ricky. "Did they find anything?"

He deflated. "I don't think so," he shrugged. "They seemed sure that he had just fallen by accident."

"What about you?" Ricky asked. "Part of being a writer is being observant, right? Did you notice anything amiss? You probably know these rooms better than anyone else."

"Dang, I should have looked more closely." Erik seemed disappointed in himself.

One of Ricky's eyebrows shot up, an even surer sign that he was looking to stir things up. "Has anything been touched in the room since last night?"

"No," Erik said slowly, looking skeptically at Ricky. "The sheriff asked us not to clean it up yet. Nobody's even been in there."

"But you could get in, right? You have a passkey?"

Erik brightened, sensing adventure. "Oh, snap! I do have a key! Do you guys want to go look with me?"

Ricky was grinning broadly. I grinned, too, knowing that my former urge to protest would have been a waste of effort and feeling liberated at giving up the pretense. Ricky had maneuvered Erik as successfully as he usually played me. I nodded my permission to Ricky, saying to Erik, "Yeah, okay, sure. Lead the way."

Erik made a show of skulking through the lobby as we passed from the lounge to the hallway leading to Richard and Rachel Rose's suite on the main floor, ostentatiously looking over his shoulders to make sure we weren't observed. He put a finger to his lips as he slid his passkey into the lock on the door, and waved us through as quickly as he could.

The room we had entered was similar to the ones Ricky and I had already seen, except that the corridor leading from the door to the main space was longer, with a small second bedroom opening off the hallway in addition to the usual bathroom and closet. I poked my head through the bathroom and bedroom doors. Rachel Rose had removed her personal belongings, and the room hadn't been slept in since Erik's last cleaning service the previous morning, so there was little to note. There was a used hand towel on the bathroom counter, but the other towels were still neatly folded, and the bathroom wastebasket contained only a single wadded tissue. The bed in the bedroom was still neatly made, as was the one in the main room at the end of the corridor.

The main room was very similar to our room, with a sitting area between the king-size bed and the windows to the balcony. There was a TV mounted to the wall above a credenza, on top of which were two stacks of books. I quickly scanned the titles, most of which seemed to be about the minutia and arcana of economic theory. Not my idea of fun bedtime reading, and probably not particularly relevant.

Erik was stalking around the room, trying to hone his powers of observation. Ricky and I met in front of the sofa in the sitting area, both of us putting our hands on our hips and looking around from this vantage point.

"Not much jumping out at me," I said.

"Yeah. But what about the music? I don't see a radio."

"Erik," I called, "Richard was listening to music before he fell. We could hear it downstairs. Do you know how he might have been playing it?"

Erik stopped mid-stalk and looked around him, then shrugged. "Maybe on his laptop or his phone? I don't see either of those, though. His wife probably has them."

Ricky reached for the TV remote on a side table next to the sofa. "Maybe he had one of those music channels on," he said as he pressed the power button.

The TV blinked on, and after a second's delay, classical music burst out of the speakers.

"Shhh!" Erik lunged for the remote, powering off the TV. We all stared at the now-dark screen.

"Guess that was it, anyway," Ricky shrugged.

I turned to Erik. "You said you let the police into the room when they arrived last night. The music wasn't playing when you came into the room?"

Erik scratched his head and thought for a moment. "No,"

he said slowly. "I remember thinking how quiet it was when we came over here. There wasn't any music."

Ricky and I exchanged a meaningful look. The music had been off, so someone had turned it off. I screwed my face up, trying to remember whether the music was still playing when I heard the splash of Richard falling into the hot tub. If it was, that would mean somebody else had been in the room with him.

My gaze drifted down to the remote next to the couch, and I could tell Ricky's eyes had followed mine when I heard him mutter, "Oh, jeez."

Oh, jeez, indeed. Maybe there had been fingerprints on the power button that could have told us who had pressed it last—Richard, or someone else. But now those fingerprints were Ricky's and Erik's. When our eyes met again, Ricky flashed me an apologetic grimace.

"Well, I guess we kind of messed up any potential evidence there," he sighed. "Does anybody see anything else?"

I realized that something about the room did feel odd, though I couldn't figure out what it was. I looked around again. Thinking vaguely of the bedroom on the other side of the wall next to the bed, I remembered something I'd heard the night before, when Lis and Mary Alice had been figuring out how to shuffle rooms.

"Last night, your mom mentioned that Richard and Rachel had a second room, for their daughters," I said. "So why did they need a separate bedroom here?"

Erik knitted his brows. "I don't know. I hadn't thought about it before, but when they checked in, Rachel made a big deal about needing this suite, which is why it wasn't available for you, and . . . well, I did have to make up both beds yesterday."

"So they were sleeping separately," Ricky mused. "Maybe that's something."

"There's something else bugging me," I said, "but I can't put my finger on it. Ricky, this part of the suite looks more or less like our room, right?"

He looked around. "Yeah, basically identical, I think."

"Most of the furniture is the same in all the rooms," Erik nodded. "Only some of the small decor items are different, like the paintings on the walls and some of the lamps and stuff."

"I feel like I'm missing something," I insisted. "Something's not the same as our room." We all looked around again.

"Would it help to go down to our room, look there, and see if you can figure out what's different?" Ricky offered.

"Maybe," I said.

We all trooped out of the room, Erik reprising his cartoon cat burglar act, then took the elevator down to our room. As we entered, I thought I caught Erik glancing jealously back and forth between Ricky, me, and the bed, but I tried to ignore him and focus on what was different from the room we had been in a moment before.

The walls were the same clean eggshell white. The couch was upholstered in the same sturdy olive-green twill, the chairs in the same dusty blue. The furniture was the same lustrous golden-toned wood. The paintings on the wall weren't identical, but were the same general sizes and color palettes.

But there was something here that I hadn't seen upstairs. The floor in our sitting area was warmed by a cream-colored sisal rug layered on top of the wood-grain laminate, and I realized that the Roses' room hadn't had a rug.

I pointed down. "Does every room have a rug in the sitting area?"

"Yeah," Erik said. "I have to vacuum them every day."

"But there wasn't a rug upstairs," I said.

"There wasn't?"

Ricky was excited. "Are you sure? Can we go back up to double-check?"

Back up we went. Erik forgot to make a show of going into the room this time, and we all rushed straight to the sitting area. Our steps echoed off the bare faux-wood floor. There was no rug, though some streaks of dust on the otherwise clean floor suggested that there had indeed been one.

Ricky was the first to speak. "Well, gang, what do we think this means?"

CHAPTER 7

Erik plunked dazedly down to the floor. He landed cross-legged and absently ran a finger through a ridge of dust left behind by the missing rug. "I can't believe I didn't notice that," he muttered.

I felt bad for Erik. "Don't beat yourself up," I said gently, lowering myself onto the edge of the sofa. "There was a lot going on. You weren't specifically looking for anything—we made you think about it after the fact, and it wasn't on your mind in the moment."

Erik nodded glumly on the floor.

"Anyway," Ricky chimed in, "I think the important question is, *why* is the rug missing? Was there something incriminating on it?"

Erik looked up at us, his eyes going wide. "Like blood?"

Ricky shrugged, looking at the floor. "Maybe, but I don't know. There wasn't a lot of blood after he fell into our hot tub. Matter of fact, I'm not sure there was any."

I had a disturbing thought. "Could he have already been dead awhile before his body fell into the hot tub? There wouldn't have been bleeding if he'd been dead long enough. Maybe he was killed in here, on the rug, and then his killer threw the body off the balcony."

We all grimaced at each other. After a thoughtful moment, Ricky said, "I wish we could find out what the medical examiner determined was the cause of death. I had assumed he died of internal injuries sustained when he fell onto the hot tub, so there wouldn't have been much blood anyway. But maybe it happened like you said. . . ."

He rubbed his chin slowly. "I don't know, though. Erik, are all the rugs the same?"

Erik nodded. "Yeah, they're all like the one in your room."

Ricky nodded back. "That's a woven fiber material, right? If there was blood on the rug, I have to think it would seep through and get on the floor underneath, too. I don't see any trace of blood here, do you?"

We all scanned the floor, which showed no stains. "The killer could have cleaned the floor after removing the rug," Erik offered.

"But then there wouldn't be any of this dust," Ricky pointed out. Erik inspected his dusty fingertips, meditatively rubbing them together.

"Okay," I said, "so we're back to asking why the rug is gone. Also, where did it go?"

Erik leaned over, peering under the sofa. I got up and Ricky and I began opening closets and kneeling down to look under beds. We ventured out onto the balcony. There was no sign of the missing rug. We regrouped in the sitting area.

I pondered this latest wild goose chase Ricky and I had set out on. We had no concrete proof of Richard Rose's death being anything but a weird accident. Were we making something out of nothing? My instincts said no, that there was too much about this situation that didn't smell right. The Rose family's immediate focus on the chain of inheritance seemed too cold, and between the music and now the rug, I was increasingly, uneasily convinced that Richard hadn't been alone in this room before he went over the balcony railing.

Maybe this was a promising tack: who could have been here with Richard?

"Erik," I said, "I'm going to test your memory and your powers of observation again. But I know at the time you weren't necessarily trying to be observant or remember anything, so it's fine if you don't have answers."

"Okay?" His expression was somewhere between eagerness and anxiety.

"Last night, when we came by the lounge, most of the family was gathered there, right?"

"Yeah, that's right. I think everybody was there at one time or another."

Ricky chimed in, "When we arrived, Richard had already gone to his room, and his sister, Lis, wasn't there, either. Right?"

"That's right," I agreed. "And while we were there, Richard's wife Rachel and their two daughters left to go see a movie. And Tawny followed us out. Did she ever come back?"

Erik thought for a second. "No, she didn't."

"It was about twenty minutes between the time we left the lounge, and the time Richard fell into our hot tub. Did anybody else leave the lounge during that time?"

"We already covered almost everybody anyway," Erik pointed out. "I think Wiley left a minute or two after you guys, which left me, my mom, and Aunt Cecilia. My mom and Aunt Cecilia talked for a minute while we cleaned up, but I'd say after you left, everybody was out of the lounge within about ten minutes."

I deflated a little. "So that's not very helpful. I suppose Rachel and the daughters are in the clear since they actually left the premises, but as far as we know, everybody else stayed here, right?"

"Nobody else drove away, anyway," Erik said. "I took some trash out after we left the lounge, and all the cars were in the parking lot except Richard and Rachel's BMW." His eyes darkened as a thought flashed across his face. "Wait a minute. Rayleigh and Rielle told me their mom dropped them off at the movie. She didn't go in with them. So we don't know where Rachel was."

Ricky and I exchanged a glance. He asked Erik, "How far away is the movie theater?"

"I dunno, five, ten minutes?"

"Maybe we should go there and see exactly how long it takes," Ricky said. "The difference between five and ten minutes could be an important one."

I knew what he was thinking. At five minutes there and five minutes back, Rachel might have had enough time to drop her daughters off and return to the inn before her husband's death. At ten minutes each way, maybe not. Did she have an alibi, or not?

We didn't exactly invite Erik to come with us into town, but as we passed through the lobby on our way to the parking lot, he breezily told his mother that he was taking his lunch break, and once outside, he clambered eagerly into the backseat of Ricky's car. He hovered between us as Ricky drove out toward the highway, leaning forward over our shoulders, offering directions and brimming with excitement to be shadowing a real travel writer, no matter how many different ways I tried to gently tell him that what we were doing was very much not normal travel writer stuff.

To get to the town of Rose Beach from the Rose Beach Inn involved taking Highway 101 up through the coastal forest for a couple of miles, until we reached a cross street, with signs pointing to a historic lighthouse to the left, on the water, and toward the town to the right, headed inland. This road wound down through the woods from the highway into a small valley. As we descended, passing only the occasional small house set back from the roadway, Erik peppered me with questions about the parts of my job that seemed to interest him most, almost none of which were actually related to the work.

Do you get to go everywhere for free? (Kinda, yeah.) *Do you get to go to a lot of parties at the places you go to?* (Not if I can help it.) *Do you get to travel internationally a lot?* (My mom took me to Vancouver once, does that count?) *Do you think restaurants and hotels give you better service than everybody else?* (Probably, which I mostly find embarrassing.) *Did you guys meet through your work?* (Yep.) *You probably get to meet a lot of hot guys, though, going so many places, right?* (Ummm . . .) *So, like, is it serious between you two, or . . . ?* (What are you getting at, kid?)

I caught Ricky's eye in the rearview mirror, and we each raised an eyebrow at each other. There were signs of a town forming around us, as the buildings became more frequent and got closer to the road, some even with cars parked in front of them that were more than yard art.

"We're looking for the movie theater," Ricky drily reminded Erik.

"Yeah, keep going. We'll hit downtown in a couple blocks."

Up to this point, *blocks* had been a loosely defined concept, but presently cross-streets did start appearing more regularly; the street sprouted sidewalks and decorative, vintage-style streetlamps, and the urban core, such as it was, of a small, early twentieth-century lumber town emerged around us. The Bijou theater was hard to miss, its moderately elaborate neon marquee anchoring one of the three main blocks that constituted downtown Rose Beach.

I consulted my watch as Ricky angled the car into a parking spot in front of the theater. The drive from the inn had taken us seven minutes.

"Inconclusive," I said. "We think it was about twenty minutes, but we don't know exactly how long it was between when Rachel and the girls left the inn last night and when Richard died. But she could have gotten here, dropped the girls off, and gotten back to the inn within about fifteen minutes. She'd have had to work fast, but she might have been able to do it."

Ricky turned to Erik. "Any idea if anyone around here might have seen them here last night, and could tell us where Rachel went during the movie?"

Erik nodded in the direction of the box office under the marquee of the theater. "I know that kid working in there. He goes to my old high school. We could ask if he was here last night. He might remember."

We got out of the car and followed Erik, stopping on the sidewalk as he ambled over to the little glass-enclosed booth. The bored-looking teenage boy inside brightened as he recognized Erik, calling out through his tinny microphone, "Yo! What up, bruh?"

"What up, K," Erik said, self-consciously lowering his voice.

"Aww," Ricky whispered to me, "looks like we've got a closet case on our hands."

I looked up and down the street at the tiny, quaint expanse of Rose Beach. "Small town life, I guess," I whispered back. No wonder Erik wanted to figure out how to travel out into the wider world.

"I can't believe I gotta spend my summer here," K was saying to Erik. "And then I still have another year. You're so lucky you graduated."

"I've just been working, too." Erik shrugged companionably. "Listen, K, were you here last night?"

"Yeah, man, it was dead," K said.

"My cousins were coming down here last night," Erik said, cocking an eyebrow at the boy. "I bet you noticed them, right?"

K perked up. "Couple of redheads, yeah? One of them was kinda . . ." He mimed a pair of large breasts in the air in front of himself. "Yo, did they say something about me? You can tell them they can hit me up, bruh. Give them my Insta."

"Sure," Erik said. "But did you see their mom with them, too?"

K gave Erik a dubious look. "Their mom? Yeah, she bought their tickets. Wait, did *she* say something about me? I dunno, man, some moms are hot, but she seemed a little . . . like, stuck-up or something."

"Uh . . ." Erik, blushing deeply, looked to me and Ricky for help. We both shrugged and grimaced. I mouthed to him, *Where did she go?* How he got that information out of this cringeworthy conversation with K was going to have to be his problem.

He turned back to his friend, cocking his shoulders a bit in an effort to regain his cool-older-dude façade. "She paid for the tickets, huh? Yeah, uh, she has a lot of money, you know. Like, a *lot*."

Some of the doubt passed from K's face. "She's really rich, huh?"

"Yeah," Erik nodded. "Did you see her car? She has a new BMW. It's sick."

K nodded appreciatively. "Is it that green one? It was parked right there last night. I was checking that out all night. That thing is fire."

Bingo! I had to admit I was impressed with how Erik had maneuvered this information out of K—or, at least, how he had stumbled onto the right tack.

Erik seemed pleased with himself, too. "So she didn't leave after she bought the tickets?"

"Nah, man, she walked off somewhere and came back when the movie was over and they all left together."

"Did you see where she went during the movie?"

K shrugged. "No, but, like, she probably went to the café. Everything else is closed at night."

Erik nodded. "Yeah, I bet you're right. Thanks, man."

K's face clouded over again. "Hey, look, you can tell your cousins I said hey, but I'm not sure about the mom. I mean,

I'm not eighteen yet or anything; I don't want to get her in trouble."

"You're probably right," Erik said, blushing again. "She'll, um, be disappointed, but I'll tell her you weren't interested." With an attempted fist bump through the ticket slot, Erik left K and returned to us. "Jeez, that got weird. But it sounds like Rachel stayed here and didn't go back to the inn until after the movie, so I guess I cleared her, huh?"

Ricky patted him on the shoulder. "Good job. But a journalist's job is also to verify the facts."

"What do you mean?" Erik was confused, and I was worried that Ricky's imagination was going to run away with him again.

"I mean," Ricky said, "that we should check at this café and see if she actually was there. What if she got a ride back to the inn, in an Uber or something, leaving her car here to establish an alibi?"

"I don't think we have Uber here," Erik said doubtfully.

"And that would be a little convoluted anyway," I said, giving Ricky's imagination an affectionate half smile. I was briefly torn between thinking he was being silly, and wanting to play along, knowing that it would tickle him if I did. Fake boyfriend duty called. I asked Erik, "Where is the café? I suppose we should check this alibi."

"Okay," Erik said with a shrug, leading the way down the street. Ricky gave me a triumphant smile, and I grinned in return as we followed.

The café was two doors down from the theater, on the corner. A hand-painted sign in the shape of a coffee cup and saucer hung out over the sidewalk above the door, bearing the name RONNIE'S ROASTERY. A bell over the door tinkled as we went in, and a short, wide-set, middle-aged woman bustled out from the back room and beamed at us over the counter.

"Well, hello, Erik," she said warmly, then a tinge of worry

entered her face and voice. "Your mom didn't order more muffins, did she? I don't think I have an order from her."

"Hi, Mrs. Wise. No, no muffins. I was just, um, showing these guys around town."

Her smile brightened again, and she turned it on Ricky and me. "New friends?"

"Well, we're staying at the inn . . ." I started.

"He's a travel writer," Erik said. "Mr. Popp. And this is Mr. Warner, he's a photographer."

One of Mrs. Wise's plump hands flew up to pat the gray-streaked bun on the back of her head. "Mercy! A photographer! And a travel writer, too. Gosh, uh, what do I have for you? I'm kind of picked over from the lunch rush, but I think there's some cake back here. . . ." She whirled around to a refrigerator along the back wall, pulling a tall chocolate cake, a few slices missing, into view.

Ricky was quick with his camera, shooting me a wink as he pulled it from his shoulder. "Hold it right there! That's too perfect." Mrs. Wise beamed, holding the cake in front of her apron-clad bosom as if presenting it to the judges on a TV baking competition show. He took a few more shots of only the cake after she set it down on the counter, and a few more as she slid a knife through it to cut off a generous slice.

"Compliments of the house," she said, handing me the freshly plated cake and a fork. "I can't believe I'm going to be in a travel . . . uh, what do you write for? A blog? Are you on social media? Do you need to make a video of me dancing? I know some of the TikTok dances." She started to shimmy a little.

"It's a magazine," I said quickly. *"Offbeat Traveler."*

"A magazine! How quaint."

I carefully cut off a portion of the cake and passed it to Erik, who ate it with his fingers. I took a couple of bites of the remainder, then passed the fork and the plate with the rest of the cake to Ricky.

"That's really delicious," I said. "What are your other specialties?"

"Well," Mrs. Wise said, bringing a tray with three glasses of milk to the table, "I started this place as mostly just a coffee shop, but there aren't too many restaurants in town anymore, so I'm doing a good business these days in sandwiches and salads for lunch and dinner. I get cheese from a local dairy farm, and bread from the bakery out on the highway, and I make my own pies and cakes and scones and muffins. I usually run out of scones and muffins within an hour or two of opening," she said proudly. "And I supply some to Mary Alice for the inn sometimes."

It was getting a little late for lunch, but was still far too early for dinner, and the café was empty of any other patrons. I wondered how busy her "good business" in sandwiches and salads made her. Would she remember if Rachel was there the night before?

Nothing to it but to ask. "How busy are you during a typical lunch or dinner hour? Like, for example, how busy were you last night?" Smooth, right?

She screwed up her face a little, thinking back. "Last night? Hmm, I'd say last night was kind of slow. I probably had seven or eight parties for dinner, and a few folks in for coffee later in the evening."

"My mom's cousin Rachel came into town last night," Erik said, gulping down some milk. "Maybe she came in. Kind of tall, red hair?"

Mrs. Wise nodded. "I think she was here. Pretty lady, very elegant, but not too friendly?"

Erik nodded vigorously. "That sounds like her."

"Yes, she was here for a little while, having an espresso. She was waiting by herself for a while, and then a man came and met her here, and they talked for a bit. Seemed like they were trying to keep their meeting very private." She seemed to consider this for a moment, then said to Erik in a confidential tone,

"It seemed like none of my business, and maybe that means it's none of yours, too. Forget I said anything."

We wouldn't forget, but we didn't need to know more. Rachel's whereabouts around the time of Richard's death seemed to be accounted for. We thanked Mrs. Wise profusely for the cake, and I took down her contact information, promising to let her know when the article went to print.

As she walked us to the door, she put one arm around me and the other around Ricky, standing between us and squeezing a little and saying to Erik, "These are good friends for you, Erik. You need to find more like them so you don't get lonely when they're gone."

He lowered his eyes and mumbled a goodbye as we tumbled out onto the sidewalk. Apparently his closet door wasn't closed as tightly as he might have been hoping, but it was nice to know that he had support waiting for him on the other side when he decided to really open it.

I looked around at the streetscape as we walked back toward Ricky's car, scanning the narrow storefronts, many of them vacant, a few housing boutique shops and small business offices. A sign across the street caught my eye and stopped me in my tracks, a guilty thought flashing across my mind.

"Ricky," I said, and he and Erik stopped and looked at me, then followed my finger as I pointed across the street at the sheriff's office. "Should we tell the sheriff what we figured out? About the rug?"

"Maybe," Ricky said, a little doubtfully. Working with law enforcement wasn't really our usual style, inasmuch as we had one, but we also usually worked more on hunches and suspicion. Having an actual, tangible—or intangible, as the case may be—piece of evidence and not sharing it felt wrong.

"C'mon," I said, stepping into the street. "Maybe we can get some information, too. Like what kind of injuries Richard died from."

This seemed to appease Ricky, and he and Erik followed close behind as we crossed the street and entered the storefront office. Behind the desk sat the deputy I recognized from last night, her long blond plait emerging from the back of her brimmed hat, winding over her shoulder, and ending with an incongruously frilly white bow.

I read her name badge. "Hello, Deputy Duncan," I said. "I don't know if you remember me. I'm Oliver Popp, and I'm staying at the Rose Beach Inn?"

She nodded crisply. "Yeah, I remember. The hot tub drop-in. What can I do you for?"

I hadn't fully worked out my approach. "I wanted to check in and see how the investigation into Mr. Rose's death was going. See if you needed anything else from us to help."

She shrugged. "Not really. Not much to investigate. He fell, looks like by accident, and broke his back and neck when he hit the Jacuzzi on your balcony."

Ricky rested an elbow on the desk. "Those were his only injuries?"

"I think so," Deputy Duncan said, keying something into her computer. After a pause, she said, "Yep, preliminary report from the medical examiner said the cause of death was consistent with how he fell and where he landed. Death was instantaneous," she added. I think she was trying to be reassuring, but it still sounded horrible.

"Okay, that's good to know," I said. "Erik, you said you had something to tell the deputy, right? What you saw when Rachel asked you to go into the room to get that . . . *thing* for her?"

"Huh? Oh, yeah," Erik said. "Yeah, I didn't notice it before. But it's weird, and I thought maybe I should tell you. The rug was missing from their room."

Deputy Duncan didn't seem too interested. "The rug?"

"Yeah, from the sitting area," Erik said.

"Are you sure there was a rug there?"

"All the rooms have rugs," Erik said.

"He has to vacuum them every day," Ricky piped up.

"Huh," Deputy Duncan said. "I'll make a note of it, but I don't know if we'll be able to do anything with that information. Maybe he moved it. Did you look in the closets and stuff?"

"Yes, we did, and we didn't find it. Anyway, we thought you should know," I said, feeling less guilt about withholding information, but a little new guilt that we seemed to be annoying the deputy.

"Okay," she said. "Let me know if it turns up. Maybe that will give us something to work with. But by itself, I'm not sure if there's anything to do."

As we returned to the car, I had to satisfy myself that we'd done our due diligence. We'd learned that Richard had almost certainly died from the fall, not earlier, in his room. We'd checked out Rachel's alibi and cleared her, which left . . . only the rest of the Rose family as suspects. We'd have to see if we could find out what the other family members had gotten up to after they'd left the lounge.

And as we rode back to the inn, Erik chattering happily again from the backseat, I had another thought, one that was worthy of Ricky's wildest flight of fancy. He had to be rubbing off on me, I told myself, as I resolved not to share this new wrinkle with him, lest he allow himself to really run with it.

It seemed so far-fetched, so silly, but I couldn't stop turning it over in my mind: Rachel had sat alone at the café, waiting. A man had joined her, and they had conferred privately. Before we knew that she had gone to the café, Ricky had speculated that she had left her car conspicuously parked downtown as a cover; we now knew that wasn't true, but what if her presence downtown was the cover? Who was this man? An accomplice? A hired killer? What did he tell her when he arrived? That the deed was done?

I looked sidelong at Ricky, who was driving and trying to patiently field Erik's questions and chatter. Maybe he had gotten too far under my skin, to the point that I was starting to think like him. I chuckled darkly to myself, and wondered how I could find out, on my own, who the man was and what he and Rachel had done.

CHAPTER 8

"I gotta get back to work," Erik said to me as he climbed out of the backseat on our arrival back at the inn. "Thanks for letting me shadow you. It was really exciting to see an actual day in the life of a travel writer!"

"You saw about five minutes in the life of a travel writer," I corrected him. "All we did that had anything remotely to do with my job was eat that cake."

"You have such a cool job," Erik said, giving me a last starry-eyed look as he turned to head inside, clearly still not listening.

I sighed. Ricky had come around and leaned against my side of the car, and he grabbed my arm and pulled me back as I started to follow Erik toward the inn. I yielded, leaning against the door next to him.

"Cute kid, huh," he said.

"I feel bad," I replied. "I think he thinks my job is always like this, and he won't listen to me when I tell him it's not."

Ricky shrugged. "He's not bad at the detective thing, though. I think he mostly wants to be a travel writer so he can escape small town life. And the fact that he has a huge crush on you isn't helping."

"Maybe," I said uncomfortably, avoiding Ricky's eye. I looked around before turning back to Ricky. "Why are we hanging out in a parking lot?"

"I wanted a minute alone. Erik's a nice kid, but we've spent enough time with him, and I want to make it clear to him that I have dibs on you."

I pursed my lips at him to suppress a smile, and leaned into his side a little. "Pretend dibs, anyway," I said.

Ricky pulled his phone out of his pocket to check the time. "We still have a little while before our spa appointment," he said. "Want to walk down to the beach? Get ourselves in the mood for our massages?"

I followed him toward the trailhead that led down the bluff to the inlet below. "What mood? You need to be in a mood for a massage?"

"For a couples massage, yeah, it helps," Ricky said over his shoulder as we began our descent. "Remember our assignment? *Romance*. A couples massage is supposed to be romantic."

"Really? Aren't you, like, lying face down during a massage?"

The trail was narrow, but broadened a little as we reached a long set of stone steps hugging the side of the bluff below the inn. Ricky paused to let me catch up, grinning at me as we started going down side by side. "You've never had a massage, have you?"

"No," I admitted.

"Okay, well, if you went by yourself to get a massage, it would probably be all about relaxation. But a couples massage"—he smirked at me—"is meant to be *sexy*."

I gulped. "Sexy how?"

"I'm not sure what it'll be like today, but a lot of the time there's a Jacuzzi or a big bathtub, and they give you time before the massage to bathe together. Sometimes they'll give you Champagne to drink in the tub."

I tried not to picture being in a tub with Ricky. An alarming thought about bathtubs came to me as I continued to try not picturing it.

As if reading my mind, Ricky continued, "And, of course, you're both naked the whole time. With a fluffy robe for modesty when you're not in the tub or on the massage table, but otherwise . . ."

I was glad I was walking on the inside, hugging the wall of the bluff. Otherwise, I might have fallen off the side of the staircase.

"*We* don't have to be . . . though, right?" I hoped there wasn't too much panic in my voice. "I don't think a pretend relationship covers getting . . . um." *Naked*. My mind was working overtime, conjuring up all kinds of exciting, terrifying images against my will.

Ricky grabbed and squeezed my hand, his eyes melting into concern that he had gone too far. "No. Oliver, I'm sorry, I was only teasing you. It's totally fine to wear a swimsuit, or keep your underwear on, or whatever you're comfortable with. And I'll avert my eyes, if you tell me to."

"Only if I tell you to?"

He grinned and shrugged, the wickedness returning to his eyes as he dropped my hand and pulled ahead of me as the trail narrowed once again. There was a final, slightly steep downhill curve before we reached the small cove far below the inn. A few scraggly trees and a low, tangled cover of bushes spilled down a short distance at the base of the bluff before giving way to a half-sandy, half-rocky beach strewn with driftwood, fallen branches, seaweed, and other natural detritus that gave it a wild, untamed feel, nothing like the broad bathing beaches I was used to. At the north end of the cove, the bluff jutted far out toward the ocean, capped by a distant lighthouse.

Ricky pulled his ever-present camera off his shoulder, snapping a few different angles of this sweeping vista. I found a large log and sat down, pulling off my shoes and socks, trying to stay clear of Ricky's camera as I crossed the beach to the water's edge and waded in. I tried to let the chill of the water, rising and falling over my toes, my feet, sometimes up to my ankles, distract me from my nerves about the massage. I wasn't sure whether to be grateful to Ricky for preparing me in advance, or resentful of him for making me anxious about it in advance.

I waded out a little further, curling my toes around the smooth rocks underfoot to keep my balance, momentarily lost in thought. As anxious as I was, I realized, I was also a little excited. There was no deluding myself; as terrifying as they were, these repeated brushes with a scantily clad Ricky also came with an exciting, sexy sense of possibility. Would the day ever come when I'd be able to bring myself to capitalize on any of those possibilities? I wished I could feel any confidence in myself on that score.

I looked around, remembering how Ricky and I had held hands as we waded in the pond this morning and wondering if I could engineer a repeat performance by coaxing him to join me here. As I turned, though, I caught Ricky snapping photos of me wading from his vantage point on the sand, grinning at me as soon as he realized he had been discovered.

"Cut that out," I called, "and get out here."

He sat down on the same log I had, removing his shoes and leaving his camera behind. He sloshed out to me, doing a slo-mo pretend run, then bending down and miming splashing me without actually kicking up any water. I waited for him with my hands on my hips.

"Why do you keep taking pictures of me?"

"You're very photogenic," he said.

"I don't buy that," I grumbled. "Maybe from behind."

"I think you can take my word for what is and isn't photogenic," he said. "I am a professional photographer, after all.

And I am myself a photogenic person, so I know of which I speak."

I remembered a stray comment he'd made earlier. "Did you say you'd been a model?"

"Only a little," he said, shrugging dismissively. "A few times in high school and college. Mostly regional stuff. I only did, like, one national campaign. Maybe two. I was always more interested in what the photographers were doing. Well, and in my fellow models. There was some fun to be had there."

I goggled at him. I mean, I could believe it—he was easily the best-looking person I'd ever seen in real life. It made a certain amount of sense. But it also made his pronouncements of my own suitability as a photo subject all the more suspect.

He narrowed his eyes at me. "Are you gonna be weird about this? It was not a major storyline in my life, just something goofy I did for a while, mostly at my mom's urging."

I recovered myself. "No, it all makes sense to me. My only question is, if our topic is 'romance,' won't pictures of me by myself seem kind of . . . sad?"

"Hmm," he said thoughtfully. "My take is, our readers, being mostly women and gay men, will see these pictures of this enigmatic, beautiful young mystery man"—I blushed and looked down at my toes rippling in the water—"and put themselves in the position of being here with you, being romanced. But you may have a point. Come here."

He grabbed my hand and marched us purposefully out of the water, back up the beach to our log. He sat me down and spent a few minutes moving our shoes, smoothing the sand in front of me, and getting more sand to stick to my wet feet. Then he caked his own feet with sand, sat down close to me, and grabbed his camera.

"This might get weird," he said. "I'm going to get a picture of the beach, with our outstretched legs and feet centered in the foreground."

"I had gathered that. What's going to get weird about it?"

"I'll probably have to kind of lean into your lap to line up the shot."

"Um, okay. I guess that won't be a problem." Unless I thought too hard about it.

It turned out to be a good core workout, me holding a controlled backward lean at about a sixty-degree angle while Ricky bobbed in front of me and snapped off a round of pictures.

"Okay," he said, turning as we both straightened up, that wicked glint back in his eye. "Let's do another pose. Stay there, I'm going to scoot over here, and we're going to angle our legs toward each other." He crossed his feet at the ankle, indicating for me to do the same. "Now, put your legs up on top of mine."

"What are we doing here, playing Twister?"

"No." He grinned as he leaned in to take a few photos in this new pose. "But we should do that sometime. Sounds fun."

I laughed nervously. After another burst of his shutter and a moment's inspection of the results on the screen, Ricky set his camera back down on the log, though he didn't seem inclined to change position. A big part of me wasn't, either, but the louder, more persnickety part of me needed to get this sand off my feet.

"Are we done? Should we . . ." I searched for an excuse to put my shoes back on, which would give me an excuse to clean my feet, ". . . take a walk up the beach?"

"Sure," Ricky said. "That sounds nice."

I was overcome by relief as, one by one, I put each foot up on the opposite knee and swiped and scraped it clean as best as I could with my hands, then gave each a finishing rubdown with the outside of my sock before shaking it out and putting it and my shoe on. Ricky was standing over me, smiling, when I finished. "Feel better?"

We set off slowly, heading south, away from the lighthouse,

following the curve of the inlet. Below the trail down from the inn, a small forest hugged the steep cliffside, with only a narrow strip of beach between it and the water. We had barely made it past the base of the trail when we discovered that we weren't alone. Coming around the cove toward us were Wiley and Tawny, their faces drawn, their shoes in their hands. Tawny brightened and gave a little wave as our eyes met, turning and saying something to Wiley, who remained stony-faced.

"Hey, guys," she called out as they got closer. Her tone was friendly, but much less aggressive than the night before. "We met last night for a sec, remember? I'm Tawny, and this is my husband, Wiley."

Wiley grunted, barely slowing as he passed us. "I'm going to keep going, okay? Nice to see you again."

Standing next to us now, her hands on her hips, Tawny rolled her eyes at her husband's back. "Sorry about him. His cousin Richard died, you know, but that's not an excuse to be rude. Remind me of your names again—you're Jeff, right?"

I suppressed a laugh. I had forgotten the name I had given Ricky the night before.

For his part, Ricky smiled diplomatically. "I'm actually Ricky, not Jeff. That was a little joke. This is Oliver."

Tawny laughed, too, a bit ruefully. "I came on kinda strong last night, huh? Sorry. To tell you the truth, I was just so excited to see some people from outside Wiley's family. I try so hard, but they all hate me. They treat me like trash."

I took in her teased platinum-blond hair and the hot pink low-cut top and stretchy white capri pants that hugged her curvaceous figure. She certainly did stand out in comparison to the restrained Roses.

"It's hard to break into a group like that sometimes," I offered. "Have you and Wiley been together long?"

"Five years," she said. "I've tried, but I guess maybe I took the wrong approach before. I used to get kinda loaded sometimes before family gatherings, to take the edge off, you know? But I think it gave them a bad impression of me."

I wasn't sure what to say to this. Tawny had inserted herself between me and Ricky, and was walking us slowly up the beach, back in the direction she had come from, away from Wiley.

"I've given that up, though," she went on proudly, apparently content to have someone other than her husband to listen to her. "But it's hard to figure out how to be social when you're sober. Maybe that's why I scared you guys off last night. I'm not so bad, though, right?"

She wasn't, really, though even this less pushy version of her was a little much for me. There was a resigned sadness barely concealed by her outgoing exterior, and I felt bad for her, understanding what it felt like to be an outsider. Fitting into a group almost always felt like fumbling in the dark to me.

"No, of course not," Ricky was saying. "Everybody in Wiley's family that we've met has been nice enough, but they're not exactly social butterflies, are they? Too much money, probably."

She laughed again, a bit bitterly. "I'll say! Their brains are poisoned by all that money. All they've ever seen when they look at me is a gold digger. And I'm not, I swear! I never went after Wiley for his money. *He* went after *me*, for one thing. And he doesn't have that much of his own money anyway. His dad got kicked out of the family business before Wiley was even born, and drank all his money away by the time he died, when Wiley was a little boy."

I remembered what Cecilia had said: *He was like a second son to me*. "He was close with his cousins, though, right? And his aunt, Mrs. Rose?"

"Sure, yeah, after his father died," Tawny nodded. "His aunt Cecilia, all prim and proper with a stick up her derriere, thought he needed their good influence. He and Richard were actually buddies, though; Richard was okay, not as stuck up as the rest of them. That's how come he's so upset."

"We saw Wiley come to the lounge last night to get you some milk," Ricky said. "He said you were pretty broken up, too."

Tawny's face colored ever so slightly. "Yeah, I surprised myself, getting all worked up like that. But, you know, Richard was nicer to me than most of them. Not that I knew him that well," she added quickly. "I felt sad for Wiley, really, losing someone he had been so close to."

Without the high heels she held in her hand, Tawny was short enough that Ricky and I could look at each other over her head. He narrowed his eyes at me, and I tried to give him the ocular equivalent of a shrug.

"Wiley didn't seem all that upset, though, last night," Ricky said.

"Probably shock," I offered, remembering the exchange between Wiley and Mary Alice in the lounge the night before.

"Yeah, I'm sure he was in shock. He's been awful mopey today," Tawny agreed, nodding. "I tell you, they were thick as thieves when they were kids. And Richard helped take care of Wiley when he was sick."

"Oh," I said, "when was that?"

"Back when they were kids. I think Wiley was sixteen, seventeen. He got cancer. Prostate cancer, actually, can you believe that! It's really rare, but it can happen that young. Anyway, his aunt did pay for all his treatments, I'll give her that much, and Richard visited him every day when he was in the hospital, and took him to all his appointments and stuff. But that was also kind of the beginning of the end for them being so close."

Ricky asked, "What happened?"

Tawny shrugged. "Richard had been at the university in Eugene, but then he went off to graduate school on the East Coast not long after that, so I think they drifted apart some. And then he married Rachel, who *really* has a stick up her butt, and they weren't very friendly with anybody after that, except

Cecilia. And Cecilia felt like Wiley owed her for paying for his treatments and everything, like that obligated him to always do what she wanted."

I thought about something else Cecilia had said to me about Wiley: *He took from me when he wanted to and rejected me when he wanted to.* I could see now how this must have felt from Wiley's side. Again, it felt like the Roses approaching relationships on purely transactional terms. "That doesn't seem very fair."

"Nope," she said. "So Cecilia's been hot and cold with him ever since he married me. Of course, he didn't even tell me about any of this before he threw me into the deep end with these people. I didn't even know about the cancer until last year!"

I wondered where Wiley, who was emerging as a more and more complicated figure within the puzzle that was the Rose family, had gone since he had left Tawny with us. I turned to look behind us, and caught sight of him, standing partway up the hill that led to the trail back up the bluff, his hands in his pockets, staring intently in our direction. He was too far away to make out his face, but his body language seemed to radiate hostility.

As if catching his aura with the back of her head, Tawny said, "Enough about my family. I need a break from them. What about you guys? What's it like in the outside world these days?"

I had no idea how to respond to such a broad question, but Ricky saved us both by checking the time on his phone again. "Unfortunately, what it's like for us right now is, we have to head back up to the inn or we're going to be late for our massages."

"Pooh," Tawny pouted. "Well, now that we're friends, come talk to me again sometime, okay?"

We all turned to head back toward the trail. Wiley was nowhere to be seen anymore. But Tawny still seemed to feel his chill in the air. After a moment, she hung back, saying, "You guys go on ahead. I don't wanna slow you down. I'll hang here for another minute."

Ricky let me take the lead this time, heading back up the long stone staircase that seemed perhaps three times longer going up than it had coming down. Once we had lost sight of Tawny down below, I said to Ricky over my shoulder, "I feel bad for her. She seems lonely."

"Yeah," Ricky said, only slightly less short of breath than me. "She doesn't really fit into the family, and she knows it. But, lucky for us, that also makes her more willing to spill some juicy gossip about them."

"What do you make of all that?"

"It's hard to say," he panted. The stairs seemed to be getting steeper. "She seemed to want us to feel sorry for Wiley, too, but he came across as more . . . angry? . . . than anything else."

"There's definitely something odd about Wiley," I agreed. "He was bothered by Tawny's reaction to Richard's death, and bothered that she wanted to talk to us. He was watching us after we started walking with her. It was kind of creepy."

"The vibes are off, for sure," Ricky said. "What she didn't give us was any hint of a motive—that is, if Wiley seems as suspicious to you as he does to me."

"I'm not sure," I wheezed, as the top of the trail finally came into sight. I knew there was something about Wiley that my oxygen-starved brain wasn't able to grab hold of. I stopped for a moment, clutching my sides and trying to catch my breath, staring up the hill at the last upward stretch of the trail back to the inn. Ricky passed me by, but I waited still, until it came to me: the will.

Wiley had been the secondary heir to Cecilia's fortune, set to inherit if Richard died before Cecilia. Had he known? He didn't know, I was sure, that Lis had, just this morning, taken his place in the line of succession; had he gotten rid of Richard in a now-scuttled attempt to claim the family fortune?

I scrambled up the last few yards of the trail and found Ricky, who had recovered from the strenuous uphill trek maddeningly quickly, in the parking lot. Before I had a chance to share my suspicions about Wiley, he was grinning and waggling his eyes at me, leading me toward the entrance to the spa.

"I don't know about you, but I'm in the mood for that sexy couples massage now." He leered at me. His voice dropped to a mock-seductive stage whisper. "I was watching your butt all the way up the hill."

Yikes. Everything else fled from my mind and my stomach made a hasty drop into some mysterious black pit in the depths of my guts. I had not been ready for that, and I was not ready for this, but in the absence of any signal from my brain, my legs were marching me straight into the spa, toward what was shaping up to be the most terrifying experience of my life—far more terrifying than murder.

CHAPTER 9

It occurred to me too late to protest. Ricky had said something about wearing a swimsuit, but we hadn't gone back to our room to get one. By the time I thought of this, I was halfway across the lobby of the spa, and Letitia, the wizened blond manager, was already hailing us.

"Well, fellas," she said, giving us a mildly suspicious look, "you ready for this?"

No.

"Absolutely," Ricky purred. "We can't wait."

"Okey dokey," she said. "I got you on the books with Shawn and Cole for a couples massage." She reached down below the counter and came back up with two neatly folded fluffy white robes, each with a pair of flimsy rubber shower shoes tucked under the waist tie. She waved us toward a door to her left. "You can change in there, and then head through the door at the other end of the changing room into the waiting lounge. We should have your room ready in a couple minutes."

I followed Ricky into the changing room, where he selected one of the wood-paneled lockers, plopping down onto the bench across from it and beginning to unlace his shoes. I hung back, hugging the robe to my chest, reaching across it with one arm to dig my nails into the other, almost focused enough on this mildly painful self-soothing to ignore the vile rub of the shower shoes against the underside of my arm.

"So . . . what do we do here?"

Ricky turned to look at me, then patted the bench next to him encouragingly. I sat tentatively, facing the opposite direction.

"Take a deep breath," he said in what I'm sure he meant to be a soothing voice. I managed a hoarse, shallow gulp. "We're going to take off our clothes—as many as you're comfortable with," he continued. "Then we'll put on these nice robes and these appalling shoes, and we'll go wait in the waiting room. If there's anyone else in there, they'll be in robes, too. And we're alone in here; if you want, I can stay facing this way and you can face the other way, and we won't turn around until we both give the all-clear. Okay?"

Oddly, the part I found most reassuring in all this was that Ricky hated the shower shoes, too. I nodded my agreement with his plan, and rose stiffly from the bench, then sat down again, realizing I had to take off my shoes and socks. As soon as we were both barefoot, we stood up, each facing our respective directions—at least, I had to take it on faith that Ricky was. I was pretty sure I trusted him . . . at least sixty-five percent sure.

To be really sure, as soon as I had pulled off my T-shirt, I threw on the robe, reasoning that I could drop my shorts with it on. I didn't think twice about removing my underwear—that wasn't going to happen. I tied the robe's belt tightly around my waist.

"I'm ready if you are," Ricky said from behind me.

"I'm mostly ready. You can turn around, anyway," I said. I was still barefoot, looking sideways down at the hateful slippers on the bench. Ricky followed my gaze as he turned around.

"Yes, you have to put them on. I'm sorry," he said, reading

my mind. "Most of the time we don't have to wear them. Only when we're walking around."

I sighed deeply and put on the sandals, which I discovered not only had a horrifyingly ridged texture to their institutional-grade rubber, but were also about three sizes too big. Ricky laughed sympathetically, pointing down to his own too-large shoes, and I tried to muster a laugh, too, as we waded into the waiting lounge, our sandals making obscene sucking and slapping noises the whole way.

I was dismayed to see that the waiting lounge was not empty, and horrified to see that its occupants were Cecilia Rose and her daughter, Lis. I was also mildly annoyed to see that Ricky had been wrong. Cecilia was in a robe, but Lis was comfortably clad in her own clothes.

Cecilia was watching us with a small smile as we trooped in. She and Lis occupied one of two cream-colored love seats in the small room, and as Ricky and I settled into the other, she said, "Hello, Junior. We meet again. Here for a little R and R?"

I struggled to find my voice, finally croaking out, "No. Yes. Kind of."

Lis, who had returned to the magazine on her lap after giving us a smile and nod of greeting, looked up again, her expression now tinged with polite confusion.

Ricky, as always, was ready to bail me out. "Perk of the job. We get to sample the spa's services as long as we write about them." I put my hand down on the love seat between us, burrowing the tips of my fingers into the cushion under his leg. I was unconsciously reaching for his protection, acknowledging my appreciation that he always seemed so ready to offer it, but I realized almost at once how intimate the gesture felt. It must have been okay, though; he in turn put his arm up over the back of the couch behind my shoulders, leaning slightly toward me.

"I thought you were a photographer," Cecilia observed drily. "I don't see your camera."

Ricky grinned conspiratorially at her. "I said it was a perk, didn't I? He has to write about it; I get to tag along and get a massage for nothing."

She grinned back. "You two have it all figured out, don't you?"

I looked shyly at Ricky, who gave me a wink and moved his hand on my shoulder to pull me closer.

A young woman with a long, dark ponytail and a set of white scrubs entered the waiting room. "Mrs. Rose, I'm ready for you. Right this way, please."

"Ta-ta, boys," Mrs. Rose grunted as she hoisted herself up from the love seat to follow the young woman. "Enjoy your perks."

After she had left, Ricky turned his attention to Lis. "Not joining her?"

"No, I'm not really in a pampering mood. She needed the distraction, though; she was very agitated this morning, and of course neither of us slept well last night." Lis was reflective, watching the door her mother had left through. "I worry about the strain on her. She wouldn't say so, but I don't think she's feeling very well. I should have made sure to tell the massage therapist to keep it gentle. Excuse me, won't you—I think I'll see if I can go make that request."

As she got up, she passed another young woman in scrubs coming into the waiting room. The young woman ignored her, saying to us softly, "Ricky and Oliver? Your room is ready, if you'd like to follow me."

Ricky squeezed my hand briefly as we stood up, then dropped it as we headed down the hall. The woman half turned toward us as she guided us, keeping up a gentle patter. "How are you both doing today? My name is Shawn; Cole and I will be giving your massages. But we have you in for the Lovers' Package today, so first you'll have a half hour in the hot tub."

I fought the urge to turn on my heel and run the other way. Ricky reached over and took my hand again, this time feeling less like he wanted to reassure me and more like he wanted to make sure I didn't flee.

Shawn opened a door at the end of the corridor, standing aside to usher us in. "The tub is already warmed up and the jets are on, but there's a button if you'd rather turn them off. And there are chocolate-covered strawberries and Champagne for you, too! We'll come back in half an hour for your massages, but we'll knock before we come in."

Her smile seemed too serenely blasé for the situation she was throwing us into. And Ricky's hand gripped mine too firmly as he pulled me into the room and she shut the door behind us. These people were conspiring to trap me in some kind of sexy prison.

I sucked in my breath and took in my cell. Two massage tables, draped in white sheets, took up most of the floor space. A countertop along one wall and a credenza on the opposite side of the room were both littered with fake candles giving off a soft, artificially flickering glow. On the far wall was the hot tub, really a glorified jetted bathtub, with a pyramid of rolled-up towels on one side, a pair of teak steps leading up to it at the middle, and an open bottle, two filled flutes, and a platter of chocolate-covered strawberries sweating on the other end of the ledge surrounding the tub.

Ricky was checking out the wine, reading the label and taking a small sip from one of the flutes. "It's Prosecco, not Champagne," he said, "but it's not bad. You might even like it, if you want to try some."

I was still frozen by the door. All I could think to say was, "I don't really drink."

"I know that," Ricky said. "Is there any particular reason why? You don't have to tell me if you don't want to."

I shrugged, feeling a little less trapped by this benign conversation. "I don't like the way most alcohol tastes. It usually tastes bitter to me."

Ricky took another sip of the Prosecco. "I don't know. You might like this okay. It has a little edge to it, but it's also fairly sweet. Most of the alcohol flavor gets covered up by the sharpness of the bubbles."

I had begun to edge closer to the tub.

Ricky smiled and set down his glass. "Well, shall we?" He reached for the belt of his robe, and I froze again, feeling all of my color flush out my toes. He stopped and laughed. "I'm kidding! I was thinking maybe we could put our feet in. You know, sit on the edge?"

I could breathe again. Sitting on the edge and putting my feet in with my robe still on I could do. He climbed the two little steps, gingerly lifting the hem of his robe to keep it out of the water as he walked across to sit on the far edge of the tub. I followed suit, crossing to sit next to him.

"See," he said. "Not so bad. And still kind of romantic, in a chaste sort of way. Do you want to try the wine?"

"Maybe I'll start with a strawberry," I said, and he presented me with the platter. I bit slowly through the chocolate coating, which crumbled from sitting in the humidity beside the tub, sucking in to avoid losing any in the water and getting a mouthful of sweet strawberry juice in the bargain. Ricky took a strawberry, too, and as I chewed my bite, I watched him tuck into his. The supple workings of his lips around the fruit, the tip of his tongue flicking out to catch the last bits of chocolate and juice, the rhythmic motion of his jaw as he chewed, the pure pleasure in his shining brown eyes . . . this tub was making me awfully hot.

"Maybe I will try that wine after all," I said.

Twenty minutes, three chocolate-covered strawberries, and a glass and a half of Prosecco later, I was feeling much more relaxed. At some point, I had loosened the tie on my robe to try to cool down, and then it came completely untied and the ends of the belt dipped into the tub, and then the robe had fallen open. I had failed to care about any of this. "Cute undies," Ricky had said, and I'd said "Thanks," and then "Woo-woo" as I waved the lapels of my robe open and shut, and then "Bloop-bloop" as I'd dunked the ends of the belt in and out of the water. I was feeling very tingly. Buzzy, even. *Buzzed?* Buzzed. I understood that one now.

The only problem was that my tongue had outgrown my mouth.

"So you like Prosecco, eh?" Ricky said.

"It'th not tho bad," I said, sounding like Daffy Duck, then I giggled at how silly I sounded.

"Wow," Ricky said.

"You're wow," I said, waggling my eyebrows at him. I slapped a hand onto his leg, reaching into the gap at the hem of his robe and drawing my hand up his inner thigh. He laughed and caught my wrist before I got too far.

"That's fun, but let's circle back to that later, when you're feeling more like yourself," he said.

I looked straight into his eyes and tried to feel serious. "I've never felt more like mythelf," I said, then dissolved into giggles again.

"Uh-huh."

We were already sitting close to each other, but I scooched closer, leaning in and nuzzling my head onto his shoulder. I had a moment of tingly clarity. "We're awfully cuddly, conthidering we're not really boyfriendths," I said, "and considering I'm not normally a cuddly person." My tongue was shrinking again. Maybe a sign I needed more wine.

"Maybe you're cuddlier than you think," Ricky said. "And it's okay to cuddle with friends. I think more guys should be physically expressive with their friends."

"You think that because you're a horndog."

"I'm a horndog? You're the one sitting here with your robe open," he said, woo-wooing the lapel of my robe to emphasize his point.

"Hmm. I'm a cuddly horndog," I said. "Thanks, wine, for revealing my secrets." I hoisted my flute and took another sip. "But are we really just friends? I mean *really*?"

He put a finger under my chin, lifting my face so I could see him. "You tell me," he said solemnly, then abruptly cut his eyes away. "But that's also probably a conversation for later."

The knock at the door seemed to agree with him. A soft voice from the hallway called in, "Let us know when you're ready."

"Oop," Ricky said, then called back, "one minute." He handed me one of the fluffy rolled-up towels and we both quickly dried our legs and feet as we scrambled out of the tub.

"What do we do now?" I hissed in a whisper.

"Take off your robe and lie face down on the massage table. And put the sheet over your backside."

I did as he said, and in a moment he called out to the hall to let the waiting massage therapists know we were ready. I tried putting my face down into the little padded donut at the end of the massage table, and discovered an impediment I hadn't considered.

"Ricky, what about my glasses?"

Shawn, walking into the room, said, "I can take those for you." I flailed a little to prop myself up on my elbows so I could remove my glasses and hand them to her, and she put them on the credenza next to one of the fake candles.

I hadn't gotten a good look at the other massage therapist coming into the room behind Shawn before I'd taken off my glasses, but I was now aware of a tall, well-built, blurry figure taking up a position by Ricky's massage table.

"Hello, Ricky, I'm Cole and I'll be taking care of you today," the blob said in one of those voices whose confidence comes from being really good-looking. I knew immediately that I hated Cole.

Shawn, meanwhile, had begun arranging my sheet, pulling it up over my back as I settled back down onto the table, now able to rest my face comfortably. She said, in her soft singsong, "Is there anything in particular bothering you today? Anything you want me to pay special attention to?"

A few things were bothering me. Cole, or at least the very handsome mental picture I had conjured up from his blurry figure, was bothering me by laying his very handsome, blurry hands on Ricky. Ricky was bothering me, too, by not letting me take advantage of my alcohol-induced loose lips to tell him how I felt, when he and I both knew how much harder it would be later without being any less true. I was vaguely bothered by how unbothered I had become about lying on this table being touched by a stranger while wearing nothing but my skivvies.

But all I said was, "No, not really."

"Any aches or pains I need to know about? Past injuries?"

I'd lived an injury-free life. Blessed, my mother would say, but I knew it mostly came down to avoiding risky situations. Getting entangled with Ricky had felt risky; he'd showed me how much fun taking risks could be, especially if you had someone to take them with. And so, once we'd parted ways at the end of our last assignment, I'd done what I always did and avoided him. But that's when I'd really gotten hurt, and I realized I'd done it to myself; I'd given myself a deep, acute ache that I was still struggling to get past, even though I was fairly certain both of us wanted to. What was wrong with me?

My buzz was veering from silliness into morose self-recrimination. But all I could say was, "Nope."

"Okay," Shawn said, "let's get started."

She pulled the sheet down, exposing my back, and I tried not to tense as I felt her hands come down and begin to work my shoulder blades. After a minute, I thought I was starting to relax.

"You carry a lot of tension in your back, don't you," Shawn said. So much for relaxation. "You've got some impressive knots here."

I sighed into my donut pillow. To my right, I heard Cole saying to Ricky, "Someone's really good about stretching after working out, huh? Everything feels really good, really loose and limber."

"I try," came Ricky's muffled voice, and I felt a horrible pang. Was Cole's gambit merely professional patter, or was he flirting with Ricky? And was Ricky only responding to be polite, or was he going for it?

Suddenly, another pang—a physical one this time. Something cool and liquid had hit my back, and as Shawn began working her hands into it, it became warm and my entire back started to feel slimy and started to smell, a sort of metallic floral mélange.

"Try not to tense up," Shawn said, gently pushing my shoulder blades apart.

"What is that? What did you put on me?"

"It's massage oil. It's supposed to relax you," Shawn chuckled.

I was *not* relaxed. The wine had taken the initial edge off having Shawn touch me, but either it was wearing off or the oil was a bridge too far, or both, because I was feeling very, very uncomfortable. Shawn was spreading her slimy, stinky mess down my arms now. Was she going to coat my whole body in this stuff? They had this all backward; I'd need the bath *after* the massage, not before, to get all this oil off me.

I was trying to forget about Cole and Ricky, but I couldn't tune them out in such close quarters. Cole asked Ricky, "Ready for the oil?" *Why did he get a choice and I didn't? Why didn't*

Shawn ask me first? Could I have said no and avoided all this? I was indignant.

"Sure," Ricky mumbled dreamily.

"Do you prefer the lavender scent, or sandalwood?" *He got a choice of scents?* Forget indignant, I was fuming. Never mind that I didn't want the oil at all; but why did Ricky get so many options, and I got none?

Shawn, about whom I was starting to mentally compose a sternly worded complaint that nobody would ever hear, pulled the sheet up to cover my back once again, the fabric now clinging hotly to my skin thanks to the glue-like coat of oil. She began rubbing oil into my right leg, pushing and pulling my leg hair in all the wrong directions. It probably didn't rise to the level of being addressed by the Geneva Conventions, but this had to be some kind of low-grade torture, right? People paid for this? They found it restful? I was grinding my teeth as I stared blurrily down at the floor through my pillow, trying not to squirm too much and resenting the way the cushion was pushing my cheeks toward my nose.

"How are we doing?" Cole purred.

"Mmm, great," Ricky said, the traitor.

Okay, I was getting too worked up. I shouldn't resent Ricky for enjoying himself. People were supposed to find this enjoyable, I reminded myself. It didn't work for me, but that didn't mean everyone else was wrong—or that I was. Besides, this was supposed to be a big part of my article, and I couldn't exactly put in my piece that I had hated every minute. I had to be able to figure out how to say that this was a wonderful, romantic experience, and I realized that I should be grateful that I could rely on Ricky to help me understand why it was for him.

Feeling like I was rising above and being the bigger person helped me unclench my jaw a little. I tried my best to relax my whole body.

"That's better," Shawn said approvingly. "Nice deep breaths, and you'll feel great."

I felt proud of myself. If I couldn't enjoy my massage, at least I could do it correctly.

Shawn was running her hands down my leg, pulling the hairs so that at least they were all going in the right direction. Things were improving. Then she began focusing on my upper leg, kneading the muscles of my thigh and—*yipes!*—making her way up under the sheet onto my butt. She kept to the fleshy areas toward the outside, but I still reflexively clenched my whole body back up.

This time, she seemed to take the hint, unhanding my rump and moving over to my other leg instead. I had been trying to regain a sense of perspective, but this had reactivated my panic responses. I tried to remind myself that she had stopped, that she had gone elsewhere and I could let go of some of this tension, but it wasn't working. Unbidden, a picture sprang into my mind, of Cole's handsome, strong, still purely hypothetical hands doing what Shawn had just done, rubbing firmly into Ricky's perfect, glorious butt, both of them loving every second of it. I felt my jealousy and rage bubbling back up.

And then the ultimate betrayal. Without warning, without any prompting from Cole, at precisely the wrong moment in my horrible vision, Ricky—the real Ricky, on the table next to me—*moaned.*

It was a sound of pure pleasure, probably totally reflexive, and I had no idea what Cole was actually doing to him. And my brain could no longer conjure up any ideas of what could have prompted it; everything in me had turned to white, a pure hot white blind rage. My prone body on the table felt momentarily frozen, and then I began to shift my arms, trying to lift myself up onto my elbows, with each movement totally unsure of what my next step would be.

Shawn tried to steady my legs, which were twitching as I rose. "Do you need something? Is there—"

She was interrupted, and my movement arrested, by an abrupt commotion in the corridor outside our room. There was a bang, a torrent of frenzied footfalls, a hand banging on the walls as someone ran down the hall, banging on our door, a voice crying out. I yelped in confusion, losing track of my anger but not sure what this fresh source of overstimulation augured.

Shawn and Cole rushed to the door, dashing out into the hallway. "Bianca," we heard them call out, following the person who had banged on our door as she ran by. "Bianca, what's wrong?"

The hubbub moved down the hall. I finished lifting my torso, swinging my legs around to sit up on the table, getting tangled in the sheet as I rose. Ricky sat up, too, and I regarded his blurry form, still confused, his transgression of a moment before forgotten.

"What's happening?"

"I don't know," he said. "Should I peek out down the hall?"

I nodded, and we both hopped down from our tables, holding our sheets wrapped around our torsos. I stumbled a little on my sheet as I tried to work my feet out the bottom and make solid contact with the floor. We huddled in the doorway, poking our heads out into the hallway, looking first in the direction everyone had gone, then in the direction from which Bianca had come.

This was a fruitless exercise on my part. "I can't see anything without my glasses. Do you see anything?"

"No," Ricky said. "Maybe they all went out to the lobby."

As we looked in that direction again, a mass of blurry bodies rounded the corner, coming toward us in a hurry. A voice came from the mass, directed at us. I recognized Letitia's reedy pitch. "Back in your room, please, for a minute. Sorry, we'll be right with you."

We shrank back from the doorway as they hustled past. I turned, groping along the top of the credenza near the door, trying to find my glasses. By the time I found them, Ricky had crossed the room and grabbed our robes from where we had hung them on the wall, handing me mine. We traded our sheets for the robes and sat down together on my massage table.

"Well," Ricky said, swinging his feet, "were you enjoying your massage?"

I was too off balance to lie. "No. But it sounded like you were."

"Yeah, mine was going good. I was almost asleep, actually."

"Cole, huh." I was starting to remember things, but feeling more dejected about it than angry by now.

"He was doing a pretty good job," Ricky agreed companionably.

"Was he . . . ?"

"Was he what?"

Ugh, don't make me say it. "Hot," I choked out wretchedly. "Was he hot?"

Ricky laughed. "I didn't notice. Honestly, Oliver!"

I blushed and studied my toes.

A movement at the door brought my eyes back up, and Shawn entered slowly, holding her left arm with her right hand. "I'm so sorry," she said softly, a tearful tremble in her voice. "We're going to have to cut our time short. We've had an emergency, and we have to close down for the day."

"What happened? What was the emergency?" Ricky wanted to know.

Shawn looked over her shoulder, out the door and down the hall, as if checking to make sure she wouldn't be overheard, then turned back and said in a low voice, "I guess you'll find out anyway, since you're all staying at the inn. . . . Bianca was giving her a massage, and she had to step out for a minute, and when she came back, she was . . . dead!" Shawn had been straining to hold back tears, and at this final word, she broke down.

Ricky was confused. "Bianca's dead?"

It had been hard to follow, for sure, but I had managed not to get lost in Shawn's word salad. "No," I said, "not Bianca. Cecilia Rose. Mrs. Rose is dead."

CHAPTER 10

Shawn tearfully ushered Ricky and me back to the changing room, where we quickly traded our robes for our clothes. I was almost too shell-shocked from the roller coaster of emotions that the afternoon had taken me on to notice my clothes clinging a little to my oily skin. *Almost*, but not so shell-shocked that I didn't desperately want a shower, right now.

This was not to be, however. As we passed back into the lobby of the spa, ducking to let a pair of EMTs with a stretcher pass, we nearly collided with Deputy Duncan from the sheriff's office. She did a double take on seeing us.

"Two days in a row, two deaths out here, and both times I run into you two?" She narrowed her eyes suspiciously. Pointing to a pair of chairs by the door, she said, "You better sit here. Don't move until I come back."

"Oh, boy," Ricky said as we sat down. "She thinks we're suspects!"

Ricky seemed to think this was amusing, maybe even exciting. At this point, having been through such a busy day, I was starting to simply feel exhausted. And I really wanted that shower. I was sitting on the edge of the chair, trying my hardest not to increase the contact between my clothes and my greasy skin. Everything I was wearing was probably ruined by now, I figured, but I didn't need to make it worse.

"Oliver, relax," Ricky said when I didn't respond. "I'm joking. She'll talk to Shawn and Cole and she'll know we couldn't have done anything. And how could we have pushed Richard onto our balcony *from* our balcony? It doesn't make any sense. We have nothing to worry about."

"I'm not worried," I said, a fair bit more crabbily than I had intended. "I'm sticky!"

"Huh?"

"She spread this . . . stuff . . . all over me, and I'm all slimy and my clothes are sticking to me, and I hate it." We had been too busy today; too much had happened. I could tell I was getting overstimulated. I had to figure the wine wasn't helping, either.

"The massage oil?" Ricky jumped up, ducking down behind the registration desk and coming back with a big, rolled-up white towel. "Here, give me your arm." He rubbed vigorously all up and down my arm, pushing up my sleeve to get almost up to my shoulder. Relief washed over me as I felt the greasy residue sloughing off my skin into the towel. I willingly gave him my other arm when he was done, and then he crouched down in front of me to rub down my legs.

"Is that better?"

My gratitude layered on top of my exhaustion to nearly overwhelm me. "So much better," I sighed. I was trying to figure out if it would be too much to ask him to go over my back as well when Deputy Duncan returned.

"I talked to the massage therapists," she said, more friendly than before but still maintaining her professional veneer of gruffness. "You're in the clear. The EMTs say it looks like a pretty clear-cut heart attack, anyway. But it's kind of like you two are a kiss of death! If I find any more bodies with you guys around, I might not arrest you, but I might have to call a priest for an exorcism or something."

Dang it. I had so nearly forgotten about my worry that Ricky and I were cursed, but now Deputy Duncan brought it roaring back. I tried to think what we had done this time to activate the curse; Ricky hadn't asked me out, but I had a vague memory of maybe trying to get him to agree to be more than just pretend boyfriends. That might be an even more serious offense.

"Oliver," Ricky said sternly, reading my thoughts, "we are not cursed. She's not serious. It's a weird coincidence, that's all."

I looked to Deputy Duncan, hoping for confirmation that Ricky was right, but she merely raised an eyebrow and shrugged. It appeared she came down more on my side than Ricky's. Cursed in the eyes of the law seemed like a major problem.

"Anyway," Deputy Duncan said, "you can go. At first glance, it doesn't look like this was a murder, either, so we'll have to talk to the family, but not much else to do unless the medical examiner finds something suspicious after all and decides to order an autopsy. Talk about coincidence." She shrugged again, and watched us leave the spa.

Ricky had reduced my need for a shower, but he hadn't eliminated it. As we began moving again, passing from the spa into the lobby of the inn, my shirt still clung stubbornly to my still-oily back. I was gritting my teeth, making a beeline for the elevator, when Erik called to us from behind the front desk.

"Psst," he said, waving us over. I reluctantly followed Ricky in heeding his call. Erik's eyes shone in excitement. "I just heard the news—the sheriff's in the lounge talking to the family. Another death! So soon after Richard," he whispered. "Are you guys suspicious of this one, too?"

Ricky and I spoke at the same time.

"I don't think so," I said.

"Maybe," Ricky said.

I looked at him incredulously. "Really? You heard the deputy. There's no sign of foul play."

I was maybe not whispering quietly enough; as I said "foul play," Tawny passed into the lobby from the lounge and her head immediately swiveled our way.

"Wait," she said in a low tone, hustling to join our little huddle around the desk. "Foul play? What are you talking about?"

"Aunt Cecilia," Erik said. "Dying right after Richard like that. It seems suspicious, right?"

"The sheriff said she died of natural causes," Tawny said. "And Richard fell on accident, didn't he?"

"Maybe someone wanted it to look that way," Ricky said. "It does seem strange—I'd believe natural causes for Cecilia, except for two things: the timing, and the fact that she was alive when the massage therapist left the room, and dead when she came back."

"Hmm," Tawny mused. "I dunno. It's weird, but maybe it's like—who was that? Debbie Reynolds! Remember? Her daughter died, and then the next day, she died, too. Of a broken heart," she said, putting a sorrowful hand to her breast.

"You spent a little time with Mrs. Rose," Ricky said to me. "Did she seem brokenhearted, like Debbie Reynolds?"

I tried to mentally compare Mrs. Rose to what I could remember of Debbie Reynolds. "She seemed old like Debbie Reynolds?"

"She was *real* old," Tawny nodded. "I lost count, like, three times trying to put the candles on her birthday cake the other day. There were *so many*."

"I heard they burned her dining room to the ground when the cake fell," Erik agreed.

"It wasn't me that dropped it," Tawny said defensively. "Rayleigh was trying to carry the cake and make a TikTok at the same time. I told her I'd film, but she said I had to help Rielle do the dance."

Tawny made more sense to me now that I realized that she saw Richard and Rachel's teen daughters as her peers.

"Anyway," she continued, "what about Richard? You think there was something suspicious about that, too? Didn't he slip and fall?"

"It's totally suspicious," Erik answered. "There's evidence that he wasn't alone in his room at the time. What if the other person pushed him? I mean, falling off a balcony is awfully weird."

"Evidence?" Tawny leaned in, intrigued.

"Yeah, and I helped find it," Erik beamed.

"Shh-hh-hh," Ricky cautioned, looking up furtively as Rachel Rose sailed out of the lounge, toward the elevator, though she altered her path when she saw us.

"Tawny," she commanded. "Give me a cigarette."

Tawny instinctively reached for her purse, which wasn't there, then fruitlessly patted her empty pockets before catching herself. "I don't have any," she said, adding proudly, "I gave them up."

"What about the rest of you?" Rachel demanded, encompassing Erik, Ricky, and me in an impatiently sweeping point. We all shook our heads.

"Fine," Rachel huffed. "For the record, I don't smoke, either." Her point turned threatening. "You got that?" she barked.

"Yes, ma'am," Erik said meekly.

Rachel took a breath to gather herself, drawing a smoothing hand over the front sweep of her auburn helmet. "It had already been such a trying day," she said, her attempt to sound calm slightly brittle. "And now, this. I suppose we all need our releases. I'll have to find one that's less self-destructive. Excuse me—you can resume your little cabal."

She stalked imperiously to the elevator, and once she had boarded, Tawny and Erik eagerly pulled us back into a huddle.

"You were saying something about evidence that Richard wasn't alone when he fell," Tawny said.

Erik bobbed his head excitedly. "Right, the evidence. *And* I was the one who knew that Richard and Rachel were sleeping in separate rooms, and that she didn't go into the movies with Rielle and Rayleigh. And then we found out that she went to the café and met someone there, but we don't know who it was."

"Yeah, the hitman," I said distractedly, trying to discreetly pull my T-shirt away from my back.

Everyone stopped and stared at me.

Delight danced in Ricky's eyes. "The hitman? What is this theory? This sounds way wackier than usual for you."

Shoot. I hadn't said my goofy hitman theory out loud earlier, I remembered, and I remembered why. "It's not a theory," I said quickly. "It's not anything."

"It sounds like something," Tawny insisted. "It sounds exciting!"

"You have to tell us," Erik pleaded.

"No, forget I said anything, please," I said, inwardly kicking myself for my loose lips. Could I blame the wine for my carelessness, I wondered? I could, I decided. No more Prosecco for me, ever again.

"C'mon, Oliver," Ricky said, grinning. "Why should I always have all the fun of coming up with crackpot ideas? Tell us yours, and we'll take it as seriously as you always take mine."

"Hey, I try to engage intellectually with your theories as best I can, even when they're totally silly," I protested. "This is not worth intellectually engaging with."

"Let us be the judges of that," Ricky said.

I sighed. "Fine. But I want to make it clear that I in no way actually believe that this is what happened. Understood?"

Everyone nodded eagerly.

"I had this goofy thought that, what if Rachel hanging around at the café was a way for her to establish an alibi even though she really did kill Richard, by hiring a hitman, and the guy who came to meet her at the café was the hitman telling her that the job was done. Okay? Are you all happy? That's the stupidest thought I've ever had."

Tawny looked from Erik to Ricky to me, her eyes wide. "Wow! You think that? That's wild!"

"No! I thought I was clear—you all said you understood, were you not listening?—I absolutely *do not* think that," I said exasperatedly.

"It's an interesting theory," Ricky said. "It would be a B-level theory coming from me, but for Oliver, it's impressive. But we're not sure Rachel had much motive. We have to investigate more, to see if we can find out."

"Ooh, investigating! I thought you were writing a travel article," Tawny said. "Being undercover detectives is so much more exciting!"

"We're not undercover detectives," I protested, my agitation mounting. "We *are* writing a travel article."

"But we're also keeping our eyes and ears open," Ricky said, nodding as if he and I weren't completely contradicting each other.

Tawny nodded, too, as if all of this was making perfect sense. "So what other theories do you have? What other motives could explain all of this?"

"We haven't had a chance to discuss this yet," Ricky said, shooting me a conspiratorial look, "but it seems like the thing that could connect Richard and Cecilia's deaths is the chain of inheritance for Cecilia's estate."

Tawny's eyes went wide again. "You mean, someone killed her for her money?"

"And killed Richard first, to make sure they inherited all of it," Erik said, putting the pieces together. "Aha, I get it. But that wouldn't be Rachel."

"No," Ricky said. "That would point right at someone else."

We must have looked ridiculous, all turning at once as a group to look as Lis rounded the corner coming out of the lounge.

I felt guilty, all of us gawking at this woman who, in a span of two days, had lost her brother and mother. Lis, for her part, looked very tired, her normally erect posture sagging at the shoulders. She gave a sad little wave, and I wondered what to do or say. Platitudes seemed especially empty in this situation. Thinking of her as a suspect suddenly felt very wrong.

Ricky stepped forward, offering his hand. "I'm so sorry again. This must be awful for you." I wondered if he felt as bad as I now did, or if he was still in his suspicious mode, trying to feel her out.

"Thank you," Lis said weakly. "It's hard to feel anything other than numb at this point. I wish I could understand. . . ."

"What did happen?" Tawny was, as usual, a model of tact.

"I don't know, exactly. Apparently, the massage therapist left the room to take a phone call, which seems awfully unprofessional to me, but maybe it doesn't matter. She said Mother spoke to her when she left, but when she returned and tried to restart the massage, Mother was dead."

"Omigod, she was massaging a corpse," Tawny gasped.

"I think she figured it out fairly quickly," Lis deadpanned. "Anyway, I was out in the parking lot, on a phone call, and didn't even know anything was happening until the sheriff's people arrived. The deputy said it looked like a heart attack. I'm sorry, all, I need to be alone."

Everybody tried to make sympathetic clucking noises as she walked to the elevator. As soon as the doors slid shut behind her, Tawny, Erik, and Ricky were ready to resume their huddle. I rolled my eyes and reluctantly joined them, tugging a little at the hem of Ricky's T-shirt to indicate that I wanted to leave. I still wanted that shower, but he didn't seem to notice my signal.

Erik still had a conspiratorial gleam in his eye. "Well, what do we think of that?"

"She was awfully anxious for us to know where she was when it happened," Tawny said. "Like she thinks she needs an alibi. That's kinda suspicious to me. I think you guys are onto something with this inheritance idea."

I was losing my patience. I liked being nosy with Ricky—up to a point, with my caution balancing out his impulsiveness—but I wasn't sure how our dynamic duo had become this feather-brained foursome in which I was severely outnumbered.

"And what is it," I snapped, "that she's supposed to have done here? The deputy said there were no signs of foul play. So she didn't sneak back into the spa and smother or strangle her mother or something."

Tawny shrugged. "It's just weird that Cecilia was fine, and then she was alone for a minute, and then she was dead. And we don't know for sure whether Lis really was in the parking lot on the phone or not."

"So subpoena her phone records, then," I said, my voice getting dangerously close to a shriek. I could feel the day finally getting away from me, the *fight* part of my overactive "fight, flight, or freeze" instincts kicking into high gear, with me powerless to stop it. "She was old! Old people die! What are we supposed to do with this? Why do we care? It's not our problem!"

Ricky was walking backward away from the desk, pulling me with him. "I think it's time to get you that shower," he said soothingly.

Tawny had shrunk back, a frightened look on her face. "It was your idea," she said, raising her hands, as if in surrender. "I was agreeing with you, that's all."

"My idea?" Ricky was steering me backward into the elevator now as I flailed my arms and screeched, "My idea? Mine? Me?"

As the doors closed and we started to descend, Ricky spun me around, holding both my arms at my sides with his hands and looking worriedly toward my eyes, which couldn't meet his. "Oliver, breathe," he said.

I heaved against his hold as I tried to comply, gulping hoarsely but getting dismayingly little air.

"Breathe with me," Ricky said, taking an exaggerated breath through his nose, and exhaling forcefully out his mouth. I tried to follow along, eventually falling into rhythm with him as he guided me out of the elevator and down the hall to our room.

He shut the door behind us, and sat me down on the edge of the bed. "Are you okay?"

I shrugged miserably, still breathing heavily. I was confused and disoriented, unsure how I had gotten into this state. All I knew was that it had been a very long, very busy, very strange day. And somewhere in the back of my mind—or maybe it was the back of my body—oh, yeah, it was my back—I knew that I still felt sticky and slimy from the massage oil.

An image popped into my head, of a magnifying glass directing a ray of sunlight on a point, intensifying the heat in the spot over time until it eventually combusts. I wasn't sure if the massage oil was the sunlight or the magnifying glass in this metaphor; all I knew was that I was now reduced to a pile of ashes.

Ricky was still regarding me, his brown eyes clouded deeply with concern. "Do you still want a shower? Or a bath? Do you need something to eat? Or do you want to go to sleep?"

"Bath," I mumbled, and heaved myself up to head to the bathroom.

As I floated limply in the tub, exhausted, I tried to visualize the oil washing off my skin, forming an imaginary slick on the surface of the water. It was maddening that the part that felt the worst was my back, where I couldn't reach to scrub. I wondered if—if I could convince Ricky to be more than my fake boyfriend—he would ever scrub my back for me.

This led me to other, less comforting thoughts about Ricky, and the status of our pretend relationship at the end of its first day. It had started off fun and flirty. There had been a fair amount of spontaneity, which isn't usually my thing, but which had felt fine at the time. Ricky had taught me to drive; we had agreed to change our appointment time at the spa; I had gone to witness Cecilia Rose's will; we had gone snooping in Richard Rose's suite with Erik, then into town to follow Rachel's alibi; we had taken an impromptu walk on the beach with Tawny; our massages had been disrupted; Erik and Tawny wanted to play detective, too. None of this had been in our plans when we woke up this morning. Also, somebody had died. Again.

When I added it all up, it suddenly looked like a lot. And, like the magnifying glass starting fires, it had been okay until it wasn't.

There was another factor, too. Ricky and I had started the day more or less alone together, but it turned out I wasn't the only one susceptible to Ricky's charisma, and by the end of the day he had roped in Tawny and Erik, and I felt less in control and less sure that his charisma was a positive force. We had, I realized, spent most of our time together up to now basically one on one. But that wasn't how real relationships worked, and I wondered what it was like to be with Ricky among his friends or family. What was it like for him to be in a group with me? Had I been a wet blanket on his fun with Erik and Tawny? Probably.

Ricky had seen me shut down before, and now he had seen me start to melt down, though fortunately—or maybe unfortunately, if this was already enough to put him off—I hadn't gone all the way to code red. So far, he had always been sweet and supportive and tried to help me through the moments when I got overwhelmed, but at what point was the reality of my autism going to be too much for him? Would today be the day he realized he couldn't—or, worse, didn't want to—deal with me? And why, I wondered for the millionth time in my life, couldn't I simply deal with myself and not get so overwhelmed in the first place?

I sank down in the water, submerging myself almost to my nostrils, and blew a few frustrated bubbles from my mouth. I was spiraling, and getting into a pity party, and getting hung up on questions I couldn't possibly answer, no matter how much I hated surrendering control over that knowledge.

So much for things I didn't know. I needed to claw my way back onto solid ground. What *did* I know?

My head was still swirly from the overwhelm of the day. I had to close my eyes and think for a long time before I could latch onto anything concrete.

Here's what I came up with: I had some strong feelings for Ricky.

I kind of had for nearly as long as I'd known him, I realized. They weren't quite *in-love* feelings yet, although I had a creeping suspicion that they were getting somewhere close. But at the core, it was simpler than that. These were feelings that I had, up to this point in my life, only really ever harbored for my parents—or maybe a more apt comparison was how I felt about my teddy bear, Chester. Ricky could be a lot, but he had been, so far, an unfailing friend to me, a source of joy, of comfort, of reassurance, of companionship. I felt possessive of him, and I wanted to know that it would always be like this between us. And I knew that I couldn't expect Ricky to be perfect, because, no matter how I tried, I couldn't be perfect for him.

And that was the problem. The big difference between Ricky and Chester was that Ricky was a person. I loved my teddy bear deeply, but I didn't have to do a whole lot to know that he'd never leave me. I wasn't sure what to do to keep Ricky happy, or interested, or not scared off. But I knew I had to try to come up with something, because I had felt about very few people the way I felt about Ricky.

What else did I know? I knew that, no matter how fine he appeared on the surface, Ricky had been deeply rattled by seeing Richard Rose fall. If he felt like he would feel better understanding how that had happened, and if I cared for him and wanted to show him that I cared for him, I knew I had to do my best to help him figure it out. But maybe we could be more discreet about it—try not to invite more involvement from Erik, Tawny, or any other members of the extended Rose family.

I knew that this was at least partially my possessiveness talking. I was fine with that.

I realized that I knew a few more things. I knew that it had to be getting late. I knew that it had been a long day. I knew that Ricky would be getting hungry. I knew that my toes were getting pruny. I knew that there was only one bed in the room out there, and that—novelty of novelties—I was craving more of the closeness I'd stolen from Ricky in our sleep last night. It was time to get out of the tub.

I drained the water, dried off, and put on my pajamas. As I left the bathroom, a foil take-out container of pasta from the restaurant next door greeted me on the nightstand next to the bed. Another, empty container sat on the coffee table, and Ricky was stretched out on the couch, fast asleep. I wondered for a moment if I should wake him up, but decided that would be selfish. Instead, I pulled a blanket off the bed, draped it over him, then sat on the bed alone, watching him sleep as I ate.

CHAPTER 11

I was roused by Ricky moving around the room. Morning light streamed in from the windows fronting the balcony, and as I blinked myself awake, I realized that Ricky was gathering his things from the drawers and packing up his duffel bag.

I had a moment of panic. Was he leaving me, abandoning our assignment because I actually had scared him off? I thought I'd at least get a chance to try to save face after my mini meltdown, but maybe he'd simply had enough of me.

I tried to keep my voice steady. "What are you doing?"

"Oh, hey," he said. "You probably want to pack up, too. We can leave our stuff here for the morning, but we should be ready to go when we get back."

"Huh?"

Ricky regarded me coolly, only a hint of a smile in the corners of his mouth. "What's happened to you, man? You used to be so in tune with your plans and itineraries. You're spacing out on me."

The grogginess of sleep and the panic of waking up to Ricky leaving were beginning to fade, and my brain scrambled to catch his drift. *Plans . . . itineraries.* Wow, I had really been a mess the last couple of days. It had completely escaped my notice that we were supposed to be leaving the Rose Beach Inn today; we were booked at another resort, about a hundred miles down the coast, tonight and tomorrow night.

My heart sank as I dragged myself out of bed and into the bathroom to freshen up. I had wanted to help Ricky figure out what was going on here—but how could we do that when we weren't here anymore? I had wanted so badly to try to make things better for Ricky, but kept getting so distracted that I'd overlooked this giant hitch in my plans. What would I do now?

I was also embarrassed that I kept falling down on the job in front of Ricky. As I brushed my teeth, I dredged my memory to make sure I knew what else our day's itinerary held, so I could save at least a tiny bit of face.

We were supposed to drive an hour or so north this morning, I remembered, to tour the facilities of a collective of dairy farmers known throughout the region, and with a growing national profile, for their cheeses, butter, and ice creams. Remembering our brief, I wondered what was so romantic about dairy products. I mean, I liked cheese and butter and ice cream as much as the next person; but if I wasn't entirely sure what would put me in an amorous mood, well, I was pretty sure cows weren't it. But maybe Ricky knew something that I didn't about the erotic allure of cheddar.

Ricky tapped on the bathroom door and said he was going to the lounge for a cup of coffee. Left alone to gather my own stuff and pack my bag, I tried and failed to ignore a gnawing little thought that Ricky seemed less sociable than usual this morning.

I was still in my head about yesterday, I told myself. *Ricky's fair and reasonable*, I thought. *He'll give me a chance to apologize. He's just not much of a morning person.*

Yet there was still a small pit in my stomach when he came back and all he said to me, a dull look in his eyes as he sipped coffee from his travel mug, was, "Ready to go?"

He was quiet in the car, too, as we set off, leaving me alone with a swirling eddy of thoughts that were determined to suck me in and drag me down. *Something is wrong. He's upset. He isn't talking to me.*

I tried to break free with a conversational gambit. "So, do cheese and ice cream make you feel romantic?"

"Not since I turned thirty," he said, looking down the road ahead but seeming to relax a bit. Or maybe I had imagined the tension. "I can't really do a lot of dairy anymore."

"Oh," I said.

He flashed a weak smile at me. "Something for you to look forward to, youngster. Meanwhile, you'll have to let the cheese get you hot and bothered for the both of us."

"Is that . . . a thing? Have I been totally oblivious to the romantic possibilities of dairy products?"

Ricky thought about this. "I guess whipped cream has its uses."

"Huh." I looked out my window and counted a few trees to clear that thought from my mind. I turned back to Ricky. "Okay, but seriously. How does this fit in with our assignment? I hated the massage, but I sort of get why somebody else might think it was nice. I don't get this one."

Ricky shrugged. "It was probably put on our itinerary at the request of the ad department. Or maybe we're trying to boost readership in the upper Midwest or something. You're overthinking it."

"Sorry," I mumbled, worried that I had annoyed him, that I was losing even more ground, having already started the day from behind.

"You don't have to be sorry," he said a little testily, then, more softly, "See, but now I do. I'm sorry I snapped. Got up on the wrong side of the couch this morning."

I tried to take his apology at face value, to let it sink in and convince me that whatever mood he was in wasn't my fault.

But there was a potential problem with that theory, and I couldn't stop myself from pushing a little deeper, giving him another chance to lay the blame on me. "Why did you sleep on the couch?"

He chewed the inside of his cheek for a minute before he answered, still keeping his eyes straight ahead. "I thought maybe you needed some space. To decompress."

There it was.

I wanted so badly to protest, to say that I'd wanted him closer, not farther away. But I wasn't sure that he wasn't really saying that *he'd* needed the space. And I wasn't sure what to say anyway.

All I could do was say again, "I'm sorry. I'm really embarrassed."

Ricky considered this for a couple of miles. "Maybe," he finally said, "we chalk this one up to a learning curve. I'm still learning to read your signs, and I missed some red flags yesterday. And you should know that you can always be up front with me about what you need."

Now it was my turn to mull a few miles away. "I'm not sure that's entirely fair," I said. "To you, I mean. You should be able to get what you need, too, even if it's not what I need in that moment."

He shot me a glance, his eyebrows slightly raised. "What do you mean?"

"I mean," I said slowly, "that figuring out if Richard and Cecilia Rose were murdered, or what happened, is important, too. You and Erik and Tawny wanted to try to talk through it, but I didn't let you, and I don't like that I made out like my problem was more important than yours. Because it wasn't."

"Murder is kind of important," Ricky agreed with a small smile. "Feeling slimy is maybe less important, but more urgent."

I was so grateful to him in that moment. I still felt stupid about the whole thing, but at least he understood.

"So," he continued, "we took care of the urgent matter last night—right? You're not still oily, are you?"

I stuck my tongue out at him.

"Now we can get back to the important matter of murder," he finished.

"Possible murder," I countered.

"You're still not convinced?"

I tried to sort through my thoughts. "I guess I'm more confused than ever. It feels like there's more of a motive to kill Cecilia, but her death looks more natural, less suspicious than Richard's. I know the timing is suspicious, but is it really so hard to believe what the EMTs said, that an old woman under a great deal of stress would have a heart attack?"

"Maybe not, but if it really is about money, about the chain of inheritance, both of their deaths make sense as murder," Ricky pointed out. "Take out Richard to move to the front of the line, then take out Cecilia to get the loot. Which points to Lis."

"Yeah," I said dubiously. "Which makes her a really obvious suspect. Plus, the sheriff's office doesn't seem to be investigating either death as a murder. They're calling Richard an accident, and Cecilia natural causes."

"That's the genius of Lis's plan," Ricky insisted. "Yeah, it would point to her—*if it looked like anybody got murdered.* But she made sure everything looked accidental or natural, so it looks like she just got really lucky."

"Okay, how did she do that?"

"Um . . ." Ricky's confidence faltered. "Well, we think Richard wasn't alone, and we don't know where she was," he said unconvincingly.

"That's true," I conceded. "And how does the missing rug factor in?"

Ricky drummed his fingers on the steering wheel as he thought. When he stopped drumming, he said, "I got nothing."

"Yeah, me too," I said. "And what about Cecilia? The deputy said no sign of foul play."

"Maybe Lis poisoned her? Put something in her coffee?"

I thought that sounded awfully far-fetched, but at least, unlike Richard and the rug, there was a theory. Something came back to me. "When we were in the waiting room at the spa, Lis said she thought her mother hadn't been feeling well. If she had given her some kind of slow-acting poison—for the sake of argument, let's say I agree with this theory—maybe she was planting a story, with us as witnesses, so Cecilia's death a short time later wouldn't seem strange."

Ricky's face brightened. "See, now you're getting on my wavelength! I like that."

I smiled, too, happy to make him happy.

The highway had meandered inland, navigating first through coastal forest, and now through lush green farmland, the valley distantly framed by hills covered in logging forests. A roadside billboard with a picture of a smiling cow told us that our destination was only a few more miles ahead.

"It's all academic, though, isn't it," Ricky said, the light dimming from his face again. "We have to leave this afternoon, so probably we won't ever really know what happened."

I felt myself deflate, too. If only there had been something more we could have done this morning, some clue we could have uncovered before we had to leave, so we could find at least a little bit of closure. Instead, here we were, miles away, and I was about to have to eat cheese for two by myself and figure out how to feel romantic about it.

It may not have been romantic, but the dairy's visitor center was much more impressive than anything I could have imagined if you'd told me that there was such a thing as a "dairy visitor center." The building, right off the highway, looked vaguely like one of those midcentury houses with an asymmetrical roofline to evoke a ski lodge, but on a massive scale and attached to a boxy, corrugated metal processing plant. From the overflow parking lot—where we had to bounce over rutted gravel to find a spot amid a surprisingly large sea of cars, mostly with out of state license plates—I was almost certain there were no actual cows on the premises, but a bovine aroma still permeated.

True to its stylish promise, the experience got a lot more polished as we approached the visitor center building. An elegantly landscaped walkway led us to the glassy entrance hall, and the cow smell seemed to weaken, making me wonder only half in jest if they were pumping something into the air to counteract it.

I'd been given the name and phone number of a member of the dairy's marketing staff, and I'd texted a few minutes ago to let him know we were coming. As we approached the front doors, we were hailed by a tall, athletic man of about thirty-five, with stylish glasses and the kind of expensive jeans and work boots that sold on "heritage" and "American craftsmanship."

"Hey, guys, you're Oliver and Ricky, right? I'm Ryan," he said, pumping our hands enthusiastically. Again, I'd never considered who might be the ideal person to do marketing for an employee-owned dairy with an Oregon-crunchy vibe, but Ryan, with his hale-and-hearty, corn-fed-meets-collegiate hipster look, made perfect sense for the role. "C'mon in, and I'll show you around," he said eagerly.

Ryan led us through a sort of hybrid museum exhibition-factory tour, talking up the network of local dairy farms that made up the collective and dropping not-so-subtle references to the company's distribution deals with a rapidly growing list of supermarket chains nationwide. I definitely smelled the work of *Offbeat Traveler*'s ad team. No money would have changed hands to get me here, I was sure; more like a hope that if we scratched the dairy's back with a little positive coverage, they'd scratch ours at some unspecified future date with some sweet, sweet ad dollars. Oh, well. I could say nice things about dairy products—after all, it wasn't as though I was touring a munitions factory or a tobacco processing plant or something.

Our tour had taken us upstairs to a mezzanine overlooking the plant, from which vantage point we could watch machines separating curds from whey and whisking the solids off down conveyor belts to another machine where they were molded and cut into blocks of cheese. Ryan gave us samples of their cheese curds, made from scraps from the molding machine, and mine were so salty and chewy and delicious that I didn't think twice about taking Ricky's, too, when he offered them to me as soon as Ryan's back was turned.

As he walked us back downstairs toward the cavernous food court that comprised most of the main floor, Ryan said, "Have a look around and take your pick. Lunch is on me."

We took a lap, checking out the stalls offering artisanal grilled cheese sandwiches, deluxe mac and cheese, salads generously topped with crumbled soft cheeses, and giant waffle cones cradling scoops of ice cream, offered in a dizzying array of flavors. Knowing what I now did about Ricky's troubled relationship with dairy, I felt bad, wondering if he could find something that would work for him. Salads seemed like the safest bet. He surprised me by getting in line for the mac and cheese stand.

He saw my look of consternation and shrugged. "What? So it's a bad decision. I make bad decisions all the time. Sometimes that's how you get more out of life." I grinned and got in line behind him. I liked mac and cheese a lot more than salad, too.

Ryan didn't wait in line with us. He caught the eye of the woman working the cash register and made a series of complicated gestures that apparently told her to comp our food, then said apologetically, "I've gotta run, but thanks for coming, and enjoy your lunch!"

"I suppose we earned it," I muttered to Ricky as we returned our attention to keeping up with the line.

He gave me a funny look. "I think I'm supposed to be the cynical one," he said.

"You are? I thought you were the fun one, or the adventurous one, or the one who can drive. What does that leave for me?"

"You're the cute one," he said. I arched my eyebrows and glared at him, and he hastened to add, "And the grounded one, and the analytical one. And you can drive, too, kind of. In a pinch, maybe."

We had reached the front of the line, sparing me from getting too analytical and reading too much into Ricky's assessment of what I brought to our team. On the one hand, it sounded like he thought we had complementary strengths, which was probably a good thing . . . but on the other hand, did I want the garlic Gruyère mac with broccoli, or the pepper jack mac with spicy linguiça?

Suddenly mindful that the day might come when I'd need to moderate my intake of greasy, spicy foods and think of my heart health, I opted for the garlic and broccoli. Ricky, despite being older and lactose intolerant, went for the zesty sausage. We took our trays of food and entered the massive dining area, looking for open seats at one of the long communal tables, most of which were packed with family groups in vacation wear. This novel world of dairy tourism never ceased to amaze me.

We lucked into two seats at the very end of the outermost table along the back wall of the hall, affording us as much quiet as we could hope for in this giant space. As we tucked into our rich, cheesy lunch, I asked Ricky, "How long do we have before this cheese starts giving you problems?"

"A couple of hours, at least," he said breezily.

"Great. So between now and then we can figure out how this place is romantic."

"How romantic is this," he said, pointing a forkful of cheesy noodles over my shoulder. "I've got a clear line of sight to that old guy's butt crack."

I ventured a peek over my shoulder at the man sitting behind me, whose jeans were riding entirely too low as he sat eating his grilled cheese. I laughed. "Yeah," I said, "but what about the beautiful music of all these screaming kids?"

"Mmmm." Ricky closed his eyes and swayed in time as a baby in a high chair down the table started wailing, as if on cue.

Ricky's mood seemed to have improved since this morning, which made me feel somewhat better, but I was still struggling to shake my fear that I had alienated him. Looking down at my food, I asked, "Are being grounded and analytical good qualities for a fake boyfriend? For you, I mean?" I looked up shyly.

He was chewing thoughtfully. "For a fake boyfriend, sure," he said as he swallowed, then winked. "A real boyfriend also has to be cute, and to own his cuteness."

"Well, so much for me, then," I said, and he laughed. "But, um," I fumbled, "what about a fake boyfriend who sometimes gets overwhelmed and freaks out a little?"

He shrugged. "Are you still worried about that? You may recall that I knew that about you before I asked you to be my fake boyfriend."

Huh. I hadn't thought about it, but this was true.

"And I'll let you in on a secret," he said, leaning across the table. "I don't always know how to react to stuff, either."

"I'll believe that when I see it," I said.

Ricky's eyes softened, holding mine intensely in that way that I'd never been able to manage with anyone else. "You have seen it, you just haven't realized it. I fake it all the time.

Everybody does. I think I understand why it's so important to you to feel like you know—like, unambiguously *know*—how to deal with everything. But what I don't think you realize is that people who aren't Autistic are maybe better at *looking* like we know what's going on or what we're doing, but we don't actually know any more than you do. Maybe less, even, since we're less concerned about always getting things right. You try so hard, and I love that you do, and I don't think you need to change, but I wish it wasn't so hard on you."

Oh, wow. It was as if the cavernous room around us melted away, and the chair vanished from under me and I plopped softly to the ground, which rolled gently into a carpet of lush green grass dotted with wildflowers under the bluest sky, and there were no screaming children, only singing birds, and it was Ricky and me and his endlessly deep brown eyes in his beautiful face, sitting in the grass, and there were cows, but, by God, the cows *were* romantic.

The hikes and the restaurants had been nice enough; the massage hadn't done it for me, but I sort of got it; I hadn't understood how the dairy fit into our allegedly romantic itinerary at all. And yet, it was here, over a bowl of cheese that he wouldn't be able to properly digest, that Ricky had finally shown me what romance really, actually felt like.

I was stunned, in a fog. I had no idea what to say. Ricky didn't seem to notice. He balled up his paper napkin, dropped it into his now-empty bowl, and started gathering all of our dishes and trash onto his tray. "I'm going to do the most romantic thing I think you can do here," he announced, completely unaware that he already had. "I'm going to buy you an ice cream."

I saved our seats while Ricky went to get me a cone with a scoop of birthday cake ice cream. While I waited, I pondered. I wanted more than ever to do something big for Ricky, to show him I cared, the same way he kept finding ways to show me—and I was having a hard time letting go of the idea that figuring out what was going on at the Rose Beach Inn was the best I could do. We had to move on, but maybe there was a way we could keep investigating from a distance, like . . . like . . .

Once again, I had nothing.

"A real cone for my pretend lover," Ricky said, presenting me with the ice cream as he returned.

"Ooh," I said, mock seductively. "It's *lover* now, is it?"

"Sure," he said with a grin. "As long as we're pretending, why not go all the way?"

Right when I had started to feel like I was back on solid ground with him, he knocked me off balance again. Why did he keep ragging on the pretend thing?

"How do we figure out what happened to Richard and Cecilia," I said, changing the subject to distract myself from my confusion, "even though we have to leave?"

Ricky stroked his chin. "We could enlist Erik to be our eyes and ears," he suggested.

I licked some rogue ice cream drips from my hand. "That doesn't sound like much fun," I said. "And besides, I'm not sure I want Erik to have my phone number or email or anything."

"Oliver, he's a kid," Ricky said. "He doesn't use email or phone numbers. He'd probably want us to communicate through Instagram DMs or something. Which, you're right, probably wouldn't work, since you're Mr. Anti-Social-Media. Plus, it does sound kind of exhausting."

"What about . . ." I said, then realized I still didn't have an ending to my thought.

Ricky gazed out the glassy walls of the food court at the cloudless blue sky. "I thought Oregon was supposed to be super rainy. It would be kind of helpful to get trapped at the inn by a major storm, so we couldn't leave."

"Good for the ambiance, too," I agreed. "Stupid climate change."

Ricky propped his chin in his hand. "So no act of God to keep us in town. Maybe we have to give up on this one."

"That sucks," I said, crunching down the last of my cone. "You said it would help you to know what had happened. And it's all so weird and confusing. I feel like there's definitely something strange about the—"

"Rose!" The cry came from halfway across the hall, echoing as if it was the voice of God himself confirming that our destiny lay with the Rose family, though I didn't think God would sound so panicky. Ricky and I both jumped and turned to follow the noise to where a middle-aged man had knocked over his chair as he jumped up, hustling around the table to the other side where a woman in a floral print sweatshirt was gasping and clutching her throat and turning blue. "Rose, I'm coming," the man hollered.

The hall erupted into action, as people scrambled from their seats, most simply trying to get a better view of what was happening. A few people started rushing toward the choking woman, presumably to offer assistance. A number of phones were whipped out; I was dismayed to observe that far more people were filming what was happening than were trying to call for help.

Ricky and I rose to our feet, too, almost reflexively, but I hesitated to move closer. I didn't know how I could help, and Ricky seemed to come to the same realization. Things were moving quickly, anyway. The man had started thumping his choking companion on the back, then made a clumsy, ineffectual attempt at a Heimlich maneuver. Several of the would-be helpers had reached the scene, and one, a short, square-shouldered woman with a boxy brown haircut, gently pushed the man aside, wrapped her arms around Rose, and quickly and efficiently expelled the offending morsel. A smattering of cheers arose from the crowd as dairy personnel carrying first-aid kits belatedly arrived on the scene.

"Ricky." I grabbed his arm, staring intently at the woman who had saved the choking Rose. "We've seen her before."

"Yes, we have," he said.

We may not have gotten an act of God to keep us at the Rose Beach Inn, but this surely felt like some kind of sign. The woman who had been talking to Lis at the trailhead about her inheritance the morning after Richard died, the one who had first planted the seeds of suspicion in our minds, had miraculously resurfaced.

CHAPTER 12

Ricky and I both stood still, keeping our eyes locked on the brown-haired woman as she conferred with the dairy employees. The choking woman, Rose, seemed to be on the road to recovery, shakily sipping from a glass of water.

I didn't know why, but I felt the need to whisper to Ricky, leaning sideways into him and hissing, "What do we do?"

"Come around to my side of the table and sit by me so we can both keep eyes on her," he said in a low voice. We both sank slowly into our chairs, not daring to look away and lose track of her.

The woman finished her conversation with the dairy staff, then gave Rose a friendly pat on the shoulder and a few words of goodbye as she turned to go back to her own seat at an adjoining table. She appeared to be alone as she dug back into her salad contentedly. After a moment, she pulled her phone out of her pocket and began scrolling idly while she ate.

Ricky and I kept our gazes fixed firmly on her. I didn't know about Ricky, but my heart was racing a little, which seemed like an awfully silly reaction to watching a woman sitting alone eating her lunch.

"We've got to find out who she is," Ricky said with an urgency that belied the woman's placid chewing.

"Right," I said. "How do we do that?"

"We tail her," Ricky said, "until . . . um, until . . . until she goes somewhere we can get someone who knows her to identify her."

"Right," I said again. I was dimly aware that this was likely a silly diversion, and that there probably wasn't much of import we could learn by identifying this woman. I'd take any excuse to try to get even a tiny bit closer to unraveling the mystery of the Rose family.

"She's getting up!" Ricky tensed with excitement, ready to jump up and follow her. "And not bussing her seat, tut-tut."

"That's because she's only getting a refill," I said, relaxing back into my seat as the woman topped off her root beer at the soda fountain. She meandered back to her spot and sat back down, resuming her focus on her phone. I looked at my watch. "Do we need to set a cap on how long we watch her, so we're not late checking out of the inn?"

Ricky broke his stare away from the woman to give me an appalled look. "You would set a time cap on solving a murder?"

"Are we sure that's what we're doing here?"

"We won't know if we don't try," he pointed out, then tensed up again. "Look! She's getting up. And she's taking her tray, so she must actually be leaving this time. Be ready to follow her when I say go."

Our eyes followed her as she deposited her dishes in a bin at the bussing station and threw away her trash, then Ricky squeezed my arm and we both jumped up and tried to be both nonchalant and quick, keeping our distance as we followed her out of the hall toward the front of the visitor center.

Straining to keep eyes on her as we pushed through the crowds thronging the various food stalls, I said to Ricky, "This would be easier if any of us was tall."

"Did you really call me short? I am *average* height, sir, thank you very much, and I can still see her," he huffed. A second later, a family of six, the parents and the three oldest teen kids all over six feet tall, all wearing matching blue T-shirts and all carrying massive ice cream cones, pushed their way in front of Ricky and me, and I saw him briefly shoot up onto his toes, his head bobbing, as we both lost sight of our target. Average height had nothing on this family, but as soon as they passed, he grabbed my wrist and pulled me full speed ahead as he homed back in on the brown-haired woman.

As it happened, we didn't have far to go anyway. She crossed the lobby, making a beeline for the gift shop.

"Act natural," Ricky hissed as we entered the shop. "Look around at stuff, maybe buy something. I'll keep eyes on her."

"I did want some of those cheese curds," I said, eyeing the refrigerated cases that lined one wall. I found the curds quickly and got in line, casually looking around to see the woman picking up stuffed cows from a rack and smiling at them as Ricky thumbed through T-shirts on a nearby display while glowering in her direction.

She seemed to be moving aimlessly through the store, in no particular hurry, which was good news for me. After I finished checking out, I handed my bag to Ricky, saying, "I have to use the bathroom. Think we have time?"

He looked again in the woman's direction, in an exaggeratedly furtive fashion that would have been totally conspicuous if she'd been paying any attention to us instead of slowly flipping the pages of a cookbook. "Try to hurry," he said under his breath.

I took care of my business, not taking any longer than necessary but not in any particular hurry, either. Ricky liked to heighten the drama of a situation, but that didn't mean I wasn't going to thoroughly wash my hands. I was surprised to find Ricky waiting impatiently for me at the restroom door. "She's rolling," he said, nodding across the lobby toward the exit doors. I could see the woman making her way down the path to the parking lot.

We scrambled to follow her, trying to keep eyes on her as she weaved through the sea of cars, while also trying to head at least vaguely in the direction of our own car. I eventually lost her as she ducked between two giant SUVs and didn't seem to reappear on the other side. Ricky was looking around, too, and it appeared he had also lost her trail.

"All right, let's get to the car quick. Maybe if we can catch up with anyone else leaving we'll be able to pick out which car she's in," he said, pulling me toward the overflow lot.

I trotted at his heels toward the little old copper-colored car, easy to pick out among the sea of modern grayscale SUVs and sedans. "Wasn't she in a little red pickup when we saw her at the park?" A bright color seemed like a good thing. Maybe that would be easy to spot, too.

Ricky hurriedly unlocked his door, got in, and reached across to unlock mine, starting the engine as I dropped down into my seat. "Was she? I think you're right," he said. "That should help us spot her. Ideally before she gets on the highway; otherwise, we don't know which direction she'll go."

As he maneuvered into the lane to exit the parking lot, however, we saw no red pickup. "I guess we go south? She was south of here when we saw her with Lis," I suggested. "And we ultimately have to go back south to the inn anyway."

"Yeah, I guess so," Ricky said, flicking on his left turn signal. "But keep a sharp eye out for her. She may even be in a different car."

I tried to scan the faces in other cars headed our way as we followed the highway south, into the town near the dairy. Traffic was moving at the slow pace we'd come to expect in small Oregon towns, but Ricky was zipping around, jockeying for position, trying to pass as many cars as he could, both to try to catch up to the woman and to give me a chance to see if she was inside a car we weren't expecting. As we crossed one intersection, I saw a police cruiser idling at the light with the cross traffic. "Better not be too aggressive," I said mildly to Ricky.

He gritted his teeth and slowed slightly, still gripping the steering wheel tightly. "I had a terrible thought," he said. "We know she's been somewhere down south, near the inn, because we saw her meeting with Lis. But what if she lives somewhere north, like Portland or Seattle or something, and she decided to stop here on her way home? What if—"

"There!" I pointed ahead to a gas station, where an old red Toyota pickup was pulling in from a few car lengths ahead of us.

"Ah! Yes! Nice work, Oliver!" Ricky put on his signal and turned into the gas station as well. He pulled up to a pump at the island across from the red truck, and we both watched as the woman climbed out and began poking at the payment screen.

I was startled by a tap on my window. I turned and cranked my window down slightly. A cute younger guy with a curly mullet sticking out from under a ball cap hunched down to smile through the window at us. "What'll it be, fellas?"

"Huh?"

"Whaddaya take for this, premium? Ninety-three? You wanna fill up?"

"Oh," I said. "We don't want anything. We're just waiting here for a second."

The attendant screwed his face up. "You'll need to wait somewhere else, then, fellas. I got other people here who actually want gas, you know."

Ricky fumbled for his wallet, handing a card across to the attendant. "We'll take premium. Five gallons, please. Oliver, you keep watch, and at least if she leaves we'll know which way she goes."

The attendant touched the brim of his cap in thanks and

turned to the pump. I rolled my window back up, turning to look back at the woman leaning against her red truck as it filled up with gas. "I didn't know that full-service gas stations even existed anymore," I said.

"Only in Hollywood period pieces and Oregon, I guess," Ricky replied. "And New Jersey, I think. I didn't notice I was pulling up to a full-service pump. Obviously," he said, nodding in the direction of the red truck, "there's a self-service option, too."

The woman's pump finished its job. She put the nozzle back, closed her gas cap, grabbed her receipt, and hopped in the cab. I heard our nozzle click off, too, and saw the attendant pull it out and return it to the pump, screw on the gas cap, and amble away.

"She's going south again," Ricky said, cranking over the engine and engaging first gear.

As he began to pull forward, I cried, "Wait! We didn't get your card back!"

He slammed the brakes and threw the car in reverse. I rolled my window down again as he backed down the island, sticking my head out and waving to get the attendant's attention.

The attendant emerged from his booth. "Yeah?"

"Can we get our card back, please? And the receipt," I called.

"Sure, sorry," he said, heading back to the till inside his booth.

I could feel Ricky looking at me. "A receipt?"

I looked over my shoulder at him. "Don't you want to get reimbursed? Gas is expensive."

"It was five gallons! I'll live! We're in a hurry."

"Here you go," the attendant said, emerging again and handing the card and receipt through the window. The car began to move before he fully withdrew his hand.

As Ricky peeled out, I leaned out the window, calling back to the attendant, "Thank you!"

Back on the highway, Ricky waited until we were clear of the town before opening it up, trying to regain sight of the red Toyota. I had a feeling we were sharing the same unspoken worry, that the woman could have turned off the highway at any time, but within a few miles we saw her again up ahead, trundling along behind a logging truck with a few other vehicles between us.

Ricky eased up, falling into the flow of traffic, still watchful but less hurried. His hands loosened their grip on the wheel, dropping down onto the spokes as we slowed to a fifty-five-mile-per-hour Oregon mosey.

"Okay," he said at length. "She's headed back south. We know she's not staying at the inn, but she met with Lis at the park not too far away. Who do we think she is?"

I tried to remember what we had heard of the conversation between the two women. "She wanted Lis to inherit, which suggests that she had a stake in it as well. A girlfriend or partner?"

"Aw, no," Ricky protested. "Gay people can't be the bad guys. It's bad representation for our community. Besides, do we even know Lis is gay?"

"She is," I said. "Cecilia told me so."

"Ooh, I thought I'd never get to learn anything from your top-secret meeting with her," he said, a touch of mockery in his voice. "But still, maybe . . . maybe this lady is someone Lis owes money to. Maybe Lis owes her a bundle, and the only way she can pay is by inheriting her mother's millions. Maybe she's with the mob!"

"Are there a lot of lesbian mobsters? That red truck doesn't look like a mobster car," I said. "Shouldn't it be a big black Cadillac or something?"

"Hey, we don't know that *this* lady is a lesbian. Haircuts can be deceiving. And I'm sure mobsters these days can be whoever they want and drive whatever they want. There's plenty of room for bodies in the bed of a pickup."

"Still, I think they're together," I insisted. "Didn't this woman say, 'this is what *we've* been waiting for,' or something like that? A mobster wouldn't put it like that."

"Dang," Ricky said. "It'll be a real bummer if, at the end of all this, it turns out the killer in the family is the gay one."

"You wouldn't kill for me?" I cocked an eyebrow and grinned at him. "Even if we could somehow make it all look accidental, and afterward we'd be gazillionaires?"

"For a fake boyfriend, no. That's definitely real boyfriend stuff. That might even have to be husband stuff. As fake boyfriends, whichever of us didn't inherit the gazillions would have no legal claim to them. That would be foolish."

"And bad representation for our community," I reminded him, trying not to think too hard about what Ricky's stance on marriage might be, or mine.

"Yeah, that too."

For miles we headed south, the red pickup remaining a few cars ahead of us as the highway wound through farmland, slowed through tiny towns, climbed hills as we approached the coast once again, and hugged the bluffs above the Pacific. We had covered much of our route back to the Rose Beach Inn. Ricky mused, "I wonder how close we're gonna get. . . ."

We were getting very close indeed, only a few more miles to go. "Or maybe she'll keep going," I said. "I wonder how much further. We do still have to get our things and check out, you know."

"Look, she's signaling!" Ricky pointed for a second, before following suit. She was turning left, off the highway toward the town of Rose Beach. We followed her down into the little valley, no cars between us now but keeping a bit of distance. As we entered the downtown commercial district, the red Toyota swung into one of the angled parking spots along the street in front of the movie theater. We slowly motored by, then pulled into a spot on the next block, both of us keeping our eyes on the red pickup in the mirrors.

The woman got out and walked toward Ronnie's Roastery on the corner. We sat in the car and waited, our necks craned toward the café. I wondered aloud, "Do you think Mrs. Wise knows her?"

"Maybe," Ricky said. The woman emerged from the café carrying a disposable coffee cup, crossing the street and walking slowly up the block toward us, window shopping as she went. "Let's find out."

We got out of the car right as the woman passed in front of it. At the sound of our doors, she turned to look, then smiled and nodded at us, continuing on her way. We hustled in the opposite direction, to Ronnie's.

The café was empty once again when we entered, the jingle of the bell over the door echoing from the black-and-white checkerboard linoleum on the floor to the high ceiling, which on closer inspection appeared to be an old tin ceiling under countless layers of thick paint.

Mrs. Wise looked up from where she was washing her hands at a small sink behind the counter. "Hi, boys! Back for another piece of cake?"

"Not this time, I'm afraid," Ricky said. "We passed a woman coming out of here a second ago, and I know we met her here in town the other day, but I can't remember her name. Isn't that embarrassing?"

"That *is* embarrassing," Mrs. Wise nodded gravely. "I'm, like, twice your age, and I don't forget people's names after just a couple of days."

"Mmm-hmm," Ricky coughed. "So you remember her name?"

"Well, no," Mrs. Wise admitted. "But that's not because I

forgot it. I never knew it in the first place. She doesn't live here in town, I don't think."

"It was worth a shot," I said. "Thank you anyway."

"You're welcome," she beamed. "Come back anytime, Mr. Popp, Mr. Warner."

"No need to rub it in my face," Ricky muttered as we left. We looked down the street to where we had last seen the brown-haired woman. She had stopped near the end of the next block to look into a store window. We hung back, loitering on the corner in front of the café.

"How do we follow someone without them noticing when there's nobody else around?" I looked up and down the small downtown, taking in its all-but-deserted streets.

"She's window shopping," Ricky pointed out. "Can't we window shop, too?"

"I suppose so," I said, and we stepped off the curb to cross the street. The first store on the opposite corner was a liquor store.

"Ooh, they have Crown Royal," I said to Ricky, looking in the window as he kept the corners of his eyes fixed on the woman down the block. "What exactly is Crown Royal? Is it whiskey?"

"Yes, it's whiskey," he said. "You wouldn't like it."

"Do you like it?"

"Not really."

The next two storefronts were vacant. The brown-haired woman was still in front of the store at the end of the block, her back to the window now, talking on her phone. I was beginning to get concerned about how quickly we'd get close enough to look conspicuous.

As we neared the middle of the block, we encountered a small shoe store. The window display was mostly dominated by women's shoes—clogs and hiking boots and sandals. "Look, Birkenstocks," I said, finding a small corner of the window devoted to shoes that were at least unisex, if not specifically targeted at men. "I've always wondered if I should get a pair."

"Those you would like," Ricky said, still looking down the street but distractedly raising a foot and wiggling his toes at me from within one of his own sandals. "Great arch support. Classic German style. You may think I'm joking, but when you get to my age . . ."

"Okay, old man," I started, but he interrupted me.

"No, look—she's moving again."

The woman was off the phone, heading across to the opposite side of the street, where she turned and started back down in our direction.

I lowered my voice to a whisper. "Should we cross, too? She hasn't gone inside anywhere else, and if Mrs. Wise is right and she's not from here, nobody else is likely to know who she is, either."

"It's a waiting game," Ricky whispered back. "If we follow her long enough, maybe she'll take us back to wherever she's staying, since she's from out of town. Then we can figure out a way to find out who she is." We started toward the end of the block, tracing the woman's path to the corner where we'd cross the street, too, but moving more quickly now.

"And what is it again," I wondered, "that we learn by finding out who she is?"

"*Something*," Ricky intoned. "Which is better than *nothing*."

I couldn't argue with that. We crossed to the opposite side of the street at the end of the block. By now, the woman had made it nearly back to the other end of this block. We moved quickly but as quietly as we could to follow her. She crossed to the next block and it looked like she was making a more direct path now, back to her car, but as we reached the cross street, one of the windows caught her eye and she made an abrupt stop.

I pulled up short, too, right before crossing the street, but

Ricky, in his zeal, was caught off guard after he had already stepped off the curb. "Oh!" he said, trying to reverse course, and then, "Ohhh!" as his classically stylish German sandal caught on a storm drain and he went down, toppling into the street, his legs twisting over each other as he fell.

He said a few other choice words as he strained to pull himself up into a sitting position in the gutter. I scrambled over and crouched down. "What happened? Are you hurt?"

"Ugh, my ankle," he sputtered, clutching at his leg and doubling over in pain. "I got caught on this stupid drain and twisted it. Cripes, Oliver, this is bad."

I looked up and around, wondering what I should do, if I should call for help.

But there was no need for that. Help was already on the way. The medical hero of the day, the brown-haired woman, was running across the street, straight toward us.

Chapter 13

"Oh my gosh," the woman said as she reached us, huffing from rushing down the street. "Do you need help?"

I was starting to freeze up with panic, which I knew was not helpful to Ricky. I probably did need help, but I wasn't sure if I should be accepting it from this particular person, who I didn't really believe was dangerous but who I did feel guilty about following all afternoon. But we were in a mostly unfamiliar place with nobody else around to rush to our aid, and Ricky needed me to help him.

"I, uh," I stammered. "He . . . he fell," I finished feebly.

"I heard that," she said. "It sounded like a doozy. What do you think, buddy? Think if we help you up you can stand?"

"God, I hope so," Ricky winced. I winced inwardly, too. It sounded like he didn't think I'd be able to help if he was really hurt. But that was probably me reading too much into things again.

The woman and I squatted down on either side of Ricky, each pulling one of his arms over our shoulders. All three of us grunted as we hoisted Ricky up into a standing position.

"What about it?" the woman asked. "Can you put any weight on it?"

Ricky gingerly planted his left foot, which he had been holding up, onto the ground and slowly tried to shift his weight off our shoulders. "Yipe! Nope!" he yelped, quickly slumping back onto us, his foot shooting back up. "Not happening."

"Oh, boy," the woman said, looking down at his suspended ankle. "That sucker's swelling up fast. You guys from around here?"

"No," I said. "We're staying at the Rose Beach Inn, out on the highway."

"Yeah, I know that place," she said, betraying no special recognition. "Look, I'm not from here either, but I know where there's a medical clinic. You need to get this looked at. I can give you directions. You want me to help you to your car?"

"Yeah, that would be great, thank you," I said, already panting under Ricky's weight. "It's over there." I indicated across the street. "The copper-colored one."

"Hey, that's neat," the woman said admiringly as we slowly hobbled across the street. "My dad had a Corvair. Rusted to bits. It's funny, I hadn't seen one in years, but there must be two around here. I saw one kinda like this being driven real slow the other day. I think it was a different color, though. More brown. But yours is real cute."

"Thanks," Ricky grunted, struggling to shift his weight entirely onto me so he could fish his keys out of his pocket. I let out a stifled gurgle as I started to buckle.

"Keep your arm up," I croaked. "I'll get them."

I almost immediately regretted this offer. Getting to Ricky's keys with his arm over my shoulders required me to twirl around in front of him until we were face-to-face, pulling his arm around me into a very close almost-hug, and then—*how had I not thought through that I would have to do this?*—reaching into his pocket. I knew Ricky was in serious pain when he let me execute this entire maneuver without saying or doing anything remotely inappropriate.

I fumbled with the surprisingly tiny keys, trying to figure out which one would unlock the door. "The octagonal one," Ricky groaned. I found the right one, turning it in the lock with a satisfying *clunk*. The three of us did a little shuffle-spin together once I got the door open to point Ricky's rear end toward the seat and lower him down.

The woman followed me around to the driver's side. As I slid behind the wheel, she leaned over in my open doorway, pointing down the road. "The medical clinic is down that way, back toward the highway. About half a mile, you can't miss it."

I nodded, going numb as I took in the dash and wrapped my hands around the skinny steering wheel, its plastic molded to look like wood grain. I had been on autopilot up to this point, but as I looked blankly at the gauges, which Ricky had told me to ignore during my last—only—driving lesson, I realized I had no muscle memory left to rely on. Ricky was moaning in the passenger seat, apparently in too much pain to realize that we had made it to a critical moment and I was failing him.

The woman shut my door, standing next to the car and looking at me curiously as I sat frozen in the driver's seat. After a few seconds, she tapped on the window. I knew how to roll down the window, I realized, so I did that much.

"Are you okay? Do you want to follow me? I can guide you to the clinic if you're afraid you might miss it," she offered, her eyes concerned under knit brows.

"Okay," I choked out.

"I'm right over there," she said, pointing down the street to her red Toyota. "I'll pull out, and you pull up behind me, okay?"

I nodded numbly, and she turned to head to her truck. I choked down a couple of breaths and resolved to do this for Ricky. I looked again at the keys in my hand. I turned to Ricky. "Sorry, which—"

"Octagonal," he moaned.

I slotted the key with the octagonal head into the dash,

planted my feet on the brake and clutch, and turned. The engine rumbled easily to life. I let out an exhale. *Okay.* I had done this much successfully.

Looking out the window, I could see that the little red pickup had already backed out into the street and was idling in front of the movie theater. I simply had to back out, too, and pull up behind her, and then follow her a half mile down the road to this clinic. A half mile didn't sound so bad. I could run a half mile in less than five minutes.

I looked down at the shift knob. I had to focus intently for a moment before the hieroglyphics inscribed there morphed into a pattern I could comprehend, but eventually I remembered how the shift pattern worked. I located the *R*, and tried to move the lever in that direction. It wouldn't budge.

"Um," I said, hating to bother Ricky, but perplexed.

"Down," he panted. "Out of first. Can't just go sideways."

Right. I pulled the lever down, toward neutral. The car bucked and died.

"Uh." I was starting to sweat.

"Clutch in," Ricky said through gritted teeth.

Oh, right. I cranked the engine over again, keeping the clutch fully depressed this time. I managed to finagle the knob over to the reverse position, started to release the clutch, and—the engine sputtered and died again.

"Too fast." Ricky shook his head.

"But I have to be fast. This is an emergency," I protested.

"Ughhh," Ricky moaned.

I reached for the key to start the car again, then paused. "It's still in reverse . . . I probably have to go back to first, huh?"

"No," Ricky said huskily.

"No? I can start it here? Wish I'd known that before." I was starting to get punchy.

"Just start the damn car," he barked.

I started the damn car, in reverse, tried to come off the

clutch, and stalled again. Over Ricky's moans, I heard a shout from outside the car. I saw the red pickup in the rearview mirror; the woman had backed all the way down the street to come check on me. I cranked down my window again and stuck my head out.

"Are you doing okay? Having some trouble?" she called from inside her truck.

I could only nod.

"Do you want me to drive you there? Hold on, let me repark." She wheeled her truck into an open spot next to me, and I climbed out and into the backseat as she came around.

"Not much of a driver, eh," she said sociably as she settled into the driver seat and, in what looked to me like one fluid motion, turned on the car and backed out into the street.

"Thank god," Ricky groaned.

"I've only had one lesson," I explained.

Her eyes flicked to me in the rearview mirror. "Didn't ace the test, huh?"

"Not yet."

With an expert—or, at least, someone with a valid driver's license—behind the wheel, it was indeed a short trip. Within a couple of minutes, we had pulled off the road into a small parking pad in front of a nondescript building that could very well have originally been built as a craftsman-style house. A sign above the door identified it as the ROSE BEACH COMMUNITY CLINIC.

Our helper and I guided Ricky up a ramp to the front porch and into the building. The receptionist jumped up as soon as we entered, and within seconds Ricky was in a wheelchair, being whisked back to an examining room.

"Gosh, I don't know how to thank you," I said to the woman when we were alone in the waiting room.

"Happy to help," she said. "I'll tell you, it's been a heck of a day. Here I've been, killing time, nothing much to do, and first I give some choking lady the Heimlich while I'm eating lunch, and now I get to help you guys. I feel like a real Florence Nightingale today."

"You saved our bacon," I said, smiling shyly. "I don't want to hold you up, though. Maybe I can see if there's a cab we can call to get you back to your car?" I really did feel immensely grateful, and felt that, if nothing else, I could repay her kindness by leaving her alone and letting her go on her way without any further suspicion from us. I owed her at least that much, probably significantly more.

But she shrugged. "I don't mind waiting, if you don't mind the company. It seems to me you'll need some help getting back to the inn. I don't think your friend's going to be able to drive you."

"Are you sure? I don't want to take you out of your way. Won't you end up stuck out there?"

"Not at all," she replied, steering us toward a cluster of chairs facing the reception desk. "Have you met any of the other people staying at the inn? The Rose family?"

"Yes, we've, uh, had an interesting few days with them."

She laughed. "I'll say you have. So you've met Lis? She's my wife. I'm Denise."

Denise offered me her hand, and I shook it, pleased with myself for correctly deducing their relationship. "Oliver. The sprained ankle is Ricky."

"So it's easy," she said. "I'll drive you back to the inn in your car, then Lis can take me back to town."

"Okay, sure," I said, wondering why she wasn't staying at the inn with her wife.

"You're probably wondering why I'm not staying at the inn with my wife," she continued.

"Well, it's not really any of my business," I demurred.

"Nah, whatever. You've met that family, you know there's lots of dirt. I'm Lis's dirt. You know how long she and I have been together?"

"No," I said.

"Fifteen years." She jabbed a finger into my arm to punctuate each syllable. "You know how many times I've been to her mother's house? Zero. When she does family stuff, I'm not invited. After fifteen years! Isn't that pathetic?"

I didn't think I should respond, but I thought it was more sad than anything. She must have loved Lis very deeply to have put herself through that kind of disrespect for so long.

Or, a little Ricky voice in my head piped up, *she must have been playing a really long game, waiting for those gazillions to make it worthwhile.* I hoped the little Ricky voice was wrong, but I had to admit he might have a point.

"So she's been trying to reconcile with her mom after that crone wouldn't talk to her for years," Denise went on, "and to my mind, wouldn't a true reconciliation include her mom accepting her fully? I'm like, if she wants to make nice, bring me along and let her make nice with your whole life, right? Lis waffled and wavered about it for a while, but when it came down to it, she wouldn't bring me, yet again. So I came on my own, and have been staying in a motel down the highway, trying to convince Lis to change her mind and let me come show them how much I love her and how proud of her I am. Anyway, turned out that was all a waste of time."

"I'm sorry," I said. "That sounds really hard. You shouldn't be treated like that."

Denise looked down at her hands in her lap. "Yeah, that's what my therapist says, too. But, like, that's the *one thing*, you know? Everything else is great. It's a really big one thing, but it's the only one. It feels like I'd be losing too much if I let that be the sticking point."

Losing too much, like a big payday now that the old lady's dead? the Ricky voice in my head wondered, dripping with suspicion.

"I feel kinda guilty, though," Denise said, still studying her hands. "I mean, now that Cecilia's actually dead—see, Lis was written out of her will a long time ago. And I thought, this reconciliation might mean more if Cecilia put Lis back in the will, like, as a show of good faith, you know? I guess I also felt like, if Cecilia still couldn't accept Lis fully—i.e., accept me, too—then at least she could paper over it by leaving us some money. Isn't that awful? I feel like such a ghoul."

I considered this. "Based on what I've observed of Lis's family this week, it seems like it might be very hard to have healthy relationships when there's that much money involved."

"You might be right," Denise nodded. "Especially when there's someone as stubborn and narrow-minded as Cecilia in the middle of all those relationships. I shouldn't speak ill of her now, I suppose, but she never acknowledged me, so what do I owe her? It's never been about money for Lis and me, anyway. She's a marriage and family counselor—that's pretty funny, right?—and I teach high school chemistry. We love our little life in Portland. We don't need all the crap that comes with that kind of money. I mean, look at what's happened. Richard probably killed himself, and Cecilia's such a drama queen, she couldn't live without her little prince. She had to go and pull a Debbie Reynolds on us."

I was shocked. "You think Richard killed himself?"

"Lis does. There wasn't any note, but he and Rachel were having a lot of problems. He was drinking a lot, he'd lost his position as department chair and probably would have gotten fired if he didn't have tenure, we're fairly sure he was having an affair, and he and Rachel were always on the verge of divorce. She was putting the screws on him to collect some money he had loaned to his cousin, you know, Mary Alice, who owns the inn? We think Rachel wanted to make sure she got her money back before she left him."

"Wow," I said. This was a lot to swallow.

The Ricky voice floated back into my head. *But how much of it is true? Any of it?*

"Anyway, now that I think about it, I think Lis mentioned you guys to me yesterday."

"She did?"

"Yeah, she called me while her mom was getting a massage, which—well, you know how that ended. She was telling me about this cute young couple at the inn, and how her mom seemed to really like you guys. I think she was starting to consider letting me come. So, thanks for that. You almost got me across that finish line."

If that had been how Cecilia showed she liked you, I was glad she hadn't disliked me. "Glad we could help, sort of," I said. "We are usually a little more with it than we have been today—well, Ricky is, anyway. Sometimes."

Denise laughed. "I think it helped her to see her mom interact with other gay folks, that's all. Our circle in Portland is queer as you like, but that had never intersected with her family before."

I smiled vaguely at her, wondering how Ricky was doing. She cut into my thoughts. "So how much longer are you guys staying at the inn?"

Oh, crud. We were supposed to have checked out by now! We were supposed to be checking into a different resort, nearly two hours away, within the next thirty minutes!

"I think I need to figure that out. Sorry. Thanks for reminding me. Excuse me," I stammered, scrambling to my feet and fumbling in my pocket for my phone. I stepped out onto the porch, my mind doing its own scramble to figure out what we could do.

Denise was probably right; Ricky almost certainly wouldn't be able to drive this afternoon, and maybe not tomorrow, either. I couldn't drive us the hundred miles to the other resort—I couldn't, right? No, of course not—so it looked like we were stuck in Rose Beach after all. I wondered, as I dialed the inn, whether there were any other rooms available at Denise's motel up the highway, in the event that Mary Alice needed us out. She was very kind and accommodating, though, when I explained what had happened. Of course we could stay, she said.

Then I called the other resort and asked if we could shift our reservation by a couple of days, catching them on our return trip to California. That worked, too. Crisis averted. I had fumbled earlier in trying to get Ricky to the clinic, but at least now I could smooth out our logistics.

I returned to the waiting room to find Ricky sitting in his wheelchair in front of Denise, looking completely wiped out, his ankle elevated and wrapped tightly in a thick bandage. "Look who's here," Denise said, beaming. "You better check in with the nurse, but then I can take you back to the inn."

The nurse met me at the check-in desk. "It's a pretty standard sprain," she said. "Keep an eye on the swelling. It should go down in the next day or two. Keep it elevated, keep him off it as much as possible, keep the bandage on with good compression, ice it as long as he can stand it. Nothing to get too excited about."

"Can he drive with it?"

The nurse shot some side-eye in Ricky's direction. "Certainly not today. It really should be nothing to get too excited about, but he got excited. You've got kind of a baby on your hands when it comes to pain, huh? We had to give him some serious painkillers to calm him down. The doctor gave him a prescription, but if I were you"—she dropped her voice to a whisper—"I wouldn't fill it. He doesn't need it. Give him ibuprofen if he needs something."

I glanced over my shoulder at Ricky. He caught me looking, so I flashed him a smile. He closed his eyes in return in a show of exaggerated suffering. Ricky having a low tolerance for pain was an interesting development. It didn't exactly *please* me, but it helped sometimes to have some reminders that this fearless, sweet, take-charge, funny, impossibly handsome devil was actually human.

"He said you'd take care of payment," the nurse said, breaking into my thoughts. Devil, indeed. "The cost for his visit today is five hundred dollars. It looks like his insurance has a high deductible. He said he's on a plan from the exchange; you know, if you have an employer-provided plan, you should consider adding him to your coverage."

Adding Ricky to my insurance seemed like a big leap for a fake relationship, never mind the major flaw with that plan. "I'm still on my mom's insurance," I said.

Five hundred bucks, though. I wondered as I looked at the cards in my wallet if it would be wrong of me to give Ricky some employer-provided healthcare anyway. I couldn't really afford it, and I did need him healthy to be able to finish my assignment. Maybe it was a work-related injury. If anyone questioned that, we could point to the photos he took at Ronnie's Roastery, right across the street from where he fell. Sure, he didn't take them today, but who would know?

I pulled out my corporate credit card. "Will this work?"

CHAPTER 14

Back at the inn, Denise and I took up our positions propping up either side of Ricky as we dragged him from the parking lot to the lobby. He was increasingly uncooperative as he grew sleepier from the painkillers. "My armpits hurt," he groused.

"We're almost there," I said. I was aiming for soothing, but it might have come out closer to a grunt.

We made it to the elevator, and when it opened, Lis stepped out, her eyes going wide as she saw Denise.

"Hey, babe," Denise said. "Look who I found."

"Oh, uh—oh!" Lis stammered in surprise. Quickly assessing the situation as we shuffled onto the elevator, she called after us, "I'll ask Mary Alice to send some ice down to your room!"

"See, she's a good egg," Denise said as we rode down the elevator.

Or eager to make us think she is, anyway, with your help, my inner Ricky intoned, as my outer Ricky whimpered on my shoulder.

Denise and I finally got him into our room, and deposited him onto the bed. I piled all but one of the pillows in the room up and hoisted his leg, shoving the pile under his ankle.

"Well, I better go find Lis," Denise said.

"Thank you again, so much," I said, relieved that, with her help, I'd been able to actually take care of Ricky in an emergency.

We met Erik at the door, bearing a bag of ice. He craned his neck to look into the room, trying to catch a glimpse of our patient—everyone loves to look at a car wreck, don't they?—but I didn't invite him in.

Ricky and I were finally alone. We had made it past the moment of crisis, and I was determined to take the best care of him I possibly could. I brought the bag of ice to the bed, arranging it on top of his ankle. He started squirming, trying to scoot up into a sitting position, so I helped shift the pile of pillows under his ankle, then pulled the pillow up behind his back so he could comfortably sit against the headboard of the bed. I went around to the other side of the bed and hopped up to sit next to him.

"Do you need anything else?" I asked.

"Can I have more medicine?"

"No," I said. "That stuff was strong. You shouldn't have any more for several hours."

He screwed up his face into a pout. "Fine. Can I have something to drink?"

"Some water?" I got up, thinking of the tumblers in the bathroom.

"I was thinking more like a beer."

"I don't think so," I said. "Not with those painkillers in your system."

"Wine?"

"No!"

"Unh," he whined. "A Diet Coke?"

"Yes," I conceded. "You can have a Diet Coke. Will you be okay here while I run up to the lounge to get it?"

He nodded listlessly, then tilted his head back to the headboard and closed his eyes.

* * *

I passed Rachel exiting the lounge as I went in, so I wasn't surprised to find Erik holding court behind the bar while her red-haired daughters, Reille and Rayleigh, sipped sodas.

The girls regarded me coolly, but Erik jumped to attention, as eager as ever. "Do you need something else, Mr. Popp?"

"*Ricky* would like a Diet Coke, please," I said.

The younger of the girls shot an amused look back and forth between me and Erik. "Who's Ricky? Your boyfriend?" She giggled, though I wasn't sure what was funny about this.

"Reille, stop. Don't be inappropriate," her older sister admonished. At least, I thought she said "Reille." She had a mouth full of soda and ice when she started speaking, which dribbled out as she spoke, so the name really sounded like "Rugherre." If asked in court to swear to whether she'd said "Reille" or "Rayleigh," I'd have had a very hard time.

"Erik's jealous of your boyfriend," the younger girl whispered while her cousin's back was turned.

"Yeah, well, you're jealous of anyone who has a boyfriend," her sister taunted. "God, I can't wait to go home and see *my* boyfriend. He won't believe what a horrible time we've had."

I figured these girls were bored and lonely and dealing with tremendous loss, and the least I could do was make a little idle conversation with them. Unfortunately, I'd never really known how to talk to teen girls, even—especially—when I'd been a teen boy. "Where is home?" I attempted. "Where are you from?"

The older girl rolled her eyes at my weak attempt, but replied, "We live in California."

"Really? Me too. Where?"

"We live in Kensington," the younger girl said. "You've probably never heard of it. It's near Berkeley."

"I know where Kensington is," I said. "I live in Oakland."

The younger girl took this in disdainfully. "Like, the poor part?"

Compared to Kensington, most of Oakland was poor, but I wasn't sure what to say in the face of this rudeness.

"Rauaughaugh!" Her sister, through another mouthful of soda, again chided her poor manners.

Erik placed the Coke on the bar in front of me. I was determined not to leave having let these girls get the best of me. They may have considered me their economic inferior, but at least we knew a common geography. "Where do you go to school? Do you go to El Cerrito High?"

"No," the older girl sniffed. "We go to College Prep."

"Ah," I said. "That's a very impressive school. What grade are you in?"

"I'm going to be a junior and she's a freshman," the girl said.

"A junior, huh. Time to start thinking about college."

"Daddy wanted me to go to Cal, 'cause it would be free since he worked there, but I don't think I'm going to college. I'm going to be an influencer."

"Hmm," I said. "That seems like a tough job to really succeed in."

"I already made forty grand last year"—the girl shrugged—"and I figure I can go to cosmetology school if I really need a backup. Like Tawny."

It struck me as odd that these girls were so fond of the misfit wife of their father's cousin. She seemed like the kind of person their mother would try to train them to steadfastly avoid. "You guys like hanging out with Tawny, huh?"

"She's so awesome," the younger girl said. "She's, like, a free spirit."

"You get to see much of her?"

"She has an aunt, I think, who lives in Oakland, so she's come to see us a couple of times when she was going to see her aunt," the older girl said.

"It's funny, though," her sister mused. "She said she was coming to visit her aunt, but then she spent all her time with us."

"She gets along well with your parents?"

The younger girl shrugged. "She liked Daddy okay, I guess. Every time she's come so far, Mother's been traveling for work. She does that a lot."

"Mmm, zip it," the older girl warned, elbowing her sister in the ribs and pointing with her eyes. Rachel had returned to the lounge and was heading our way.

"What are you talking about?" It was less an effort to join into the conversation than an imperious demand. The girls rolled their eyes at their mother.

I jumped in. "We just discovered we're neighbors."

"We're not neighbors," the elder daughter corrected me. "He lives in *Oakland.*"

"Like Tawny's aunt," her sister added, which earned her another shot to the ribs.

Rachel glared at all of us. "Tawny has an aunt who lives in Oakland? How fascinating. But why," she demanded, "are you talking to that woman about her undoubtedly appalling family?"

"She was staying with us," the younger girl said. "It would have been rude not to talk to her."

"Staying with us here, we mean," her sister added quickly.

"Mmm-hmm," Rachel said through pursed lips, her eyes flashing. "From now on, rude or not, you are not to speak to that woman, do you understand? Now go down to the room and start packing. I need to find out if there's going to be a reading of your grandmother's will, but I want to be ready to leave as soon as we can."

"Yes, Mother," the girls said in concert, slipping down from their bar stools. As they neared the door, the younger girl called back to me, "Hey, tell your boyfriend I think Erik *should* be jealous of him, 'cause he's so hot he melts my butter."

"Reyuhhh!" her sister chided, her voice trailing off as they ran through the lobby before I could be sure what name she had said.

Rachel sighed in exasperation at her daughters, then turned to me. "They lied to me there, didn't they," she said curtly. "About Tawny. What did they tell you? Did they give me the same story they gave you?"

I squirmed uncomfortably on my stool. I didn't want to lie to Rachel, but it didn't seem like my place to get involved.

"Never mind," she said. "I can tell by your face they lied to me. That woman was in my house, wasn't she?"

She sank down onto the stool next to me and put her forehead in her hands. After a second, she looked up again to ask me, "Do you have a cigarette?"

"No, I don't," I reminded her.

She eyed Erik, wiping down the counter along the back of the bar and trying not to get involved in our conversation. "No use asking him, either, I suppose. Nobody smokes anymore. Not even Tawny all of a sudden, who you'd think would be the kind of person to puff her way right through the third trimest—" She cut herself off, staring into space for a beat, then straightened up. "Of course, I don't smoke, either. It's a disgusting vice. Erik," she called, "give me a vodka rocks."

Erik turned reluctantly to join us. "I told you, I can't serve you alcohol. I'm not old enough."

"Seriously? Who's going to tell?"

"I'm sorry," he said with a shrug. "My mom might be back in a minute. She could do it."

"Look," Rachel snapped. "Give me the bottle. I'll pour it myself."

"I don't think—"

"Give me the bottle! Until your mother pays me back, I own half this place anyway. Give it to me, or I'll . . . I'll repossess your hot tubs!"

This was getting ugly, and Ricky's Coke was at risk of going flat. "Excuse me," I mumbled, slipping off my stool and making a break for the lobby as Rachel stood on the rungs of her stool and started leaning over the bar, slapping the air in Erik's direction with one hand and reaching for the vodka with the other.

Ricky accepted his Coke with a reproachful, "Took you long enough."

"Sorry," I said. "I was practicing my small talk at the bar with Richard and Rachel's daughters. It may please you to know that, while Erik is jealous of you, the teen girl contingent around here is jealous of me. They think you're a hottie."

"Darn right," he grumbled.

I climbed up next to him on the bed, sneaking a peek as I went. His face was haggard, with bags under his eyes, his hair in disarray, his body language cranky and petulant, and yet still, somehow, he *was* hot. Those girls were right to be jealous, I thought, though only of the pretend me, not the real me.

Ricky sipped his Coke, then said, "So, we ever gonna talk about your new friend? My rescuer, slash possible mob bag lady, slash murder accomplice?"

"Be nice to her," I said. "She helped us both in your hour of need."

"It hurt so bad," he whined.

"I know," I said, dropping my head onto his shoulder.

"So," he asked my hair, "who was she?"

"Oh, yeah," I said, popping back up. "She's Denise. She's Lis's wife."

"You were right," he yawned. "Did they bump everybody off?"

"I don't know about that," I said. "I don't think so, but I tried to look at it like I thought you would, too, and that side of me still thinks there's a chance."

"You tried to think like me?"

I smiled at him. "I didn't even have to try that hard. It was as if you were already there in my head. You have a tendency to be very suspicious, you know that?"

"That doesn't sound like me," he grumped. He looked around the room, his eye landing on our packed bags on the sofa. "Weren't we supposed to leave here today? What happened there?"

"I arranged with Mary Alice to stay tonight and tomorrow, since you can't drive. And I pushed back our reservations at the other place."

"Okay, that's good," he said blandly, taking another sip of his Coke.

"I know it's not the one we wanted, but it's kind of like we got that act of God to keep us here." I grinned, trying to lighten his spirits with a joke.

"That's not very funny," he said, yawning again. "This really hurts. And I'm so tired."

"Do you want to take a nap?"

He nodded, and I climbed off the bed to help him maneuver back down into a prone position. I pulled a blanket out of the closet and spread it out over him.

"How's that?" I said. "An acceptable level of pretend boyfriending?"

"Oliver," he mumbled sleepily, "enough with the pretend stuff. We're not doing that anymore." He clutched the blanket up around his neck and tried to turn onto his side, facing away from me.

I stood over him for a long moment, stunned. Trying to gather myself, I looked around the room, wondering where to go, wondering when everything had gotten so blurry, realizing that the blurriness was the tears gathering in my eyes. I walked stiffly, unthinkingly to the couch and sat down, looking blearily down at our bags next to me.

Where had this come from? I had failed, obviously. I had been so thrown by Ricky's sudden reappearance in my life and I had never recovered my footing. I'd been teetering on the edge of total meltdown for days, unable to remind Ricky of any reason why he might ever have possibly liked me.

He, meanwhile, had been trying everything, I realized. He'd tried the fake boyfriend gambit to put me at ease, but it had put me in my head instead. He'd tried to teach me to drive to give me a way to help him, but when the moment came when he really needed that help, I couldn't do it. He'd tried giving me Prosecco to lower my inhibitions, and I'd lowered them too far.

Ricky had never been unkind to me before, but apparently he'd finally given up. Whatever fun we'd had together in Washington had been lightning in a bottle that we couldn't recapture. I tried to think of what to do about the rest of the trip. Try to be professional, get through it. Maybe start looking for a new job when I got home, so I wouldn't always have to be reminded of how humiliated and hurt I felt right now.

I looked around the room again, trying to gather myself. Ricky's back was rising and falling, his breathing heavy. If he had so completely given up on me as to be able to cut me loose so cruelly and then fall asleep without a hitch, so be it. I'd be professional the rest of the week, starting now. Only—maybe not in the same room as him. I dug my laptop out of my duffel and headed for the door.

I trudged my laptop down the bluff to the beach without thinking much about where I was going. I sat down on a sunbleached log, opening my computer in my lap and staring numbly at the blank screen. It was windy down here, and as the wind buffeted my face, a stinging in my eyes informed me that tears were forming again.

I shut the computer and set it down next to me. Who was I

kidding? In my best moments this week, I'd struggled to focus on my job even a little bit. Surely trying to be professional in my lowest moment was a fool's errand. I leaned forward and rested my elbows on my knees, propping my chin up in my hands and letting the wind fly through my hair and beat at my face.

I had been a bit heartbroken since my last trip with Ricky, but that had snuck up on me slowly as I'd realized I didn't know how to maintain our long-distance friendship. Now I felt my heart breaking in a whole new way as Ricky had abruptly ended whatever confused hope I'd managed to scare up from our reunion, and this one was a much sharper, more acute pain. I hunched over, folding my arms as I dropped them to my knees, and dug my fingernails into the skin on my arms to try to feel anything other than the pain of knowing that my resolve to show Ricky that I cared for him hadn't been strong enough to defeat my ability to self-sabotage by being too anxious, too easily overwhelmed, too . . . me.

A pair of bare feet with cheetah-print toenails padded through the sand in my peripheral vision, stopping in front of me. "Hey, Oliver," Tawny said in a flat voice. My eyes traveled upward, past her short black shorts, the pair of red patent leather peep-toe heels hanging in her hand, and her surprisingly loose-fitting, tasteful linen peasant blouse, meeting a face that looked only fractionally happier than I felt.

"Still having a bad day today, huh," she said, dropping down onto the log next to me.

I shrugged, wiping the back of one of my hands across my eyes. "I'm sorry about yesterday. I didn't mean to yell at you. I was upset about something else."

She shrugged in return, the heels in her hand, now hanging between her legs, clicking against each other as they rose and fell. "It's okay. I'm having a bad day, too," she said. A finger swiping underneath one of the lenses of her sunglasses told me that she'd been crying, too.

We sat together in silence for a while, the wind whipping around us, Tawny hunched in a similar posture to mine. Eventually, she dropped the shoes down into the sand, stretched out her legs, and leaned back on the log. "Well, this is depressing," she said. "Should we get it off our chests? What's going on with you? Trouble with Jeff?"

"Ricky," I corrected her, not wanting to answer otherwise.

"Oh, yeah. Anyway, you guys'll work it out," she said, pushing back some hair that had blown into her face. "I can tell he really loves you."

I thought I had been miserable before. I tried to hide my face in my hands, but I couldn't hide the heave of my shoulders as I started full-on weeping. How badly I wished I could believe Tawny more than I believed myself, but the hurt of Ricky's words was too fresh and too deep to overlook.

I felt Tawny put one arm around my shoulders and the other on my arm, and heard her worried voice near my ear. "God, is it that bad? What happened? Did you mess up? You musta messed up pretty bad."

She released me and took up another hunched position, her arms wrapped around her legs, as I struggled to compose myself and wipe my face again. She blew out a sigh. "I've been there, too. I've messed up a lot, and now—well, let's just say, the way I've messed up now, at least you'll never have to worry about doing what I've done."

I looked curiously at her through puffy eyes. She pushed her sunglasses up onto her head, using both hands to wipe her eyes, smearing her mascara slightly. "You won't judge me, right? You've messed up, I've messed up. You won't judge me. I gotta tell somebody."

She took a deep breath, looking away, then turning back to me. "I'd be a good mom, wouldn't I?"

I was too much of a mess to come up with anything more convincing than a weak nod.

"I wanted it so bad," she continued, her voice quavering a

little. "A baby. I knew if I had a baby, it would all be okay. I kinda thought it would just happen, you know? Wiley and I, we used to party a lot and have a lot of fun and we were really into each other, right? I mean, we were doing it *all the time*. So finally, one day, I ask Wiley why he thinks we haven't had a baby yet. And he gets all serious and acts like he's better than me, and is like"—she deepened her voice to do a Wiley impression—" 'I've been making sure that doesn't happen, because you shouldn't have a baby unless you get clean.' "

She seemed to want validation. "That's hypocritical, if he was using, too," I said, my voice still a little wobbly. "But if you wanted to be parents, you should probably both have been clean."

"Yeah, I know," she said in a small voice. "He always thinks he's so in charge, so I guess he thought he could stop anytime he wanted to, but I was so weak and stupid that I couldn't. But I did stop. I even finally quit smoking. Do you know how hard that is?"

"You should be proud of yourself," I said. "I've heard it's really hard."

"It is," she said, the pride in her voice rising triumphant over the wind. "I don't even use the gum no more, or vaping, or anything. I haven't been this much of a goody two-shoes since I was nine. So then I go back to Wiley, and I'm like, what about it? And he's all, 'Tawny, you're so dumb, I can't get you pregnant 'cause of the cancer.' You better believe I was mad."

"He had been lying to you?"

"Yeah, can you believe it? That manipulative son of a—" Tawny cut herself off with a yelp, raising her hands in an unsuccessful attempt at a catch as a gust of wind blew the sunglasses off the top of her head. We both jumped up, scrambling over the log, looking at the patch of thick, untamed brush that we had been sitting in front of.

"My Dolces!" Tawny cried. "Can you see them anywhere? Wiley'll definitely kill me now if I lose them."

We were both stepping gingerly through the growth, pulling branches apart and pawing through leaves. I stopped, struck by Tawny's last words. "What do you mean, 'definitely kill you now'? Were you worried he would kill you before?"

"That's what I was telling you," Tawny said, lowering her face into a bush. "He's been acting so weird the last couple of days, I think he found out what I did. I'm really scared of what he's gonna do."

We were getting further and deeper into the brush than I thought the sunglasses were likely to have gone, but Tawny's frantic searching had me convinced that this was truly important to her. I headed toward an odd indentation in the ground cover, as though there had been a small sinkhole, wondering if there was water here and the glasses had rolled down toward it. But there was no water, and no sunglasses, either. The impression had been formed by something flattening the bushes in this spot; something that looked like a big piece of garbage, which struck me as odd for this wild, inaccessible, unpolluted beach. I leaned in for a look.

"Eek! I found them," Tawny screamed behind me. I turned to see her arm joyfully waving the designer shades aloft. I was still curious, though. I turned back, taking another step closer to the foreign object that had crushed the brush. It was, I judged as I approached, about five feet long, thick and oblong and sort of imperfectly cylindrical. It looked heavy. How had it gotten here? I looked up the bluff. Far above, the balconies of the inn jutted out from the stone facing.

I crouched down next to the object, laying a trembling hand on its rough surface.

"Oliver, what are you doing over there? Did you find something?"

"Yes," I called back. "I did! I found it! The rug!"

Chapter 15

Tawny plodded unsteadily over to me, putting her sunglasses back on as she went. "This would probably be easier if I wasn't barefoot," she said. "Though maybe not, considering the shoes I have."

Finally, she made it, looking down with me at the rolled-up sisal rug from Richard and Rachel Rose's suite at the inn.

"Holy crap," she said, looking from the rug up to the balconies soaring hundreds of feet above us, her face white. "This went *far*."

"Yeah," I said, excitement pushing a bit of my earlier anguish aside. "It came from Richard and Rachel's room, and it was missing after he fell. I wonder what it means that it's down here."

"The cops told you it was missing? What did they think it meant?"

"No," I corrected her. "We discovered it was missing. Ricky and I did. We reported it to the sheriff's deputy, but she didn't seem that interested."

"Wait, you were poking around in Richard's room? How come?"

"Looking for clues. Trying to figure out what happened."

"Gosh, I thought you guys were joking around last night.

You really are investigating. And you really don't think he was alone. Well, what do *you* think this means?"

"I don't know," I admitted. "I really wish I did."

Tawny pondered the rug for a few seconds, then said, "Yeah, but, like, what's it to you? Why investigate at all? I mean, like, this is definitely weird, but if there's nothing else—nobody else—saying that anything happened, why waste your time?"

"For Ricky," I said, without hesitation. "He saw Richard fall. He saw him *die*. He doesn't show it, but it really freaked him out, and he'd feel better if we knew what had really happened."

Tawny nodded, as if this made sense to her. "Okay, but if you find something . . . If, say, you find out who was with Richard—if he really wasn't alone, I mean—are you gonna tell the police?"

My thoughts had wandered back to Ricky, but they had taken on an even more jumbled and distracted, slightly numb form, and as her question registered, my brain struggled to spit out a coherent answer. "Probably? If that person pushed him, yeah, I guess we'd tell the police, right? Wouldn't you? But if that person was there, but he fell by accident and they didn't see it happen, or couldn't help him or anything . . . well, I don't know exactly what we'd do in that case. That person would have been a witness who didn't speak up, which is morally wrong, and maybe illegal, I'm not sure, but maybe the police wouldn't need to know."

"Gosh," Tawny said, looking back down at the rug.

"What are you two doing in there?" We followed the somewhat artificially chummy voice to see Wiley staring at us from back near our log, a smile not quite reaching his eyes. He was supporting Lis on his arm; her bemused smile seemed more genuine.

Tawny clutched my arm as we tramped through the bushes

back to the beach. I didn't love that she kept touching me, but I reminded myself that supporting a barefoot woman tramping through bushes was the gentlemanly thing to do, and that flinching or yanking my arm away would be very ungentlemanly, plus if she fell, she'd probably lose her sunglasses again.

"We found something," I said as we joined Wiley and Lis, not sure I wanted to be more specific, or if it would upset Lis.

"The rug from Richard's room," Tawny chimed in, blowing my attempt at tact and discretion.

"What? Down here?" Lis said, her smile gone.

"We had discovered that it was missing from his room," I said. "It appears to have ended up down here somehow."

Lis had tensed up, her eyes narrowing. "What—what do you think it means?"

"I don't know," I said again. I was starting to wonder if I knew anything. My thoughts were becoming very slippery.

"I bet I do," Wiley said, his voice cutting through my befuddlement, his tone still blustery and still at odds with the hard glint in his eye. "I bet Richard got drunk and thought the rug was talking to him, so he took it outside and threw it off the balcony. Hey, I bet that's how he fell—he went down with the rug! Right, Tawny? Don't you think that's what happened?" He laughed unpleasantly. I found myself more confused than ever by his bizarre scenario.

"That's not funny, Wiley," Lis said sharply. "None of this is funny."

"Yeah," Tawny said. "Not funny."

"Okay," he said, putting up his hands in surrender, then lowering them to his hips. "Should we pull it out? Take a look, see if there's important evidence on it? Maybe something he spilled?"

"No," Lis said—nervously? Was it nervously? I couldn't quite tell. Maybe the quiver I thought I heard was a trick of the wind. "Maybe it is evidence. In which case, we shouldn't touch it, right?"

I looked around at the group. Everyone was shifting their weight around uncomfortably. Maybe we were all cold. Being cold was one of the few things I was sure of; I was too distracted to get a handle on what was happening or what to do. "We probably need to tell the sheriff's office," I finally said. "Ricky and I already reported the rug missing, so we should tell them we found it."

"You did? How efficient," Wiley said.

"I agree," said Lis. "We should tell the sheriff's office. This is very . . . perplexing."

"Yeah, okay," Wiley agreed.

"I'll do it," Tawny offered. "I was ready to go back up to the inn anyway, and you gotta go back up there to get any reception. I'll tootle on up right now and give the sheriff a call." She didn't wait for a response, stomping barefoot double-time across the sand to the trail back up the bluff. As she started to climb the rise, she called back, "I'm on it!"

"She's on it," Wiley said, raising a cynically arched eyebrow.

I shivered, cold from the wind, but also unable to shake my persistent discomfort around Wiley. I wanted to be somewhere warm, somewhere else, away from him. I still had a hint of a notion that there had been a reason I had left our room to come down here, but the events of the last several minutes had pushed exactly what that reason was out of my mind. Being around Wiley made me want to go be with Ricky instead, though I couldn't put my finger on why that desire had a dark tinge around its edges. "I'm about ready to head back up, too," I said, reaching down to retrieve my computer from atop the log. "I should check on my patient."

My head buzzed all the way up the bluff, thinking about the rug, wondering what it meant that it had ended up in that remote spot down on the beach. Had someone hidden it there, or had it truly fallen? Wiley seemed like he had been joking, but was it really plausible that Richard Rose had thrown the rug off his balcony and accidentally gone with it? Why would he have done that? I tried to remember what Tawny and Lis and Wiley had said and done. I knew the whole conversation about the rug had felt weird and uncomfortable, but even just a few moments later, the specifics were fuzzy in my mind. Had their behavior seemed suspicious? Did Wiley's behavior ever *not* seem suspicious? Why had I been so distracted?

What would Ricky think?

I was growing too excited to put my finger on any reason why that shouldn't be my primary thought.

As I emerged from the top of the trail and crossed the parking lot to the inn, I noticed a tall, broad-shouldered guy about my age sitting on the bench by the door, a book in his lap. He noticed me, too, and looked up and flashed me a dazzling smile.

"Hey," he said. "Oliver, right?"

I recognized that voice. I hated that voice. *Cole*. Ricky's massage therapist yesterday, who I hadn't been able to see but who I had imagined was very handsome and unnecessarily flirty with Ricky. I cursed myself to discover that he was almost even more handsome than I had imagined. Model handsome, all muscly and chiseled and tan and cheekbony. Like, distractingly handsome. Where had I been going?

"I'm Cole," he said, mistaking my stunned stupor for a lack of recognition. "I was massaging your . . . partner? . . . yesterday. Ricky. We don't get a lot of couples like you guys in around here."

"Oh?" It wasn't very articulate, but at least I'd been able to get something out.

"I hope you don't mind me saying so," Cole said, feigning modesty, giving me a beguiling blue-eyed look from under a Clark Kent curl that fell perfectly across his forehead. "You know, that I noticed you guys."

"Oh," I said.

"So, are you . . . ? Where is . . . ? What are you up to?"

Was he flirting with *me* now? "Huh?"

"Looks like you're on your own right now," he said, trying out a shy smile that, like his Hugh Grant stammering act, I felt certain had in fact been painstakingly honed in front of a mirror and deployed to great effect many times before. "If you need something to do, maybe I can help."

"What do you mean?"

He laughed his appealing, handsome-guy laugh. "I mean, I'm from around here, that's all. I can show you around if you want. Go to town, hang out. There's a park where me and my friends go—we got pickleball courts, only, like, five years late this time instead of ten. Or we could go to a movie . . . ?"

Suddenly breaking through the fog of Cole's beauty, I found myself incensed. He had been flirty with Ricky yesterday, and now he was trying to pick me up. Who did this punk think he was? What gave him the right to presume anything about Ricky's and my relationship? Our admittedly pretend relationship, I reminded myself, coming dangerously close to remembering that it was now a defunct pretend relationship. But still.

And what if it had been Ricky who had chanced by instead of me? Would Cole have made a play—another play?—for him, too, like some kind of indiscriminate himbo? Or had he been flirting with Ricky only because it was his job, while really being interested in me? Either way, I was offended, and if it was the latter scenario, I questioned his judgment, since Ricky was clearly the better-looking of the two of us.

I pulled myself up to my full five feet, eight inches and, no longer finding anything particularly appealing about Cole, said icily, "No, thank you. I don't have time to see your pickleball court. I need to get inside to Ricky."

"Is he in there?" Cole said, tensing as if to rise from his bench. "Do you want me to come—"

"No!" I barked as I sailed haughtily past him into the lobby.

My line of sight into the lounge as I entered the lobby brought my curious gaze to rest on Cecilia Rose's attorney, Bradley Benson, sitting at one of the tables in close conversation with a woman who had her back to me. My first thought was that it was Lis, which made sense as she was Cecilia's heir, but the hair was more auburn than red, and besides, I had left Lis down on the beach. What was he talking about with Rachel Rose?

I knew Ricky would want a report, and I had by now completely forgotten that Ricky had decided that he and I were no longer a team. I mentally scrambled for an excuse to loiter, hoping I could overhear something. I ambled over to the desk, where Mary Alice was working at the computer and Erik was reading in a chair behind her.

"Thanks again," I said, leaning an elbow on the desk. "For letting us keep the room, I mean. Really helped us out in a pinch."

"It was my pleasure," Mary Alice replied with a smile. Rachel and Benson had to be talking extremely quietly; no sound had carried in from the lounge so far. Of all the times for Rachel to discover discretion.

"Thanks for the ice, too," I said, leaning further toward the partition with the lounge, straining to hear.

"Not a problem," Erik piped up, looking up from his book. "You need some more?"

"Sure." Thanks, Erik. A good reason to be here at last.

"I can bring some more down to your room."

"No, no," I said quickly. "Don't do that. I'll wait here, and then I can take it down."

"O-o-okay," Erik said, giving me a funny look as he got up from his seat.

I still hadn't caught a peep from the lounge, which apparently meant I'd missed the conclusion of the meeting, as at that moment, Rachel swept out toward the elevator, followed shortly by the attorney, who joined me at the desk.

"Why hello, Mr. Popp. Hi, Mary Alice," he said, turning quickly from his cordial but perfunctory greeting of me to flashing a warm smile at Mary Alice.

"Hi, Brad," she said, beaming back.

"Hi," he said again, still smiling. Something was going on between these two.

"Do you need something, Brad?"

"Mmm, yeah," he said huskily, then, following her darting eyes and turning briefly to remember that I was there, he gave a little jump and said, "Yes. Right. I'm wondering if you have a room available for us to use tomorrow morning. I need to read Cecilia's will. I'd do it at her house, but the fire marshal's still not letting anyone in, and everybody's already here, so . . . ?"

"Hmm," Mary Alice said, consulting her computer. "We've still got a mostly full house. . . ." I felt a pang of guilt. "I have two empty rooms," she said, "but I'm not sure how everybody would feel about them. One is the suite where Richard and Rachel were staying, and the other is the room below it, where Mr. Popp and Mr. Warner were staying until Richard fell."

"You probably don't want to use the suite," I said. "The sheriff's office might want to come back for another look—you know, now that we've found the rug."

Mary Alice and Brad both looked at me as if I was spewing gibberish.

"Didn't Tawny say anything? About the rug? Down on the beach?"

"I haven't seen Tawny," Mary Alice said. "But I suppose if the sheriff comes back, the suite will be off limits." I wondered if perhaps Tawny had made the call to the sheriff from the parking lot, or if she had passed through the lobby when Mary Alice wasn't around. *The sheriff would be coming, right?* Tawny had seemed so eager to help, but it occurred to me now, too late, that maybe I should have stuck around long enough to make sure the report of the rug made it to the right place. Where had my head been?

"Maybe downstairs is better anyway," Brad offered. "Folks might not even realize it's the room where Richard fell."

"Okay," Mary Alice said. "Do you mind—can I run down there and see if we ever cleaned that room? If not, I'll need to ask Erik to do it tonight. Excuse me a second," she said, hustling to the elevator.

Brad turned his back to the desk and leaned against it with his elbows up behind him.

"So," I said slowly. "Is that what you were meeting with Mrs. Rose about? The will?"

"I can neither confirm nor deny, your honor, what I was meeting with Mrs. Rose about," he chuckled. "But, no, not about the will—at least, not directly. I've been consulting on a little matter for her."

"Were you the attorney for Richard and Rachel as well?"

"No," he said. "They live in California, so that wouldn't have been very convenient. No, Rachel's had a few questions about something that's come up since they've been up here, so she asked me for some advice."

I remembered something about Rachel meeting with a man while her daughters were at the movies, the night her husband had died. I wondered if this, not some far-fetched caper with a hitman, was the missing piece of that puzzle.

"So was this your first meeting?" I ventured, trying to still sound casual.

He gave me an amused grin. "You're very curious. No, we met once before—the night her husband died, as a matter of fact, though before we knew about it. We had this little follow-up because that particular incident rather changed the contours of her problem, as you might imagine."

"Aha," was all I could get out before, at the same moment, the front doors opened, admitting Wiley and Lis, and the elevator doors opened, bearing Mary Alice and Erik.

"Brad, we're all set for tomorrow," Mary Alice called.

"Wonderful," he replied, turning to Wiley and Lis. "Mr. Rose, Ms. Rose, this concerns both of you—especially you, Ms. Rose. We'll be reading Cecilia's will tomorrow morning, downstairs. Ten a.m., okay? Mary Alice can give you the room number." He gave a cheery wave and headed for the doors.

Lis turned to Wiley as they walked to the elevator, a look of confusion on her face. "Did he say especially me? He said 'Ms.,' not 'Mr.'?"

"Yes, that's what he said," Wiley said gruffly.

"Here's your ice, Mr. Popp," Erik said, holding out a dripping bag.

"Thanks," I said, my head swirling as I tried to keep up with everything happening all at once.

"It's no problem," Erik shrugged. "But I really could have delivered it myself. The ice machine's right next to your room."

Chapter 16

"Ricky," I called as I burst into the room, catching myself as I slipped on some drippings from the bag of ice in my hand. "Are you awake?"

I caught myself again, mentally this time, as the door closed behind me, shutting out the light from the hallway, and my eyes adjusted to the dim light of the room. I pulled up short as I neared the bed and suddenly, painfully remembered what had happened there before I had left the room.

"Mmf," Ricky snorted. "Wha?"

"Sorry," I said in a half whisper, my bubble thoroughly burst. "Never mind." I looked at the bag of ice I was carrying, sighed, and started to replace the bag on Ricky's ankle, now mostly full of sloshy water, with this new one.

As I reached for the bag of water, Ricky started pulling himself up into a sitting position, giving me a sleepy smile. "No, I'm up," he said. "Aw, you brought me fresh ice. You're so sweet."

I looked up at him in confusion, but he didn't notice, wiping the sleep from his eyes.

He went on, yawning out, "Mmm, those are some good painkillers. Anything else happen?"

"Yes, but . . ." I didn't understand what was happening

here. Had he forgotten what he had said? Had those painkillers really been *that* strong?

He was looking more alert now, still smiling at me. "You're going to start holding out on me *now*? Out with it! What happened?" He pulled one of the pillows out from under his ankle, propping it up against the headboard next to him and patting the mattress in invitation for me to sit.

I cautiously sat down, not committing to the pillow against the headboard, but instead folding my legs under me and holding my knees in a protective pose. "We—Tawny and I—found the rug. From Richard's suite."

He bolted upright. "What! Where?"

My excitement was returning, too, in spite of my confusion. "On the beach. It almost—it almost looked like it had fallen all the way down there, like it had been thrown off the balcony."

"That's so far," Ricky marveled. "Was there anything on it? Any clue as to why anyone would have thrown it overboard? Or who did it?"

"It was rolled up," I said. "I don't know if there was anything on it. We thought we shouldn't touch it, let the sheriff's office examine it as we found it."

"Tawny thought that? That sounds like you, but not really like her." Ricky grinned. *Why was he so smiley?*

"Wiley and Lis came by, too. I think it was one of them who said we shouldn't touch it."

"Probably Lis, I bet," said Ricky. "Because she knows what's on it and didn't want you to see. But what did the sheriff say when they came out?"

"Umm." My heart sank as I remembered the critical error I'd made in my desire to get away from Wiley and my misguided excitement to share this news with Ricky. "I didn't wait for the sheriff. But Tawny went up to call them, so I imagine they'll come soon. Maybe we should be ready to talk to them?"

"Yeah, probably." His eyes were shining. He didn't seem

too bothered by my carelessness. "What else did Lis say to try to throw you off the scent?"

I thought back. "She said . . . that the rug being there was 'perplexing.' She seemed confused about it."

"Convincing, huh?"

"Yes," I said absently, still thinking about the conversation on the beach and feeling boneheaded for leaving the rug. Wiley and Lis hadn't stayed down on the beach much longer after I'd left, but what might they have done in that short time? "Honestly, they were all kind of strange about it."

"Strange how?"

"Tawny wondered what we'd do if we found out what happened to Richard, or who was with him. Like, she asked if we'd call the police." Tawny didn't strike me as a particularly law-and-order type of person, and the more I thought about it, the more I wondered where the question had come from.

"What did you say?" Ricky was still rapt, leaning in as close to me as his elevated ankle would allow.

"I said it depended. If there was another person and they pushed Richard, obviously we'd tell the cops. But if there was another person and Richard fell on his own, it would maybe depend on whether that person had a good reason for not coming forward as a witness."

"That sounds about right," Ricky said, nodding. "So Lis pretended to be confused, and Tawny wanted to know if we'd squeal if we found something. What did Wiley say?"

"Wiley always seems to act like he thinks everything is funny, but in a weird, mean way, like he's keeping you out of some joke he's in on. He made a weird crack about Richard being drunk and trying to throw the rug and going over with it."

"That . . ." Ricky paused, thinking. "That actually sounds plausible, though, kind of. But why would Richard be throwing the rug? Why would *anyone* be throwing the rug?"

"That's what I still don't understand. The other possibility is that someone carried the rug out of the room and hid it on the beach, though it was more or less out in the open, just back in the bushes."

"They would have had to move fast to get the rug out of the room," Ricky pointed out. "And they would have faced a good chance of someone seeing them carrying a rolled-up rug out of the building."

I nodded. "And it's a long, treacherous walk to the beach. It would have to have been someone really strong—like, I don't think anyone here is that strong—or, more likely, two people to carry it down there. It feels more likely that it did fall there, but harder to understand *why*."

I had relaxed into the spot Ricky had made for me, sitting next to him now, leaning on the pillow he had placed there. "Okay, let's review our suspects," he said, grabbing my wrist and starting to count off names on my fingers. "We have Lis, Wiley, and Tawny. There's also Rachel—or, rather, Rachel's hit-man, killing Richard for her, then meeting her at the café."

"I think that theory's out," I said. "I know who she met with at the café."

"How long was I asleep? You've been so busy," Ricky said admiringly. "Who was it? What was the meeting about?"

"I don't know what the meeting was about," I said, "but I know it was with Brad Benson, Cecilia's attorney."

"Hmm, something to do with the will?"

"No, he said he was advising her on a personal problem."

Ricky played with another finger. "Wild card: Mary Alice? Any reason why she might have killed Richard? If only for the sake of argument?"

I furrowed my brow. I'd never considered Mary Alice, but something floated to the front of my consciousness. "She did owe Richard money."

"That's right!" Ricky waved my hand at me in excitement,

then paused to think again. "But, didn't we hear Rachel telling her she'd still have to pay it back? And Mary Alice didn't seem that surprised or upset about it. If she'd killed Richard to clear the debt and it hadn't worked, I feel like she'd have had more of a reaction—or tried to kill Rachel, too, or something."

I looked at Ricky incredulously. "Are you clearing a potential suspect? I don't think you've ever done that before."

"I am capable of personal growth." He smirked. "Or at least of occasional rational thought." He rested his head on my shoulder, still playing with my fingers. He folded down all but my index finger. "I still think Lis makes the most sense. I don't know how she did it, but the only clear motive we have goes back to Cecilia's will."

I studied the whorl of my fingerprint, my mind following its loops and dead ends. Something was sticking in my craw, but it was floating out in the ether beyond my finger's reach. There was something wrong with the will, something I had forgotten or overlooked.

Maybe Ricky could help me get closer to it. "You keep talking about Cecilia's will," I said. "What do we know about Cecilia's will?"

"What do *we* know? Not a whole heck of a lot," he said, pursing his lips at me. "You know something, I suppose. I've only guessed."

Of course. I'd been so stupid.

"What have you guessed? Remind me," I said slowly, dreading the confirmation of my colossal brain fart.

"What I've guessed, which I kind of assumed you'd confirmed without actually saying so, is that, as Cecilia's children, Richard and Lis stood to split her estate, but with Richard dead, Lis became the sole heir. Are you telling me that's wrong?"

The bed vanished with a *poof*, replaced by an endless black void into which I was falling, falling, falling, spiraling downward on my own embarrassment. I couldn't believe I'd been so . . . so . . . ugh.

"Oliver," Ricky said, his mildly worried face popping into my void. "What's wrong? You've gone pale."

I stared balefully at him through the blackness, which slowly faded away under his light, bringing me back to my spot next to him on the bed. No wonder he'd broken it off with me, even if he seemed to have forgotten that now. I'd utterly failed him.

The concerned crease between his eyebrows was deepening as he waited for any response from me. "Are you okay? What about the will? Was I wrong?"

"Yes and no," I finally managed, breaking through the embarrassment threatening to paralyze my brain and mouth.

"Okay?"

"Yes, Lis is now the sole heir. But the rest of it was all wrong."

"Can you tell me? I know you were sworn to confidence, but I figure maybe now . . ." He grabbed my hand again, lacing his fingers between mine, raising his eyebrows hopefully. "Maybe now you can let me in on it, and it can be *our* confidence?"

What now? I was already too consumed by recriminations to try to understand this confusing new gambit. But it seemed obvious that the only way out was to let Ricky into my confidence about Cecilia's will.

"I . . . you ended up with the right heir, and I never questioned how you got there. I assumed you knew, because I knew. Does that make sense?"

"Not really," Ricky said gently.

"I try *so hard*," I said, pleading. "Usually I do better. I can't believe I did this."

"Oliver, I know you try hard. It's okay if you made a mistake or if there was some misunderstanding," Ricky said, placing his other hand over the hand he was already holding.

I took a few deep, shaky breaths through my nose, gathering myself to try to explain to Ricky. "You know how I'm Autistic, right?"

"Yes, Oliver, I do," he said evenly, still rubbing my hand between his.

"So . . ." I wasn't sure how to put this. "There are a lot of ways I've tried to learn how to be . . . less Autistic, I guess? Or, to adapt, maybe, to thinking more like a neurotypical person? But, sometimes, when I'm not feeling too sharp, I forget some of those adaptations."

Ricky gazed thoughtfully straight ahead, nodding slowly. "Hmm. Kind of like code switching, but for how you think. That sounds awfully challenging, Oliver, like a lot of pressure to carry. I feel like if it was me, I'd get overwhelmed by that pressure and forget all the time—but I also feel like maybe I'd wonder why I put that pressure on myself in the first place. It seems like you shouldn't have to."

"Maybe not, in an ideal world," I shrugged. "But it's what people expect. If I don't do it, they don't know how to interact with me. Or I make assumptions or mental leaps I shouldn't. Which is what I did this time."

"Okay, I think I understand what you were saying. I said that Lis was Cecilia's heir, which is true, right? And since that's true, you assumed I had arrived at that conclusion based on the same information that you have."

"Yes," I admitted red-facedly.

"The information you're going to share with me now?"

"Yes. Ugh, I feel so dumb!"

"Oliver, please stop beating yourself up," Ricky said, putting his head back on my shoulder.

"I was just so—they asked me to keep it confidential, you know? But then it seemed like you knew, but of course you didn't know, and I should have told you, but I always take things so seriously or literally or—" My irritation and agitation were threatening again to spiral out of control.

"Oliver." Ricky's voice was firm, but with a note of pleading. "You've been distracted. Drea put this dumb pressure on us with this whole 'romance' thing, and we've both been a little freaked out about it. People have been dropping like flies here. You had every right to be distracted; it's okay to not do everything perfectly. God knows I've been a mess."

Now I was distracted again. "You have?"

"Obviously. Look at me! But that doesn't matter right now. Tell me about the will."

"The will. Right. Okay. Well, first of all, Lis is gay."

"Right," Ricky nodded. "We established that when we were chasing her wife."

"I told you that Cecilia was a homophobe, didn't I?"

"I think you did mention it." Ricky's voice betrayed only a tiny hint of impatience.

"Denise said Cecilia liked us, though, did I tell you that?"

"How could she not," Ricky said drily. "We are a delightful combination."

"Anyway, Cecilia and Lis had a big falling out when Lis came out. They were estranged for a long time, and had only recently started to reconcile. I got the impression that the estrangement had mostly come from Cecilia's side, and the reconciliation was mostly coming from Lis's side."

"Because Lis wanted to get in good with her mom to keep her claim on those millions," Ricky said insistently.

"I don't think so," I said. "Cecilia had cut Lis out of the will, and I think Lis knew that. She had made Richard her sole heir."

"But then, what if Richard died before Cecilia?"

"In that case, there was a secondary heir," I said. "Wiley."

Ricky's eyes went wide. "Wiley?"

I nodded slowly. "And I get the impression he knew about it, too. When the lawyer, Benson, told Wiley and Lis about the reading of Cecilia's will tomorrow, I got the distinct impression that they both expected that it would be good news for Wiley, not Lis."

"But the new will that you witnessed?"

"It disinherited Wiley and reinstated Lis as the sole heir. Cecilia's dislike of Tawny seemed to outweigh her homophobia. So, as you correctly assumed, Lis is the primary beneficiary of Cecilia's will. But as far as everyone in the family knew, it would be Richard, or, after he died, Wiley. Denise and Lis were talking about trying to get back into Cecilia's will when we saw them at the park—Denise told me so, she was embarrassed about it—but they had no guarantee of that happening, and probably no way of knowing that it *had* happened in the very short time between Richard's and Cecilia's deaths. Killing Cecilia, if indeed she was killed, especially so quickly after Richard, would have been a very risky move for Lis."

Ricky rubbed his chin. "Whereas . . . if I'm Wiley and Richard drops dead—maybe I helped him, maybe I got lucky—I suddenly have a golden opportunity to inherit and might want to make sure that happens before the reconciliation with Lis gets her back into the will."

"We can't place him anywhere near the spa around the time of Cecilia's death," I pointed out.

"Can we place him much of anywhere? He seems elusive. Where was he the night Richard died, after everybody left the lounge? Where was he during Cecilia's massage? How is Wiley spending his time here?"

I pondered this. "How can we find out?"

Ricky waved at his bandaged ankle. "I'm not sure *we* can, unless we invite him over for cocktails, and if we did, I'm not sure he'd come. But maybe *you* can wander around a little, see if you bump into him. In fact, I wonder . . ."

Ricky reached over to the room phone on the bedside table, punching the button for the front desk. "Hello? Hi, Erik, this is Ricky. Yes, but you don't have to call me that. Anyway, I'm wondering if the bar in the lounge is open if we wanted something? What do you have that's good for a sprained ankle?

Mmm, yes, I think a milkshake would be good medicine. Okay, thanks, Erik, Oliver might be up soon."

His eyebrow shot up as he turned back to me. "We know one way Wiley's been spending his time. Someone was playing the piano in the lounge. That will almost certainly be him. I think my ankle is acting up, and the only thing that'll make it better is a nice, frosty milkshake. You choose the flavor—you'll be the one drinking it anyway."

Chapter 17

My stomach twisted into a knot as I made my way to the elevator and rode up to the top floor. The soft tinkle of the piano greeted my ears as I emerged into the lobby.

Erik was sitting with his feet up on the desk, a book in his lap. He straightened when he saw me. "Hi, Mr. Popp. You here for that milkshake?"

"Yes, I guess so," I said. "If you're not too busy." I realized too late that what I had meant as polite may have come off as sarcastic.

Erik didn't seem bothered. "It's no problem. What kind do you want? I can do vanilla, chocolate, or strawberry. Sorry I don't have anything more exotic. I suppose I could throw some bar pretzels in if you want."

Pretzels sounded about right for the state of my gut. Come to think of it, though, they sounded pretty tasty, too. "How about a chocolate shake, and you put some of those pretzels in?"

"Sure," Erik said as we rounded the partition into the lounge together. The room was empty except for Wiley sitting at the piano, skillfully playing a jazzy instrumental of "Fly Me to the Moon."

Target acquired. Now to execute my mission.

I had hoped thinking like a spy would help soothe my nerves, but it mostly reminded me that I had no training for this, and perhaps even less natural aptitude for it than most people. So, I knew it was going to be awkward and feel completely fake. Might as well get on with it.

I stepped over to the piano, wondering if it would be too much for me to lean casually on it. I decided that trying to pull off "casual" might be a bit too ambitious, so I settled for my usual "uncomfortably stiff" instead. After a moment, Wiley's eyes rose from the keys and he gave me a curt nod of greeting.

"That sounds great," I said. "You're really good."

"Thanks," he said, his voice low and flat. "I worked my way through college playing at Nordstrom. Now it's my party trick. You go to a party and sit at the piano all night. Everyone knows you were there, you helped everyone have a great time, but you don't actually have to talk to anybody."

Maybe Wiley was a genius. I wished I had a skill like that to get me through social obligations.

"I heard you playing the other night, too. Before Richard died," I tried.

There was no real reaction. "Alas, poor Richard," Wiley said theatrically as he played a flourish with one hand, holding out an imaginary skull in the other. "I knew him."

"Have you been spending a lot of your time here playing?"

He shrugged, his hands still steady on the keys. He segued into a new tune, something vaguely familiar that I couldn't quite place.

"Keeps me out of trouble. But I only play after the sun goes down," he said, nodding behind him toward the window, through which I could see the last echoes of daylight bouncing off the distant edge of the Pacific. "During the day, we find other ways to play. Like today, I was helping my cousin Lis interview morticians. Doesn't that sound fun?"

"Not really," I said, clumsily seizing this opportunity. "Hopefully you did something nicer yesterday."

He didn't respond right away, and when he did, he didn't answer. "Do you know this song?"

"I can't put my finger on it," I said.

"It's called, 'Get Me Away from Here, I'm Dying.' Make of that what you will."

I had no idea what to make of it.

" 'Yesterday,' " he went on, a faraway look in his eyes. "That's a song, too." He started to play the Beatles tune, still keeping the arrangement jazzy. "Yesterday, after our walk on the beach, which you crashed, I went with my lovely wife to get a late lunch in town, from the venerable Ronnie Wise. She knows me well, having been my third-grade teacher once upon a time, so she can surely confirm that we were there. We got back right as all the commotion was happening at the spa. You can check with Erik, or Mary Alice, or Rachel, or either of her daughters—they were all here and they all saw us return, together. That's what you want to know, right? Where I was when Cecilia died? Now you know. How about when Richard died? Where was I then? You've got me there; I was in my room, alone, reading a book. I can show you the book, but it can't say a lot on my behalf. So I'm still a suspect for that one, right?"

I didn't know how to respond. Wiley didn't seem any angrier than usual, but his baseline was unpleasant enough that I was leery of provoking him any further. Erik waved to me from across the lounge. "You want whipped cream on your shake?"

"Sure," I said, then returned my focus to Wiley, deciding to be straightforward with him. "Maybe you are still a suspect. But we don't actually know whether Richard was murdered. Or Cecilia. What do you think happened?"

"I told you what happened to Richard. He was throwing that rug and he lost his balance. I guarantee you that's what happened."

He had changed songs again. It took a few bars for me to identify this one: "The Lady Is a Tramp."

"You seem so sure of that," I said. "But why was he throwing the rug?"

"Someone else will have to tell you that," Wiley said, humming along to the song.

"Where was Tawny while you were reading your book alone?"

"Aren't you perceptive. Tawny was walking on the beach," Wiley hummed. "She takes a lot of walks on the beach, haven't you noticed? And she always takes her shoes off. But you want to know something funny? Before yesterday, she never came back with sand on her feet."

I couldn't figure out this obscure comment, either. "What about Cecilia? You and Tawny both have an alibi. So what do you think happened to her?"

"I think she got lucky," Wiley said. "She got to get away. She lived a long time, sat on a great big pile of money most of her life, made a lot of people miserable with no inconvenience to herself, and got to die halfway through a massage. Now that's what I call a happy ending."

Yikes. Rachel had entered the lounge, joining Wiley on the piano bench and giving me an impatient look, and Erik was waving my milkshake at me, so it was time to extract myself. I wasn't sure exactly what I had learned, or how much I could trust Wiley. "Well, thanks for indulging me," I said.

"It's your dime," he replied blandly. "Not really any of your business though, you know? You might want to keep out of it."

"Richard died on our balcony, in front of my friend." I shrugged as I walked over to retrieve my shake, wondering what Rachel wanted with Wiley.

At the bar, I leaned in close to Erik, whispering, "Pretend we're talking about something."

He leaned in, too, whispering back, "About what?"

"Whatever," I hissed, "but we're not actually talking. I want to eavesdrop." I shot my eyes in the direction of the piano.

Erik nodded, then began gesticulating and silently moving his lips. Wiley had kept playing, the music masking his own whispered conversation with Rachel. Whatever he told her was too much for her to keep her voice down, however; he tried to increase his volume, but couldn't entirely drown out her yelped response. "Are you serious? I knew it! God!"

"Keep it down," I heard him urge, but a second later, his playing stopped abruptly. I shot a glance back over my shoulder to see Rachel still swatting at his hands to get him to stop.

"I don't need to keep it down," she said, her voice rising almost to a yell. "This is a problem, and you need to deal with it! What are you going to do? Tell me," she demanded, then, her eye catching me and Erik looking her way, she raised an angry point toward the lobby. "You two! Out!"

"Rachel, calm down," Wiley said testily. "Why don't you and I leave. Erik is working, and the other one is snooping. This is too public."

She glared at us all the way out as Wiley led her by the arm through the lobby and out to the parking lot. I turned back to Erik, flashed him a grin and a shrug, collected my milkshake, and headed for the elevator.

The sweet and salty combo of chocolate and pretzels was a solid choice, I decided, sucking on my straw as I reentered our room.

"How'd it go?" Ricky called from the bed, not waiting for me to even close the door behind myself. "What did you find out?"

"I'm not very good at this stuff," I said, "so I don't know how much to believe. Wiley said he was alone when Richard died, reading in his room, and that he and Tawny were coming back from the café in town when Cecilia died. He still thinks Richard fell while throwing the rug off his balcony."

"Did he say why he believes that? Why would Richard be throwing the rug? It's so weird, and weirdly specific," Ricky said, eyeing my milkshake as I sat down next to him.

"He didn't say, but he seems really sure about it." We both thought hard for a moment, me slurping up more milkshake through my straw.

Ricky got distracted by my slurping. "What flavor did you get?"

"Chocolate with pretzels."

"That sounds good," Ricky said, still covetously eyeing the cup.

"It is," I said, sucking more down.

He watched me for a few more beats, then gave up waiting. "Jeez, Oliver, can I have some?"

"I thought you said it was for me," I protested. "And you're lactose intolerant."

"I can have a sip," he said. "If this is how you're going to be, I might have to reconsider things."

I handed over the cup, then was struck by what he'd said. Ever since I'd come back from the beach, he'd acted as though nothing had changed between us. If anything, he'd been cuddlier again. I'd let it ease some of the hurt I'd been feeling, but it sure wasn't helping the confusion. "Reconsider what?"

"You know," Ricky said, smiling as he handed the cup back. "Dropping the whole 'pretend' thing."

I furrowed my brow, trying to puzzle through his bizarre, callous approach to all this.

"You look confused," he said. *Well, duh*. "Did I imagine that conversation? Did we not finish that conversation?"

I finally snapped. "What conversation? You told me you didn't even want to be my pretend boyfriend, and then you went to sleep like you didn't have a care in the world! And now you want to go back to being friends, and I guess that's okay, but it really hurt me."

"Oh, boy," he said, his brow furrowing this time. "First of all, I was in a lot of pain and on some strong drugs, so I don't think it's fair to say I went off to la-la land for no reason or like I didn't have a care in the world. And secondly . . . I was on some strong drugs, so I . . . maybe didn't say it exactly the way I meant to."

"What did you mean to say?"

He squared up to look me fully in the eyes, earnestly and eagerly. "I think I was trying to say that we weren't pretending anymore, because it's silly to call something pretend when it's obviously real. But I'm also realizing it's not for me to make a unilateral decision. So, Oliver, I'm asking you. Can we drop the pretend stuff and be boyfriends already? For real?"

I'd had no idea it could be that easy. Like *that*, my stomach unknotted. Like *that*, all my confusion and agita over everything that had gone wrong this week and my lingering embarrassment about not being better about keeping in touch with Ricky while we'd been apart—all gone. I felt light and peaceful and free, like when I was—wait, no, I'd always been kind of a ball of anxiety. I don't think I'd ever felt like this before. Could I always feel like this, from now on? Probably not, I thought, but I could chase the feeling now, while I had it.

So I did the first thing that popped into my head.

I leaned in.

And I kissed my boyfriend.

It wasn't the first time Ricky and I had kissed—that moment, in the airport in Washington, half serious, half joking in an attempt to get rid of some unwanted company, was stamped indelibly on my memory. But this one would be, too, I knew. For one thing, there was nothing performative about this one. It was for us alone, and there was no joke about it. For another,

I had initiated it this time, something I'd never done before in my life.

There was also the little matter of it being incredibly hot. Ricky was surprised at first, I could tell, but almost immediately he raised his hands to my arms, holding me there lightly for a brief second before lifting them up to hold my face to his. I usually hate having my face touched, but, as always, Ricky was my exception, his touch somehow both calming and exciting as I felt his sweet, seductive, fully, magically *alive* energy seep from his hands into my soul. I put my hands on his shoulders, his chest, his sides, feeling him, greedily claiming as much of him as I could as fast as I could.

Finally, we broke apart, sitting side by side, me facing him, both grinning at each other like idiots.

"Really?" I said. "Are you sure?"

He laughed. "If you'd asked me before you did that, I might have pretended to change my mind. Are *you* sure?"

"I've never been more sure of anything," I said. The look of radiant joy that broke across his beautiful face was almost too much. He couldn't possibly feel that way because of *me*, could he? But in my new, elevated state, I discovered, I could take it on faith that he did.

"Are you done with your milkshake? You should probably finish it before we keep making out, so it doesn't get all melty," Ricky said.

I peered down into the cup. "All that's left is some of the whipped cream."

"Whipped cream!" He sat up. "I completely forgot. Oliver, what happened to the bag from the dairy? Your cheese curds?"

In the excitement over Ricky's ankle, I'd completely forgotten my gift shop purchase, too. "It's still in the trunk of your car."

"Dang," he said. "It's probably gone bad by now, but we could have used it."

"The cheese curds?"

"No," he said, grinning sheepishly. "While you were in the bathroom, I bought a can of whipped cream."

I didn't have too much time to dwell on this tantalizing lost opportunity. We had barely started kissing again, laughing and smiling and nuzzling and teasing as we came together and pulled apart, when someone banged on our door.

"Hey guys," came the plaintive voice from the hall as the hammering continued. "Guys? Are you in there? Please open up."

I whispered to Ricky, "Can we pretend we're not here?"

He smiled and shook his head. I sighed, getting up off the bed and walking to the door. Looking through the peephole, I was greeted with a fish-eye distortion of Tawny's disheveled face as she raised her hand to keep banging on the door.

"Oh my god," she exhaled, tumbling in as soon as I opened the door. "Thank god you're here. Quick, close the door." She tottered on her red patent leather peep-toe platform pumps over to the bed, heaving down next to Ricky's ankle on its pile of pillows. She looked in the direction of the bandaged leg next to her, but I wasn't sure it registered. Her eyes were wild, her chest heaving as she tried to catch her breath, her platinum hair a jaggedly half-eaten cotton candy swirl around her head.

Ricky looked at her back, then shot me a wide-eyed look. "What's the matter? Are you okay?"

"Shh," she hissed. Then, her voice in a whisper, she waved her index finger at me, pointing me back toward the door. "Look through the peephole. Is he out there? Did he follow me?"

I looked out into the empty hallway. I watched for a long moment, but there were no shadows, no movements, not even an untoward flicker of the lights. "There's nothing there," I reported.

She heaved a sigh. "Okay, that's good. Listen, I don't got a lot of time. I gotta get out of here."

I took another peek out into the hall. Still quiet. "Is it Wiley? What did he say?"

"He didn't have to say anything," she said, her agitation rising back up. "He knows. He knows what I did, what I was gonna do, what happened. . . ." Her voice broke and tears began to well in her eyes. "I've been so dumb!"

Ricky's voice was gentle. "What did happen?"

Tawny finally turned to face him. "Hey, look, Jeff," she said, her voice wobbly. "I'm real sorry you had to watch Richard die. That'll mess you up. It's sure messing everything up." She got up and started to pace the room, alternately chewing on a fingernail and fussing with a tendril of hair sticking out over her ear, but stopped after her second lap. She looked down at her noisy shoes and quickly stepped out of them before quietly resuming her pacing at a much lower elevation.

"I'm so messed up," she said, making another loop around the coffee table. "I figure the least I can do is help you guys before I go, so you don't have to wonder no more. We were being so dumb, but we were desperate. Rachel . . . he didn't have any money without her, unless Cecilia . . . and then what would happen when Wiley found out? You gotta promise not to tell—it doesn't matter now, I had nothing to do with Cecilia actually dying, I swear. I don't know if we would really have done it, you know? We were desperate and got carried away. I want you guys to know, so you don't hafta be as messed up as me. But I can't do it here. I gotta get out of here, now."

Ricky and I exchanged a perplexed look.

She finally stopped pacing, stooping down to pick up her shoes and coming back up to face us. "Here," she said as she bent, first to one side and then to the other, to put her heels back on. "You seen the lighthouse, right? You go up the highway like you're going to town, but instead of turning right, you turn left, toward the ocean. Wait half an hour before you leave, and make sure nobody follows you. I'll wait there, and I'll tell you what happened. Don't let Wiley see you."

She crossed the room, took a long look through the peephole, and slipped out the door.

CHAPTER 18

Ricky and I stared at each other, dumbfounded. "What did that all mean?" I wondered.

Ricky leaned forward, thoughtfully hugging his knee. "It sounds like Tawny has some things she wants to get off her chest. To clear her conscience, maybe?"

"As in," I said slowly, "you think she killed Richard? Or Cecilia?"

"I don't know about that," Ricky said. "She was so agitated, it was hard to understand her. It sounded more like she knew what had happened, not necessarily that she had done anything, but she certainly seemed to feel guilty about *something*."

My mind was a jumble. I realized that, all day, Tawny had been giving me fragments, cryptic, half-finished thoughts, tiny pieces of a story that seemed too big even for her to wrap her head around fully. She'd wanted to know what we'd do if we found out who had been in the room with Richard. She had, I now realized, been asking for assurance that she could talk to us. She'd apparently weighed what I'd told her, and decided it was safe to tell us her story—or, at least, maybe safer than the alternative.

I grabbed the notepad and pen from the coffee table, desperate to get as much as I could remember out of my head. Before I could start, Ricky muscled in on my thoughts. "What was it that Wiley kept insisting had happened to Richard?"

"That he fell while throwing the rug off the balcony," I said distractedly. "We have to figure out how that ties in. Give me a sec." I took a second to reorient myself, and started writing as fragments of what Tawny had just said came back to me.

We were desperate—who is "we"?

He didn't have any money without Rachel or Cecilia = Richard. "We" above = Tawny and Richard?

<u>*Tawny in the room with Richard!*</u>

I had nothing to do with Cecilia dying.

I don't know if we would really have done it. We got carried away. . . . What is "it"? What were Tawny and Richard planning?

I looked up, gnawing on the end of the pen. Ricky was watching me intently. "Come up with anything?" he asked. "Show me what you've got."

I handed him the pad as I sat back down next to him on the bed. "I feel like I'm circling the what, but I'm forgetting something that would tell us the why."

"So that's what we have to get from Tawny," he said, beginning to nuzzle and softly kiss my neck.

"What are you doing? That tickles," I giggled.

"Mmm, I'm thinking," he said between kisses. "About Richard and Cecilia, of course. And about Tawny. About how she crashed our moment. Our *romantic* moment. Isn't that what our job here is supposed to be? Something about romance?"

I laughingly pulled him up, gave him a single kiss on the lips, then pulled back before he could come in for more. "*Now* you care about our job? Anyway, I see the point you're trying to make, and it's a very good one, but we might have to come back to it later. We have some logistics to figure out."

"Logistics? Like, who sleeps on which side of the bed? I'm easy," Ricky said, trying to pull me back to him.

"No!" I scurried to the far corner of the bed, out of his reach. "Logistics like getting to this lighthouse meeting with Tawny. It's probably going to involve some walking. How are you going to walk?"

"Oh," he said, deflating. "We probably also need to talk about how we're getting over there. I can't exactly drive us there." He waved to his bandaged ankle. "This here's my clutchin' foot. That requires a certain amount of finesse that I don't have at the moment."

I gulped. "Maybe Erik could drive us?"

"Can Erik drive? Does he have a car? If he doesn't, can he drive a stick? Can we trust him to stay in the car and not follow us?"

"That's a lot of questions," I said.

"The alternative to asking him all those questions is you driving."

"I'll go ask him," I said quickly.

"Ask him if he has any crutches or something, too. Maybe they have first-aid supplies," Ricky said as I headed for the door.

Erik had returned to his book behind the front desk. He gave me a conspiratorial smile as I approached. "Nobody in the lounge to eavesdrop on now," he said. "Wiley and Rachel never came back. I haven't seen Lis tonight, and Tawny left a couple of minutes ago to go into town."

"Good looking out," I said. "On a totally unrelated note, do you know how to drive?"

"Yeah," he said, his smile turning quizzical. "Can't get much of anywhere around here without driving."

"I suppose so," I said. "Do you have a car?"

"No," he said. "I can usually borrow my mom's car, though.

And I'm gonna get one before I go to college. I've been wondering what I should get. What do you think? A Jeep?"

"I don't know. I tend to think Jeeps are a little excessive, but I live in the city. What about your mom's car?"

"It's a Honda. It's okay, I suppose," Erik said dubiously.

"No, I mean, is it here? Could you give us a ride? Ricky can't drive with his sprained ankle."

He leaned over the desk, a suspicious look in his eye. "And he won't let you drive his car? Is he kind of a control freak?"

"No!" I didn't want to admit to Erik that I couldn't drive, so I settled on half the truth. "I can't drive a stick shift."

"I got you," he nodded. "I can't, either. Anyway, I can't give you guys a ride. Sorry. My mom's out on a date, so I can't leave the inn."

"Aha," I said, disappointed at having to endure this silly conversation and come away empty-handed. I turned to leave, then remembered the other half of my mission. "What about a crutch?"

Erik looked confused. "What *about* a clutch? I told you, I can't drive stick."

"No, a *crutch*," I corrected. "Do you have a crutch Ricky can use? You know, for walking?"

"You guys are going to try to walk somewhere? Even in the daytime, I wouldn't recommend it, especially with an injury."

"No, we're not going to walk somewhere," I said, my impatience starting to leak out. "For general mobility, so he's not stuck in bed. Do you have anything?"

"Actually, I do," Erik said, rising from his seat behind the desk. "I have the crutches I used when I broke my leg. Turned out *that* was my last gymnastics meet. I can go get them right now and bring them to your room."

"That sounds great, thank you," I said, relieved to return to Ricky with something useful to show for this excursion.

* * *

Coming down the corridor toward our room, I encountered Wiley charging up the hall toward me. He pointed accusingly as soon as he saw me, his face red and his eyes wild. "You! Where is she?"

His intensity raised the hairs on the back of my neck. I keyed open our door, hoping that if Ricky could hear what was happening, he could be prepared to act as backup if I needed it, then tried to summon an innocent tone. "Where is who? Who are you looking for?"

"My wife, you jackass," Wiley roared. "I know you've been cozying up to her, though god knows why. So where is she?"

Ricky hobbled into view, his own expression fierce under a thin veneer of control. "We don't know where Tawny is," he said, calmly but firmly.

"I think you're lying to me," Wiley hissed, his snarl swinging back and forth between me and Ricky. "I think you're a couple of lying busybodies. If I find out you knew where she is, you'll be sorry." He stormed off toward the elevator, where he nearly collided with Erik, emerging with the crutches for Ricky.

"Hey, kid," Wiley snapped, holding the elevator door. Erik looked back at him over his shoulder as he handed me the crutches. "I'll go back up with you. I need your help, because these two won't tell me the truth."

"Be careful," I warned Erik under my breath.

"I'll be okay," he assured me quietly before saying more audibly to Wiley, "Sure, I'll see what I can do to help."

I watched them disappear back into the elevator, hoping Erik was right that he'd be okay, then turned into the room to give Ricky the crutches.

"Hey, sweet," Ricky said, reaching for the crutches and limping uncomfortably on them over to the bed, where he sat down and began to adjust their height to better suit him. After a moment of fiddling, he hoisted himself back up, saying, "Let's take these babies for a test drive."

As he took a lap, swinging himself around the room on the crutches and his good right foot, he said, "Speaking of driving, what about our other problem?"

"No dice." I grimaced. "Erik's mom is on a date, so he can't leave the inn."

"Mary Alice has a date? Good for her," Ricky said, still circling the coffee table. "I wonder who with."

"If I were a betting man, I'd guess it's with Cecilia's lawyer, Brad Benson," I said. "They seemed to have some kind of thing for each other. Anyway, what are we going to do?"

Ricky crutched his way over to me and planted a kiss on my cheek. "That's for courage. You know what we have to do—what *you* have to do."

"Oh, noooo," I moaned.

"Would another kiss help? Gee, it feels good to be able to ask you that," he marveled. "I think I'll do it anyway." He landed one on my other cheek.

"I'm not saying I don't like it, because I do, but it's not helping," I said mournfully. "You're really going to make me drive us there?"

"Nobody's making you," he said. "We don't have to solve this mystery. We got close, but maybe the more important thing is we got each other. You can nurse me through my night terrors about not knowing why Richard died right in front of me."

"Is that an attempt to guilt me? Because it sounds like a reasonable trade-off for not having to drive right now."

"C'mon," Ricky said, crutching his way to the door. "We'll do a few practice laps around the parking lot. You'll be fine."

We stopped to check with Erik on our way out to the parking lot. "Where's Wiley?" I asked in a whisper. "Is he gone?"

"Yeah," Erik nodded. "He was looking for Tawny. I told him she went to town. I don't think he believed me, but he left a few minutes ago."

"Okay, good," I said.

"Hey, are you guys going somewhere after all? I thought neither of you could drive?"

Ricky clapped my shoulder. "Did he tell you that? He's such a kidder. This one's a regular driving fool."

"No, but you said you can't drive stick," Erik reminded me.

Ricky waved a dismissive hand. "Anybody can learn. I can teach you, too, if you want. Maybe tomorrow."

"Really?" Erik brightened. "That would be cool. I was telling Mr. Popp, I need to get a car soon. He didn't think I should get a Jeep, so maybe I should learn stick and get something sporty, like a Mini Cooper or an MX-5."

"Sure, those are fun choices," Ricky said, steering me out of the lobby. Once we were outside, he added, "How that kid is still even remotely closeted is beyond me."

Ricky opened the passenger door of the car for himself, then leaned over to unlock the driver door for me and stuck the key in the ignition. I plopped into the driver seat once more, my innards automatically coiling tightly into a protective ball at the memory of this place.

"Clutch in, engine on," Ricky said cheerfully. "And we'll need lights. It's the silver knob, top left."

I groped around the upper corner of the dash, landing on a metal knob. I gave it a push, and washer fluid sprayed onto the windshield.

"A clean windshield won't hurt, either," Ricky chuckled, leaning over me to twist the knob, turning on the wipers to swipe away the fluid, then pulling the other knob, the one that I hadn't seen next to the wiper knob, to turn on the lights.

With much better coaching than Ricky had been able to provide earlier in the afternoon, I was able to back slowly out of the parking spot. In the wide, sparsely populated lot that served the inn, the spa, and the bistro next door, I was able to make wide, slow turns, getting a feel for the steering and the brakes and stalling only a few times. Then Ricky had me drive a loop around the bistro building, accumulating enough speed to finally get into second gear.

"Okay," I said, panting nervously as I sped around the building, the tires making squealing noises that may or may not have been audible outside my head. "Changing gears is easier than getting started, but I don't know about this kind of speed."

"Oliver, you're going ten miles per hour. Fifteen, tops. We have enough room here, you should try to get it into third, but you're going to have to go faster."

"Faster?"

I gathered all my courage, eventually working myself up to twenty-five miles per hour and a slightly boggy shift into third. "Very good," Ricky said. "Now see if you can bring it to a stop from here."

I remembered that I could go into neutral as I braked, bringing the car to a smooth stop that impressed even me. This was apparently enough to satisfy Ricky that I was ready for the open road. He surveyed the driveway that led up the short, steep hill to the highway.

"Gosh, I hope there isn't much traffic at this hour," he mused, sending what little confidence I'd been able to muster into a tailspin. "To get up this hill, you're going to need to keep it in a low gear, probably second, but give it some gas. Don't stop at the top until you're on level ground. We have to turn left onto the highway. Ready?"

"Nope," I said, putting the car in gear and starting to roll toward the hill.

Ricky's prayers were answered—mine, too, if you didn't count the ones about not having to drive in the first place, which had very much not been answered—and there were no lights coming down the highway in either direction at the top of the hill. I didn't make a complete stop, rolling slowly into my wide left turn across the two southbound lanes.

"Never even driven in California, and you've already started doing the California roll," Ricky chided me.

"What's that?"

"It's where you don't stop for stop signs. You'd better get in the right lane."

"Don't we need to turn left?" I protested.

"Yes," Ricky said evenly, "but my lights aren't very bright and you're doing twenty in a fifty-five. If someone comes up behind us, we're toast."

I cautiously dipped my foot into the accelerator as I steered a bit more sharply into the right lane than I had intended, the needle on the speedometer jumping to a dizzying thirty-five as I popped the gear lever into third.

"Look at you," Ricky said admiringly. "Changing lanes and shifting gears at the same time. You're learning quickly."

"Don't patronize me," I said, leaning forward over the wheel and squinting at the darkness ahead. "Where's that turn? What's that?" A pair of lights emerged over a small rise in the road up ahead, rapidly growing larger and brighter as they approached, creating dazzling, blinding glare in the streaks left by the washer fluid on the edges of the windshield where the wipers didn't reach. "Ricky, I can't see! What do I do?"

"Look down," he said calmly. "Look at the white line along the right-hand edge of the lane until the other car passes."

"Okay," I said, my eyes readjusting as the light shifted to my peripheral vision. "But what if I miss our turn?"

"You won't," Ricky said soothingly. "Our turn isn't for—shoot. There it is."

"What? Where?" The other car barely completed its pass as I jerked the wheel to the left, my own headlights catching the sign pointing to the lighthouse in their arc. Unfortunately, the sign was a little farther away than I'd judged, and I discovered that I had turned a few yards shy of the cross street, bumpily cutting the corner, whizzing narrowly between the post for the street sign at the corner on my right and a couple of large trees on my left before bouncing back up onto the asphalt of the road down to the lighthouse, slewing a bit as I corrected my path back into the proper lane.

"Oh, boy," Ricky said, the corner of my eye catching his hand bracing against the dashboard. If I'd been less busy driving, I might have appreciated that I was finally paying him back for some of the white-knuckle rides he'd taken me on in Washington. As it was, I was worriedly noticing that as our altitude decreased heading down the hill to the parking area for the lighthouse, our speed seemed to be *increasing* in inverse proportion.

"Eep," I said.

"Brakes, brakes," Ricky responded urgently. "Put it in neutral!"

Right. The parking area was directly ahead, a lone car, Wiley and Tawny's Porsche SUV, glittering in the moonlight bouncing off the water in the inlet below. I rode the brakes the rest of the way down the hill, putting the car in neutral and swinging wide to park on the other side of the Porsche. But yet again, I misjudged. Hiding behind the Porsche was another, smaller car, and I saw it almost, but not quite, early enough to adjust my angle to go around it.

Almost.

They were so brief, the *thump* and the *tinkle*, that I could almost try to convince myself that they hadn't happened. "Hey," Ricky said dazedly from the passenger seat as I pulled on the parking brake and turned off the engine. "We made it, and got your first accident out of the way. Big night."

Aw, crud. They had happened. "I'm so sorry," I said, collapsing into a pile of spent adrenaline and frayed nerves and remorse, gripping the steering wheel to barely keep myself upright. I hadn't wanted to drive. I didn't have a license, didn't have insurance, and, most of all, hadn't wanted to damage Ricky's car.

"It happens," he said amiably. "No time to worry too much about it now."

As he gathered his crutches and slowly lifted himself out of the car, I hopped out, flicking on the flashlight on my phone and inspecting the corner of the other car's back bumper. There was some cracked plastic trim, a broken reflector lens, and a small scrape and wrinkle along the corner. I snapped a photo of the damage, absently thinking it might be needed for an insurance claim, and realizing that I had no idea how insurance worked. I moved to the front of Ricky's car. The chrome bumper gleamed smoothly under the glow of my flashlight, with only a small streak of paint transfer where it had come into contact with the other car interrupting its solid-metal perfection. I snapped a photo of that, too, then tried a fingernail on the paint, finding that it came off easily.

"Good news is, your car's fine," I said, straightening up. "The other one has some boo-boos. Should I leave a note? I took pictures for your insurance. Was that the right thing to do?"

"Hey, Oliver," Ricky said impatiently. "You notice how there are two other cars here? That means that Tawny might not be alone. She might be in trouble. We gotta boogie here."

I bolted to attention. "Oh my god, you're right," I said. "Come on!" I started toward the wide gravel trail leading to the lighthouse, almost breaking into a run before I remembered that Ricky was on crutches.

He started out at a reasonably good pace, all things considered, but I was already having to strain to slow my pace to match his, and that was before the trail started heading uphill. The farther we went, the higher and further away the lighthouse seemed to loom up on the bluff in the distance. I alternated between forcing myself to take long, slow strides, and dancing nervously around Ricky to keep myself from getting ahead of him. He kept pushing ahead, grunting a little now and then, until finally, with the lighthouse somewhere around a dark curve up ahead, no longer even in view, he brought himself to a stop.

"Go ahead if you want," he huffed. "I need a second. I promise it'll be short, but I need a second."

"I'm not going to go without you," I said. "We're a team. I wouldn't know what to do on my own. I wouldn't feel safe, and I wouldn't feel right leaving you."

"You'd be fine, and you'd figure out what to do," he said, giving me a wan smile. "But it is more fun when we're together. And you'd be right to feel guilty about leaving me."

I looked around, taking in for the first time how dark and quiet it was here. The moon, almost full, hung low over the inlet, its reflection shimmering on the water before breaking up on the small waves where the Pacific met the shore. Off in the distance, through the trees, I could see the occasional pinprick of light moving along the highway, and closer in, the inn glowed tiny and snug on the edge of the bluff across the water. And if I strained my eyes and caught the timing just right, I realized, I could make out one more source of light, a tiny white circle on the beach below the inn, bobbing and flickering like a drunken firefly.

I pointed it out to Ricky. "What is that?"

He leaned forward on his crutches, squinting. "I think it's a flashlight? Someone's walking on the beach below the inn with a flashlight."

"Huh," I said. "Maybe Mary Alice is finishing her date with a moonlit stroll on the beach."

"Going up and down that trail with a flashlight? That sounds more treacherous than romantic."

I threw my hands up. "I'm never going to know what's romantic or not, am I?"

Ricky's teeth flashed white in the moonlight as he grinned at me. "Of course you will. I'll see to that. Anyway, come on. We've got our own moonlit stroll to finish."

We started back up the gravel-lined hill, hugging the edge of the bluff around a couple more turns before the lighthouse burst back into view, suddenly only a few hundred yards away. Moonlight glittered off the glass at the top of the tower, but a soft, flickering light emanated from within the small attached keeper's cottage on the ground floor.

"Shh!" Ricky stopped short, putting a hand to my chest to stop me, too. We hung there for a moment watching. A low murmur of voices drifted out to us. "I have to try to make these things as quiet as I can," Ricky whispered, wincing as started toward the lighthouse again, shifting some weight onto his injured left leg to help quiet his heavy, metallic crutch-assisted footfalls. I crept silently by his side.

The voices within the building rose and fell. We inched closer and closer, moving painfully slowly to minimize noise. Finally, when we were within about a hundred feet, one of the voices rose high enough in pitch to become familiar. It was Tawny, speaking loud and high and fast, and then, not speaking at all. The lights in the keeper's cottage flickered out at the same moment that a shriek, Tawny's, tore through the darkness.

We broke into our best approximation of a run, closing the last short gap toward the building, Ricky yelping every few steps. The main entry door to the lighthouse stood ominously open, the interior inky black and frighteningly silent. The doorway to the keeper's cottage, immediately to the right upon entering the building, was open, too, and I rushed in to see if there was any sign of Tawny or where she might have gone, Ricky tumbling in shortly behind me. The lone, small room of the cottage was cold and quiet and dark, with a strange, close, stale smell.

As my eyes adjusted to the darkness, I did a quick scan of the space, my body still tensed. "Nothing," I said, wondering with growing dread what had become of the people who had just been in here, but as I turned to muscle past Ricky out the door, it slammed in my face with the metallic *clank* of a bolt being locked.

"Wha—" I sputtered, jiggling the handle in vain. "We're locked in!"

Ricky hobbled to the lone window that looked out toward the front of the building. "I don't see anyone—wait, no, there they go!" I rushed to join him, catching a fleeting glimpse of a dark figure running around the curve and down the hill, hugging the tree line to minimize their exposure.

"I think they ducked down under the window so we wouldn't see them until they were clear of the building," Ricky said. He gripped the latch on the side of the window frame, caked over with a hundred years' worth of paint, trying fruitlessly to turn it. It wouldn't budge.

"Getting that open wouldn't help us much anyway," I said, pointing to the metal bars on the outside of the window. "We're stuck in here." I pulled out my phone. "I'm calling 911. There was more than one person here, but only one person left. We're trapped, and who knows what trouble the other person is in, right?" I punched in the numbers, putting the phone to my ear.

"What's that smell?" Ricky wondered, poking around in the dark for a moment before pulling out his own phone and turning on the flashlight.

My phone gave no indication that my call was going through. I looked at the screen. *Calling* . . . I had no bars, no Wi-Fi signal.

"Here it is." Ricky bent down and came back up with something pinched between his thumb and forefinger. A smoldering cigarette butt. "Someone was smoking in here."

"Ricky," I said, "I don't think this is going through. I don't have any service here. Do you?"

He consulted the screen of his phone. "No, but I'll give it a try. This thing is out, right?" He passed the butt to me.

I looked at it, but I didn't know what to look for. "I think so. It's not still smoking."

"So why does it seem like the smell is getting stronger?"

I looked around in the dark, sniffing the air. It had been stale before, but now it was bordering on stifling, something that curled up into your nose and set up camp there and you couldn't quite get it back out. It wasn't cigarette smoke, though, it was . . . what?

Ricky's flashlight was still on, and as he tried to call emergency services, its beam hit the door of our prison, catching a shimmery tendril snaking in through the crack at the bottom.

It wasn't cigarette smoke. It was *smoke* smoke.

CHAPTER 19

"Ricky!" I yelped, pointing at the door. "We're on fire! The firehouse is on light! I mean, the houselight is on fire! The lighthouse! It burns!"

He looked up from his phone at me, smirking in the face of my panic. "It burns? *It burns*?"

"Not the time!" I waved my arms around. "We're trapped! There's someone else somewhere in here! We have to do something!"

"I'm still trying 911, but I can't get through," Ricky said, the note of consternation in his voice still maddeningly mild, considering our circumstances.

I started pounding on the door with both fists. "Help! Help! Let us out!" I channeled everything I had through my fists. I pounded for my life, which hadn't been long enough, and hadn't had enough Ricky in it yet. I pounded for my mom, pounded so I could go home to her in one piece, more truly whole than I'd ever been before in my life. I pounded for my apartment, which was mostly empty, but which was *mine*. I pounded for my job, where, for all I'd been totally distracted from it this week, it felt like I was finally getting the hang of things and finally getting a foot in the next, bigger, better door, and where I had made a true friend in Drea, who had wanted more for me than I had known to want for myself and had brought me together with Ricky. And I pounded most of all for Ricky, my boyfriend of all of two hours. Of all the things in this life that an Autistic kid like me wasn't supposed to want, wasn't supposed to be able to get, wasn't supposed to be able to keep—but that I *had* wanted, that I *had* somehow managed to get, that I desperately wanted to keep—he was the one that I'd wanted the most keenly, that I cherished the most fiercely, that I wanted more than anything to protect.

I pounded until I felt Ricky's arms wrap around me, gently pulling me away from the door. "Oliver, the door's going to get hot. You could burn yourself without even noticing."

Already I was starting to choke on the smoke, tears running down my face, though whether that was the smoke, panic, anger, anguish, or something else, I couldn't say. We stumbled back, landing seated on the wide old wood planks of the floor. Ricky scooted to rest his back against the wall, but I jumped up again, looking wildly around the room. Through the thickening smoke, I could see the glow of the fire coming in through both windows in the room, one each directly across from each other on the front and back walls of the cottage. Each one was caged on the outside with iron bars, but I wondered, on a building this old, how solid the metal, or its attachments to the wall, could still be.

I seized one of Ricky's crutches, shoving its foot through the front window with a surprisingly loud crash.

Ricky raised his hands to shield his face as glass shards flew to the floor, coughing out, "Oliver, what are you doing?"

"Whatever I can!" I swung the crutch in a spiral out from the initial hole I'd made, clearing as much of the remaining glass as I could. Then I pulled the crutch inside, spun it around, and used the wide top end as a battering ram against the metal bars outside, thrusting as hard as I could, which wasn't as hard as I would have liked, given that I could barely breathe. There was no movement.

I repeated the pattern on the second window, to the same result. I charged desperately back and forth across the room for a minute, hammering on each set of bars in turn, but nothing seemed to give or loosen. Initially, breaking the windows had seemed to help clear the smoke a little, but eventually the smoke outside was every bit as thick. Coughing and gagging, worn out from my burst of exertion, I sunk to the floor in front of Ricky and hugged my knees.

It was unbearably hot now, and sweat poured down both our faces. I reached out for his hand, pulling him away from the wall and into my arms. Over the rising roar of the fire, I said into his ear, "Can we count the pretend days?"

He leaned in close, his voice drifting into my ear. "I count them all, since the first day in Washington."

"Good," I said. "Then it's not too soon to tell you I love you."

Oh, boy. The heat and fear must have melted my brain. Or maybe they had melted my inhibitions, and I really meant it? There wasn't time to figure it out, but something in Ricky's eyes as he held me in his gaze slowed the world and extinguished the flames for a split second.

"Oliver, I—"

The world snapped back into terrifying, hot, imminent-death-and-danger focus as he broke off, his head swiveling toward the window at the front of the cottage. His voice was suddenly tense and urgent. "Help me up. Look out there. I think I heard something."

I scrambled to my feet and helped Ricky up. I thought I heard it, too, a high whine over the crackle of the flames above and increasingly all around us. The glow out the window, illuminating the broad, flat lawn and gravel paths between the lighthouse and the edge of the bluff in an eerie strobing fire-yellow, had acquired a flashing red undertone.

Even before enough of the fire engine was in sight for it to fully register, I was yelling again, Ricky joining me this time, both of us sticking his crutches as far out of the window as we could and waving them around. "Help! In here!"

Doors flew open before the wheels had fully stopped, boots hitting the gravel and running our way. A couple of rapid blows to the door of the cottage, and a swarm of reflective bodies descended on us.

"He's injured," I coughed, pushing Ricky in front of me. Two of the firefighters picked him up in a sort of makeshift chair and hustled him out, just as the largest person I'd ever seen in my life scooped me up, flung me over their shoulder, and followed them out the door.

An ambulance had rolled up the hill behind the fire engine, and a team of EMTs began taking our vitals as the firefighters ran back toward the burning building. I tried to call after them, "There's someone else still in the building!" But I choked on the words, devolving into a coughing fit. As soon as I could recover a little bit of my voice, I croaked to one of the EMTs, "There was someone else in there."

"I'm sure they'll find everybody," the woman said. "All you need to do is focus on breathing."

One of the other EMTs knelt at Ricky's ankle. "I'm guessing based on the bandage that this didn't happen in there," he chuckled, flashing an appealingly dimpled smile up at Ricky, who shook his head. We were huddled together in the open rear doors of the ambulance, our legs dangling down, the fire out of sight behind us. The EMT stood up, stretching a muscular arm up along the side of the door to pull his snug T-shirt even tighter over his well-formed chest. "Need anything else, handsome?"

Ricky looked up at him, incredulous. "Seriously? Right now? I'm taken."

The EMT coughed, embarrassed. "No, sorry, I meant him," he said, pointing at me.

I matched Ricky's icy stare. "I'm the one who took him."

"Let me get you guys some water," the EMT mumbled, turning on his heel and disappearing around the side of the truck.

I hopped down and peered around the other side, back toward the commotion of the fire. Water arced toward the flames, which were now most intense on the roof of the keeper's cottage where Ricky and I had been trapped moments ago. Another knot of firefighters emerged from the building, forming a circle as they carried a small figure out onto the lawn several dozen yards away from the building. The massive firefighter who had carried me out of the building turned from the outside of the circle and waved a summons to the EMTs, who started running up the hill toward them.

In the brief opening created by the firefighter turning to wave, I saw, limp on the ground, illuminated in the glow of the flames and the sirens, a singed red patent leather peep-toe platform pump on the end of a horrifyingly charred leg.

I was briefly stunned, my mind not wanting to believe what I had seen. Finally, slowly, I returned to Ricky at the back of the ambulance.

"It was Tawny," I said numbly. "She was still in there. They just brought her out, but it . . . doesn't look good."

Ricky blanched. "God. Was it . . . do we think it was Wiley? He couldn't have followed us, right?"

"I don't know what to think. She was definitely scared of him. And he was definitely scary the last time we saw him."

A pair of headlights underneath a set of flashing red and

blue lights rolled up the hill, coming to a stop behind the ambulance. Deputy Duncan stepped out of the cruiser, doing a wide-eyed double take when she saw us.

"Are you friggin' kidding me? Third day in a row, third dead body, third time you two are the first people I lay eyes on. And this time you burned down only the most important historical landmark in the county while you were at it. You two better not move a stinkin' muscle before I come back to deal with you, got it?"

"Yes, ma'am," we both said obediently.

"Well, that answers that," Ricky said in a low voice as we listened to the deputy's boots crunch away up the gravel. "Tawny didn't make it. Tawny, Richard, and Cecilia. Bad week to be a member of that family."

"I'm not sure there was ever a particularly good time to be in the Rose family," I muttered, my mind elsewhere. I inspected my fingers, looking without seeing. In the glow of the deputy's headlights, something glittered green under one of my fingernails. I wondered for a second what it was, before my mind wandered on.

I had started making notes before we'd left the inn, trying to capture all of the strange hints Tawny had dropped. I wished I'd gotten more of them down. Now I'd never be able to ask her what she'd meant. There had been other hints, too, from other members of the Rose family. What had Denise said about this bunch? *There's lots of dirt.* That was for sure.

"There's no question this time," I said, rousing myself. "Tawny had to have been murdered, right?"

"Yes, that much seems clear. And there's no question this time about a second person. We both saw that person. We just couldn't see who it was."

"I'm going to start brain dumping," I said. "I feel like we

have almost all of the pieces. We only need to figure out how they fit together."

Ricky rested his head on my shoulder. "Lay it on me."

"From my notes before. We're fairly certain that Tawny was the other person in Richard's room when he went over the side of the balcony. Why were they together?"

"They were desperate, she said, right?"

"Right," I said. "Richard needed money. They got carried away with something, which led to Richard's fall. And if that hadn't happened, she didn't know if they really would have gone through with whatever it was they were planning."

"Richard and Tawny do seem like an odd pair, though," Ricky said, snuggling further into the crook of my neck. "I mean, we never met Richard, but a man who would marry Rachel—you sort of make some assumptions about that person. Do we know what Richard did?"

"Yes," I said, gazing distantly into my memory. "He was a professor at Cal. I might have seen him there a hundred times and never known it. And they lived in Kensington. There was something about where they lived. . . ."

"Who told you all that?"

"Their daughters," I said. "That was it! Tawny had come to visit them. She claimed to have an aunt in Oakland."

Ricky popped up, looking at me. "She came without Wiley?"

"Yes, and always when Rachel wasn't there. And the girls said they never actually saw her go visit her aunt."

"I smell an affair," Ricky said.

"Wiley said something strange, too. He said that Tawny took lots of walks on the beach, and she always took her shoes off, but before the day Richard died, she never came back with sand on her feet. He didn't say it exactly that way—he didn't mention Richard—but now that I think about it, it seems like that was the implication. She wasn't doing what she said she was doing, she was with Richard."

"So Wiley knew," Ricky said.

"It seems that way." I thought a minute longer. "Even Denise said she and Lis thought Richard was having an affair, though if they suspected it was with Tawny, she didn't say so. She said he and Rachel were always on the brink of divorce."

"Didn't you say Rachel was meeting with a lawyer when Richard died?"

"That's right," I said. "And Rachel had the money in their marriage, until Richard would inherit from Cecilia. So if she was going to leave him, that would explain why he and Tawny needed money."

"I think I'm almost seeing something," Ricky said.

"Almost," I nodded.

A pair of footsteps crunched toward us down the hill. Deputy Duncan rounded the back of the ambulance, glowering at us, her plait, tied tonight with a green velvet bow, swaying in a pendulum effect for a second even after she had stopped.

"Okay," she growled. "This time it's one coincidence too many. Hey!" she yelled to an approaching EMT. "You need to do anything else to these two?"

"No," the woman said. "Keep monitoring them for symptoms of smoke inhalation, but for now they seem okay."

"Got it," Deputy Duncan said. "I'm monitoring. I'm taking you both with me."

"That's a good idea," I said. "We could use your help with a couple of things."

At precisely eight thirty the following morning, well in advance of the reading of Cecilia Rose's will at ten, Erik taped a piece of paper to the door of room 202 at the Rose Beach Inn. It read:

This morning's will reading has been moved to the Lounge. The Inn will be closed today to prevent any interruptions.

Neither Ricky nor I were there to see him, or to read the note. I only know about this, and about what was going on at the inn that morning, from talking later to those who were there.

One of them, Wiley Rose, was already in the lounge. He had been there for hours, since he had returned from the sheriff's office in town at around four a.m. He stared straight ahead, dark bags under his eyes, his fingers resting, but not moving, on the keys of the silent piano. Erik left him alone as he entered the lounge and busied himself cleaning all of the cocktail tables and chairs and bar stools and putting on a pot of coffee.

At a couple minutes past nine, there was a knock on the locked front door of the inn. Erik opened it to admit Ronnie Wise, bearing a large box of muffins and assorted pastries. She set the box down on the bar, walked over to the piano, and wordlessly laid a caressing hand on the side of Wiley's face, letting the memory of a sad, lonely little sandy-haired eight-year-old boy linger between them for a moment. Then she left.

At about nine fifteen, Mary Alice wheeled a vacuum cleaner into the lounge. When she saw Wiley sitting at the piano, she said, "Oh. Well, I'm sure it's okay," and took the vacuum cleaner back to the closet.

At 9:36, there was another knock at the door. Neither Mary Alice nor Erik were in the lobby, and the knocking continued sporadically for the next three minutes until Mary Alice, having received a text message, bustled up to let Lis and Denise in.

"Sorry," Lis said apologetically. "I spent the night at the motel with Denise. I'm sure you can understand."

"Of course," Mary Alice said. "There's been a little juggling of plans. We'll be in the lounge today. And there's something I think I need to tell you before you go in there. . . ."

The three women were still huddled around the front desk when, at around a quarter to ten, Rachel Rose and her daughters, Reille and Rayleigh, stepped out of the elevator and strode around them into the lounge. The girls hovered over the box of pastries while Rachel poured herself a cup of coffee. She sat down at a cocktail table near the piano, not really facing Wiley, saying to nobody in particular, "Horrible night, wasn't it."

A moment later, Lis, Denise, and Mary Alice entered the lounge. Lis briefly sat on the piano bench next to her cousin, laying a hand on one of his. He never moved. After a long moment, she got up, accepting a cup of coffee from Denise. The two of them selected a table of their own, with a table between theirs and Rachel's, where she still sat alone, her daughters having draped themselves over their customary bar stools.

Minutes dragged by. Mary Alice fussed nervously over the box of pastries, rearranging them every time someone took one. Erik was nowhere to be seen.

"Where the hell is that lawyer?" Rachel complained to the room a few minutes after ten. "I think it's in awfully poor taste to be doing this today, but if we must, let's get it over with. I'd like to be getting out of here."

"Why *are* you still here?" Lis's tone wasn't unkind, but there was a pointed edge not far below the surface. "You won't be in Mother's will. Anything Richard was going to inherit doesn't go to you."

"No, of course not, but I'm sure there'll be something for the girls," Rachel said confidently. "Cecilia wouldn't overlook her only grandchildren."

The two girls whispered something between themselves. The younger burst into loud giggles, then abruptly stopped herself at a glare from Rachel.

At about ten fifteen, Erik appeared briefly in the doorway of the lounge, shrugged to his mother, and left again.

"Brad *is* coming, isn't he?" Lis asked Mary Alice.

"Of course he is," Mary Alice said. "We spoke only a couple of hours ago, about changing the room. He's probably tied up with something he was working on in town."

Finally, ten minutes later, Erik, waiting in the parking lot, unlocked the doors to let in the group he had been waiting for. Deputy Duncan strode in first, followed by Brad Benson. Ricky and I brought up the rear, Ricky limping but moving more easily than yesterday, no more crutches needed. A flurry of confused chatter greeted the deputy and the attorney, but the room fell silent when Ricky and I appeared.

Suddenly, Wiley's fingers slammed down where they had been resting on the piano keys, banging out a single, long, cacophonous chord. His hands frozen in place, he half rose, his face going a deep scarlet.

"Th-th-*them*," he spat out. "Why are they here? Why aren't they locked up? Why aren't they dead, for what they've done?" He was roaring now, nearly hysterical, a vein bulging in his forehead.

Deputy Duncan rushed toward Wiley, in a stance that suggested that she planned to restrain him, using force if necessary. "Calm down, sir. We talked about this last night. We have no basis on which to charge these two."

"Honestly, Wiley," Rachel chimed in. "You can drop the act. It was not bad, though. But everyone knows you killed Tawny. Probably Richard and Cecilia, too!"

"Folks, folks," Brad Benson said, waving his hands to quiet the room.

Rachel couldn't help herself. "What *are* they doing here, though, Brad? Surely they're not in Cecilia's will? She was a horrible racist and homophobe, after all. No accounting for taste, mind you," she added, cocking a hungry eyebrow at Ricky.

"We'll get to the will," Brad assured the family. "But Deputy

Duncan here and I have asked Mr. Popp and Mr. Warner to join us this morning to clear up what's been going on around the inn this past week."

He turned and waved a hand, as though presenting the room to us. "Gentlemen, the floor is yours." I gulped as we stared down what was left of the Rose family, which included at least one killer.

CHAPTER 20

My mouth was dry. I curled my fingers in and out, forming them into a sort of gnarled, stiff ball, then releasing them.

Ricky, who had lowered himself into a chair along the wall behind me, softly put a hand to my lower back. "Do you want me to start?"

"Spit it out," Wiley snarled from the piano bench. "I assume this is going to be your confession."

I found my voice. "No," I said, more clearly and steadily than I'd expected of myself. "Ricky and I have nothing to confess." I swept a meaningful gaze across the room.

"I think I should start," I continued, "by making it plain that, all appearances to the contrary, I am not naturally the kind of person who likes to involve himself in other people's business." Denise chuckled softly, and behind me, Ricky, the traitor, stifled a snort. I turned to glare at him.

"Sorry. Trying not to sneeze. Carry on," he grinned.

I took a second to remember where I had been going. "Ricky and I came here to gather material for an article about travel on the Oregon coast, but on our first night here, Richard Rose fell to his death on our balcony. On our second day here, Cecilia Rose died on the massage table in the room next door while we were getting massages. And on our third day, Tawny

Rose was murdered while waiting for a meeting she had requested with us. It wasn't our intention to intrude on your family gathering this week; I think it's fair to say instead that your family gathering kept intruding on our work."

"I'm sorry, Oliver," Lis said. "I wish you hadn't gotten caught in our mess."

"I appreciate that," I replied with a slight smile. "But it seems like your family's mess has gotten too big to contain. Someone was bound to get caught in it; it ended up being us, and for our own peace of mind, it's become important to us to sort through and understand your mess. I think—with the help of Brad Benson and Deputy Duncan and, in your own ways, most of you—we've been able to get close to understanding what's been going on here. Some of this is guesswork, but I think a few of you here today can fill in the last gaps."

The younger of Richard and Rachel's daughters, leaning forward on her bar stool and waving her arms mockingly, cried out, "I don't know nothin'!"

Her sister devolved into a fit of giggles, but their mother silenced them with a sharp look and a sharper tone. "Reille! Rayleigh! If you can't be mature, I think you'd better leave. Go wait for me in the room." As the girls sullenly trooped out of the room, Rachel turned her attention back to me. "I'm sure none of us knows anything that we haven't already told the proper authorities. Which *you* are not."

"No, I am not," I conceded. "But Deputy Duncan is, and we are here with her permission and this meeting is happening under her supervision. And I don't think it's true that everyone here has told everything they know. Isn't that right, Wiley?"

He rolled his eyes, but his convictions, and with them, his rage, seemed to be wavering.

"So," Denise wanted to know, "what's the story? What's it all about?"

"Ultimately, it's all about two things: money and sex. Let's start with sex," I said.

From behind me, I caught Ricky mumbling, "Why haven't you ever said that to me?"

I stifled a laugh, straining to maintain a serious expression, and pressed on. "Ricky and I never met Richard, but we did hear something of his final moments in the room above us."

Denise gasped. "You heard him having sex?"

"No," I said, blushing, "but we did hear something that led us to believe that he wasn't alone. He was playing music in his room, but the music was turned off *after* he fell off the balcony. That tells us that someone else turned off the music before leaving the room, because the room was empty and no music was playing when the sheriff arrived. We knew that that person was not his wife or one of his daughters; the three of them had gone to town, the girls to a movie and Rachel to the café. So we wondered who the other person could have been. There were a number of clues that it was Tawny."

Rachel made a snort of disgust.

I went on. "The relationship between Richard and Tawny could have been innocent, but we suspect it was an affair. The first, and biggest, clue came from Richard's daughters." Rachel shot another angry look toward the bar before realizing that she'd sent the girls out of the room. "They mentioned to me that Tawny had made multiple visits, without Wiley, to their home in California, and always when their mother was away.

"Wiley, you all but told me about Tawny's affair with Richard, didn't you? You insinuated that Tawny often told you she was taking walks on the beach, but she was actually doing something else. You even suggested that Tawny was taking one of her fictional 'walks' at the time of Richard's death."

I looked his way, but Wiley remained seated on the piano bench, his shoulders slumped, staring vacantly into the distance.

"That definitely suggests that Tawny was the other person in the room with Richard when he fell. I think you know about their affair, but that perhaps you learned about it this week. The night Richard died, you expressed surprise at Tawny's strong reaction. What changed? How did you learn what was happening?"

Wiley finally seemed to come back to himself, though it was a weak, dejected version of himself. "I don't know nothin'," he shrugged in a meek imitation of his young cousin.

"I think you do," I said, "but we can come back to that. I've heard it said that happy people in healthy relationships don't cheat, and Ricky and I know that Tawny was not a happy person, and she was not in a healthy relationship with you, Wiley. She all but forced her friendship on us, because she was so lonely, feeling like an outsider in your family, especially once Richard was gone. She confided in me that she desperately wanted to be a mother. She told us that she hadn't known until only a year ago—well into your marriage—about your boyhood cancer, and even then didn't know, until you told her, that it had left you sterile. She dropped other hints, too—this woman that you all knew as a hard-living party girl spent this week entirely sober, having even completely given up nicotine. The medical examiner confirmed it from her records this morning. Wiley, when did you find out Tawny was pregnant?"

The piano made a discordant *plunk* as Wiley put his elbows up on the keyboard, resting his forehead on his hands. He sighed deeply, then, pulling his head up halfway, said from behind his fingers, "The morning after Richard died. I found the ultrasound, or sonogram or whatever, in her suitcase."

Ricky leaned forward. "Did you tell her you knew?"

"No." Wiley shook his head. "But I think she figured it out. She asked if I'd been in her suitcase. I probably wasn't very careful about putting it back in exactly the same spot."

"And you knew the baby wasn't yours," Denise said, piecing it together.

"Obviously not," Wiley said, shrugging.

"So Wiley killed Richard and Tawny over their affair," Denise announced to the room triumphantly. "But what about Cecilia? And where does the money come in?"

"I don't think it's that simple," I said. "And we're not quite through with sex yet." I shot Ricky a preemptive look of warning. He gave me an angelic smile. I kept going. "There was one more thing, which Erik helped us learn. He mentioned that he'd had to make up both beds in Richard and Rachel's two-bedroom suite. And you, Denise, mentioned that their marriage had long been on the rocks. We know that, on the night Richard died, while their daughters were watching a movie, Rachel met with Brad Benson, Cecilia's lawyer, at the café in town to discuss a personal matter. Brad, I won't ask you to violate attorney-client privilege, but I suspect that Rachel, too, had discovered Richard's infidelity and was asking for advice about initiating a divorce."

Rachel spun to look at Brad, who had taken a bar stool behind her. He gave an affable smile, putting a finger to his lips—but as soon as Rachel turned back around, he also winked.

"And *that*," I said, "brings us to money. Cecilia Rose and her late husband had a vast fortune, but their children, Richard and Lis, had no trust funds or other support from their parents after finishing their education. Most of the money in Richard and Rachel's marriage came from Rachel and her family. Richard and Tawny, fearing discovery by their respective spouses, or maybe simply wanting to run off and start a new life together, were, in Tawny's words, 'desperate' to figure out how to get some money. Aside from Rachel, Richard had one other avenue to wealth: he knew that if she died, he would inherit his mother's millions. Lis, you had been written out of your mother's will a number of years ago. You knew that, correct?"

"Yes, I did," she said calmly.

"Can you tell us why?"

"Because I was—am—gay. Because my mother thought love and money were the same thing, and she withheld both as a means to get you to do what she wanted," she said sadly. Denise reached over and took her hand. "And because she couldn't fathom a gay daughter as anything other than an embarrassment."

"Thank you, Lis. I'm sorry to bring up such a difficult subject. And apologies to all for the detour back into sex," I said.

I could feel Ricky getting ready to jump. "I'll—"

"No, you won't," I said firmly. "Back to money. Richard was Cecilia's primary heir," I said. I looked around the room. "Wiley, were you aware of that?"

He nodded.

"Rachel, did you know that?"

"Yes, I did," Rachel said icily. "Not that it mattered to me. Personally, I thought Cecilia was wrong. Lis, I'm sure I would have convinced Richard to give you what you were owed, if he'd ever have listened to me."

"So, we can conclude that it was common knowledge within the family that Richard stood to inherit the bulk of Cecilia's estate. This will be key to understanding Richard's death. But trying to figure out Cecilia's death, and how *it* might have related to money, threw us for a loop. To all outward appearances, Cecilia's death seemed to be a natural one. But coming right on the heels of Richard's, it was hard to believe that explanation. Especially with Cecilia's fortune providing such a ripe motive for killing her. The question is, if everybody knew that Richard was the primary heir, with Richard dead before his mother, who was next in line to inherit?"

"You didn't ask me if I knew Richard was the primary heir," Denise piped up, "but I did, and I know the answer to this one, too."

"Okay, who was it?"

"If Richard predeceased Cecilia, Wiley would inherit," Denise said, casting a reproachful look toward the piano. "Which means he had a motive to kill *her*, too!"

I smiled indulgently. "I suppose you're right that he could be construed as having motives to kill Richard, Tawny, and Cecilia. I'm not saying that he did. Rachel, did you know that Wiley was the secondary heir?"

"Yes, I did," she said, narrowing her eyes in his direction. "It does seem awfully convenient that Cecilia should drop dead and ensure his inheritance the moment Richard was out of the way."

"Ignoring that for the moment," I said, "we now know that it was also common knowledge in the family that Wiley was Cecilia's secondary heir, if Richard should die before her. Brad," I said, looking to the lawyer, "not to steal your thunder too much for the will reading, but is Wiley *still* Cecilia's secondary heir?"

Brad pretended to hem and haw for a moment, then, with a dry chuckle, said, "No."

There were multiple gasps.

"No," I agreed. "He's not. *I* knew that. The morning before she died, Cecilia executed a new will, for which I was one of the witnesses. We'll get to the will later, but Ricky will confirm that, unlike all of you, I can keep a secret."

"Yes, he can," Ricky said. "It's a little annoying, to be honest."

"I didn't even tell you about the old will, did I?"

"No. I assumed—logically, I thought—that Richard and Lis both stood to inherit, and that if Richard died before Cecilia, it would all go to Lis. Which led me to suspect Lis for a while. I'm sorry," he said, addressing her table.

"If that means I'm not a suspect anymore, I forgive you," Lis said with a sad little laugh.

"Anyway," I said, "trying to connect Cecilia's death to the money led us down some dead ends. There's a good reason for that.

"We still haven't gotten to Tawny's death—was she a victim of sex or money? And, more to the point, which one of *you* was she a victim of? Because Tawny was clearly murdered. According to the medical examiner, she had been savagely hit on the head with something heavy, and if that hadn't killed her, the fire would have. And, Ricky and I, too, were left to burn alive, probably for simply being in the wrong place at the wrong time, though the killer might have also seen it as an opportunity to frame us for her death, however weakly."

"Yeah, Wiley, it was weak," Rachel jeered.

I ignored her. "But before we can answer that, we have to establish how many murders there actually were. I believe I know the answer, and I believe the number was almost higher. Neither Richard's nor Cecilia's deaths were ever investigated as murders. The police didn't seem to know what we did, though, about anyone being in the room with Richard when he fell. Did you know anything about that, Deputy?"

Deputy Duncan's braid, finished off today with a mustard yellow bow to complement her green uniform jacket, swung back and forth under her broad-brimmed hat as she shook her head. "Negative. You didn't say anything about it, though," she said reproachfully.

"That's true," I conceded. "We did tell you about the other strange thing, which we discovered with Erik's help: the rug from Richard and Rachel's suite was missing. We also told you—or, at least, intended to tell you—that we found the rug, down on the beach, far below the balconies of the inn. Did you get that information, Deputy?"

"No," she said, the braid shaking again.

"No. I'm not entirely surprised. Tawny volunteered to call in that we'd found the rug, and I admit, I was careless in making sure that she had; the fact that she didn't further suggests that she didn't want to call attention to the fact that she'd been in the room with Richard, or to what they were doing in there.

I think we can reconstruct what they were doing, but it's a fair bit of guesswork. Though I think there is someone here who knows. Wiley, you seemed insistent that you knew how Richard had died, and when I asked you how the rug factored in, you said I'd have to ask someone else. I think that someone else was Tawny, and that she'd told you what happened. See how I do."

"Sure," said Wiley, still leaning one elbow on the piano keys, his chin in his hand.

"I said that money was an important factor in how Richard died. Tawny said that they were desperate for money, and she suggested that they were planning a way to get it when Richard died. Wiley, you said repeatedly that Richard was throwing the rug over the side of the balcony, lost his balance, and fell. Let's assume that's true. What about the rug? As ridiculous as it sounds—they said they were desperate—I suspect that Richard and Tawny were rehearsing a plan to kill Cecilia to get to Richard's inheritance, with the rolled-up rug standing in for Cecilia. In which case, Richard was *not* murdered, though if he'd lived, Cecilia might have been."

"Or she might have been murdered *sooner*," Ricky chimed in.

"Right. What about Richard and Tawny's intended victim, who did in fact die the very next day? There seemed to be no shortage of people with possible motives to kill Cecilia, but did anyone actually do it? For Cecilia, we can probably trust the medical examiner's preliminary verdict, which says . . . *no*, she was not murdered, either. She died of a heart attack, likely brought on by a combination of the stress of Richard's death and a vigorous massage."

"You mean . . . she died of a broken heart," Mary Alice gasped, putting a hand to her chest. "Like Debbie Reynolds."

"You could say that," I said, "though she might have been less brokenhearted if she'd known what Richard was up to when he died. Which leaves us with Tawny. She was at the center of our story about sex, having an affair with Richard and becoming pregnant by him, apparently planning to leave Wiley and start a family with Richard. She intersects with our story about money, too; she and Richard planned to kill Cecilia for the inheritance. And that's not entirely the end of her involvement with the money story. With Richard dead, if she managed to stay with Wiley, she still stood to benefit from Cecilia's money—at least, as far as the family knew."

"And even if you divorced her after inheriting, you might have to split some of the money with her," Denise said, again looking over to Wiley at the piano. "Either way, she knew her bread had been good and buttered."

"That raises a good question," I said. "*Did* Tawny know, after her plot with Richard had failed, that she still potentially stood to gain from Cecilia's death? We know Wiley's status as secondary heir was common knowledge within the family, but, Wiley, did Tawny know?"

"No," he said softly. "I never told her. It was such a remote possibility anyway, and she was so impulsive. It just seemed better for her not to know."

"You probably felt vindicated after you found out what she and Richard had been up to. Did I get it right?"

"Pretty much." He nodded.

"And when did you find out about their plan?"

"The morning after Cecilia died. Yesterday morning, I guess. Seems longer ago. She was terrified that someone would somehow think she *had* done something, since she and Richard had been thinking about doing it."

"She gave you a lot to think about over the last couple of days, didn't she?" I said gently.

Wiley laughed ruefully. "Yes, she did. And I didn't react well to most of it, in the moment."

"You really scared her."

"I know I did," he admitted. "I scared myself. I went looking for her after she left last night, on the beach, but of course I didn't find her."

"What had you decided to do?"

His face was back in his hands, but his voice drifted out to us. "It's so stupid, but I'd decided to raise the kid with her. Or to try, anyway. Maybe it wouldn't have worked. Maybe we would have split up—it probably would have been better if we did split up. But she wanted it so badly, and I decided I wanted to try. I was going to try. . . ." His voice trailed off as his shoulders heaved with a sob.

"Oh, come on," Rachel said, rising to her feet. "Give it a rest. You killed her so you wouldn't have to share the money with that tramp and Richard's bastard! Alone on the beach—great alibi!"

"No, Rachel, it's not a great alibi," I conceded. "But he wasn't alone on the beach—that is to say, I can corroborate his story. So can Erik. Erik gave him the flashlight, and I saw its beam on the beach when we were going up to the lighthouse. I suppose he could have faked all of that, but I know that Wiley didn't kill Tawny. I know that you did."

CHAPTER 21

"Me?" Rachel sputtered, her face red, her eyes wildly darting from me to Wiley to Deputy Duncan. "Me? Why would I kill Tawny?"

"I think you just told us," I said softly. "You couldn't bear the thought of Tawny having Richard's baby, and raising it on Cecilia's millions. The infidelity, the loss, the betrayal—I imagine it all became a bit too much for you."

She lunged forward into one of her savage points, thrusting a finger wildly in my direction. "*Think! Imagine!* You have no proof! You can't point the finger at me without proof!"

"It's funny you should say that. I do have proof, and the proof is actually on my finger." I raised my right index finger up, looking at it and realizing there was no longer anything to see there. "That is, it *was* on my finger. Under my fingernail. It was still there when we went to the sheriff's office last night, but Deputy Duncan got it out and sent it off to be analyzed. I have photos, too, from the scene of the accident. And we verified the damage when we got here this morning, out in the parking lot."

"What on earth are you talking about, you stupid boy?" Rachel screamed, clutching the sides of her face in her hands.

"You probably didn't even notice in the dark last night," I

said. "I hit your car. The green BMW—that's yours, right? The deputy retrieved fragments from your reflector from the ground in the parking area at the lighthouse, too, did I mention that? And I had paint from your car under my fingernail, where I had scraped it off Ricky's bumper. Beautiful color, by the way."

Rachel's face had gone pale, her hands frozen to her head. Only her eyes still shone wildly, flashing as they bored into me, searching, denying that what I was saying could possibly be true, that she could possibly have been caught.

"It was only his second time driving," Ricky added in my defense. "He doesn't even have a license, so I'm kind of relieved we're not gonna have to report this to insurance, honestly. My car was fine," he assured the room.

"That's good news," Denise said, sounding genuinely relieved. Rachel swiveled wildly in disbelief that anyone else would dare to speak. Denise was unmoved. "Your car is so cute. And, Oliver, good for you for getting back on the horse and driving! Sounds like it went a lot better this time."

"Oh my god," Rachel half shouted, half moaned, slumping back into her chair and bringing her hands down on the table with a loud slap. "Fine. Make it stop. I did it. I killed her." In defiance of her usual brittle poise, she had fallen into a truly magnificent slouch, her sharp, still-disapproving eyes daring anyone else to challenge her.

The room hung suspended in an electric silence at this confession. Even Denise was finally cowed into wide-eyed submission. Deputy Duncan was edging toward Rachel, but seemed unable to break through the thick atmosphere to make a more rapid approach. Not that it mattered; Rachel wasn't going anywhere. She seemed as frozen as the rest of us.

Finally Erik, his natural curiosity getting the better of him, coughed and said, "So was that really why you did it?"

The fire in Rachel's eyes was flickering lower. I saw a woman who had been so tightly wound for so long finally starting to unspool in recognition of what she had driven herself to. "Basically, yeah, I think," she sighed. "Richard was such a drain on me. He was bleeding me dry, cleaning out my inheritance. I'm sure he gave Tawny money. He made that loan to Mary Alice without even consulting me. He kept taking and taking, and then—to betray me? With *that*? I had tried to hang on, to see it through until Cecilia died so I could at least recoup what was mine, but that old bag simply would. Not. Die. And then Richard had to go and die in such a stupid way, and the second her money was out of reach, Cecilia finally drops dead? And that *thing*, that awful creature, would get the money and wave Richard's betrayal baby in everybody's face for the rest of our lives? I don't think so. She didn't deserve that. She couldn't have that."

Deputy Duncan had made it to Rachel's side. She put a hand on Rachel's shoulder. "Ready to go, Miz Rose?"

"Don't have much of a choice, do I?" Rachel stood, her posture still uncharacteristically loose, only recovering a little bit of her usual poise when her gaze landed on the bar stools vacated by her daughters.

"Deputy," she said, the hauteur creeping back into her voice. "My girls. I have to see my girls, but I need a moment to figure out what to tell them. We have to call my sister to take care of them. I won't have them stuck in this family a minute longer."

"We'll see what we can do," the deputy said, leading her toward the lobby. "But it'll have to be at least a few minutes longer, until someone from Child Protective Services can come."

I thought Lis and Denise could probably be perfectly capable caretakers, especially with the inheritance coming their way, but maybe getting out of the orbit of the Rose family wasn't an entirely bad idea, either.

Thinking of the inheritance reminded me that the family had purportedly gathered this morning to hear Cecilia's will being read. I was ready to turn the room back over to Brad. Maybe I didn't want to be stuck with the Rose family much longer, either.

I helped Ricky out of his chair, and we each wrapped an arm around the other's waist to support his weight as we hobbled into the lobby. Rounding the desk, we nearly stumbled over Wiley. Nobody had noticed him get up from the piano bench and leave the room, but now, here he was, sitting cross-legged on the floor, weeping into his hands.

I crouched down next to him. "Wiley, I'm sorry," I said. "I'm sorry you've had to go through so much in such a short time, and that—what Rachel did was horrible, no matter what else Tawny might have done."

He looked up at me, his face streaked with tears. "Why did I tell her? Why did I think Rachel needed to know? I thought she'd be mad at Richard, like I was at Tawny. I didn't mean to—"

Ricky bent down awkwardly to lay a hand on Wiley's shoulder. "Nobody thinks you did. None of it is your fault."

Wiley sniffled for a minute. "Thanks for being her friend. You were right, we had a deeply unhealthy relationship, but I did love her. At least, last night, I really hoped I still did." He looked blearily from me to Ricky, craning his neck as he shifted his gaze. "We made things too complicated. Try not to do that in your relationship, you know? Keep things simple, and you'll keep the romance alive."

We'd never managed it before, but Ricky and I tried to keep things simple for the next couple of days.

We'd spent one more night at the Rose Beach Inn, spending a good chunk of our day after the will reading with Deputy Duncan, making additions to the statements we'd already given the night before. In the evening, Ronnie Wise came back to the inn bearing a tray of sandwiches and a big bowl of salad, and she, Mary Alice, Erik, Lis, Denise, Ricky, and I all ate together in the lounge.

"I wonder what I should do about my loan from Rachel now," Mary Alice said, absently rooting around in her salad bowl with her fork. "Do I still need to pay? What happens to someone's money when they go to prison? I guess there'll need to be some money to support the girls. Maybe I should ask Brad." She pulled her phone out and began composing a text.

"Rachel's not in prison yet," Lis pointed out. "And I think you'd feel better if you fulfilled your obligation."

"You're probably right," Mary Alice sighed, looking up from her phone.

"Would you feel even better if, say, a modest inheritance from your late Aunt Cecilia helped you fulfill your obligation?" Lis smiled shyly at her cousin.

"I wasn't in Aunt Cecilia's will," Mary Alice said.

"Maybe not on paper," Lis said. "But there were a lot of people, and organizations, and causes, that weren't named in the will, per se, but are definitely in the will, as far as I'm concerned. Starting with you."

Mary Alice leapt up and hugged her seated cousin's startled head.

As we finished dinner, and Mrs. Wise produced and began slicing a giant chocolate cake, Brad Benson joined us, dropping into a chair next to Mary Alice and draping an arm around the back of her chair. I gave Ricky a little kick under the table and a triumphant smile. He responded by putting his arm around the back of my chair.

"So, Erik," I said as we tucked into our cake, "with the caveat that what you saw is in no way what my job is usually like, are you still interested in being a travel writer?"

"Are you kidding me? Of course I am," Erik enthused, his eyes lighting up. "Your job is so incredible! I can't believe the stuff you get to do. Solving murders, nighttime rendezvous, chasing suspects . . . I never knew being a travel writer would be so exciting!"

I sighed. "Again, none of that is a typical part of my job."

"Oliver," Ricky said, "how many feature assignments have we been on?"

"Two," I said.

"And how many of those have we spent most of our time chasing a murderer?"

I put my head in my hands, trying to choke down my frustration. "Two," I admitted grudgingly.

"Maybe this *is* what your job is typically like," Ricky said. "I mean, at this point, I feel like I expect it when I'm assigned to one of your stories."

"No! It's not," I howled in protest.

"God, I can't wait," Erik said.

The next day, we left the inn and the village of Rose Beach, driving a couple hours down the coast to another, larger resort on the beach. Ricky's ankle was sufficiently healed for him to do the driving, which definitely kept things simple, though I resolved to keep practicing so that someday it would be even simpler because we'd both be able to drive with equal ease.

We kept things simple at the resort, sharing gourmet dinners in their lovely restaurant overlooking the Pacific and swapping our scheduled massages at their spa for a private couples yoga lesson instead. I grinned indulgently at all of Ricky's inappropriate cracks about the erotic benefits of stretching, and exulted with him after the lesson when he said it had helped his ankle feel significantly better. I definitely enjoyed the yoga more than the massage, and it probably helped that our instructor was a pleasant but entirely unthreatening middle-aged woman; no Cole redux to throw me off.

I let Ricky take pictures of me on the beach, on the nearby dunes, of my hands during our oyster-shucking lesson with the restaurant's executive chef—though I insisted on also getting one with both our hands in it as well.

We kept things simple, or at least tried to avoid too much complication too soon, by keeping both of the rooms Drea had reserved for us. Though whether both rooms were occupied for the entirety of both of the nights we were there—well, that's none of Drea's business.

Keeping it simple was nice. And it did feel romantic, though I wondered as Ricky drove us south, heading back to California at last, whether that wasn't merely the honeymoon effect of finally knowing that Ricky was my boyfriend.

I looked Ricky over out of the corner of my eye, then remembered I could ogle him openly now, so I did. He looked so summery and cool in his sunglasses and pale blue shorts, the short sleeves of his linen shirt rolled even shorter, the top several buttons undone, all to show off more of his gloriously sun-kissed golden body.

"Like what you see?" A grin broke out across his face. "What are you thinking?"

"I'm thinking, I found it," I said dreamily.

"Found what?"

"Romance. On the Oregon coast."

"Well, whaddaya know? You're right, we did. That should make writing your piece a breeze."

I shuddered to think about how distracted I'd been from my assignment when we were in Rose Beach. The week had been unforgettable, for better or worse, so I knew I'd be able to pull an article together, but it would be hard work, that was for sure. "I don't know about that . . . I guess I'll figure that out, but finding romance definitely took a while. Like, until the last two days maybe," I said.

Ricky feigned shock. "What are you talking about? It was very romantic, the whole time."

"I demand proof," I said.

"Let's see," Ricky said thoughtfully. "The very first day, I held you in my arms and soothed away your tears. That's romantic, in a Byronic sort of way, I think. Then you went to sleep for, like, a full twenty-four hours and, I assume, dreamed of nothing but me. That's straight out of a fairy tale or something."

"Yes, I dreamed only of you," I said, remembering how wonderfully romantic it had seemed when Ricky had given me that pillow.

"Then, on our first evening in Oregon," he continued, "we shared an intimate dinner for two, of everything on that restaurant's menu, then were serenaded from above by what I can only guess was the most romantic composition in the classical canon, and then decided to take a hot tub with very full tummies, which, I'm realizing, might have been romantic, but would not have been in line with water safety recommendations, so maybe it's as well that we didn't."

"I think that swimming on a full stomach thing is a myth," I said. "We never did use a hot tub at the inn, though, did we?"

"I think the shine wore off after Richard dropped in on us," Ricky said drily.

He was right, I was sure. I thought about what had happened later that night, when I'd held Ricky as we slept. That had certainly been something.

"And then the next day, I taught you a new life skill, which is maybe kind of romantic if your love language is 'acts of service.' And we agreed to become lovers."

"Fake lovers," I interjected.

"It was never that fake, and you know it," Ricky said, raising an eyebrow in my direction. "And you decided we were cursed—or cursèd, should I say, because that's a very Shakespearean kind of romantic. What ever happened to the curse?"

"Well, Tawny did die right after we decided to drop the fake thing," I said, only a little nervously. "But I'm hoping we broke the curse by figuring out what had happened and bringing Rachel to justice. I mean, nobody died nearby in the last couple of days, right?"

"That we know of," Ricky said ominously. "And I wasn't going to say anything, but I think I saw a swimmer getting eaten by a shark when you were busy climbing that dune. You know, the morning after we—"

"You did not," I said firmly.

"No, I didn't," he said, grinning. "The only thing we're cursed with is the hots for each other. And that's pretty romantic, I think."

I contemplated this for a few miles. This was a curse I could get behind.

I'd never taken the curse thing too seriously, anyway. I'd cared much more about making sure Ricky got a modicum of closure on what had led Richard to fall right in front of him. It had ballooned into so much more than that one accidental, but not at all innocent, fall, but we had managed to chase all of it down.

"Do you feel better? Knowing what happened, I mean," I said.

Ricky thought for a bit. "A little bit, yeah, I think so. And it helps knowing that we did something about it. Was that really what drove you to keep poking into the whole thing? To make me feel better?"

"Yes," I admitted.

"Look," Ricky said. "It'll never be perfect. I'll never forget what I saw. But knowing that goes a long way to making me feel a whole lot better."

"I had to show you that I—"

"Oh, yeah," Ricky said, smiling. "You said it. You love me."

"I did say that," I said a little sheepishly. I knew it had been way too soon, but I was fairly certain that, after all we'd been through already in our short time together, I'd meant it. Leave it to me; I didn't know how to get close to many people, but when I did, I went all the way. No matter how certain I was, though, I still felt the need to give Ricky an out. "You don't have to say anything about it."

"I was going to say something at the time, but I didn't get the chance," Ricky said. "What was it?"

I felt my heart start to race. Did Ricky feel pressured to say something he didn't mean?

"Ah, right," he said at length. "I was going to say, I think you're real cute."

"I hate you."

"And you love me. That's how we know this thing was always real."

I turned and looked out my window to hide my smile.

As he drove, Ricky reached over and twirled a finger through the hair behind my ear, bringing my attention back to him.

"It just occurred to me how prophetic I was," he said.

"About what?"

"Back when we became fake-not-fake boyfriends, I said we could be one of those couples that solves mysteries together. Like Batman and Robin."

I looked at him sternly. "You've named several twosomes, but only one that I can recall that were actually a couple who actually solved mysteries."

He untwirled his finger from my hair, returning his hand to the steering wheel. After a moment's deep thought, he half shouted, "The Hardy Boys!"

"*Ricky.* They were *brothers.*"

He turned and tilted his head down so that he could look at me skeptically over the tops of his sunglasses. "*Were* they?"

I sighed deeply. If he was going to be my boyfriend, he was going to find out eventually about all of the weird things I shouldn't or didn't need to know but did anyway.

I started counting on my fingers. "Nick and Nora Charles, I'll give you that one. *Moonlighting. McMillan & Wife.* Mulder and Scully, sometimes. *Columbo* and *Mrs. Columbo*, although they never appeared on each other's shows, so maybe technically they didn't solve mysteries together. . . ."

"See," he interjected. "This is what makes us a powerhouse mystery-solving couple."

I rolled my eyes at him, making only a tiny effort to suppress my smile.

I decided to change the subject. "So are you still planning to stick around awhile when we get back?"

"I thought I might," he said.

"And you're coming to stay with me, right?" It had seemed so impossibly presumptuous, such an embarrassing indictment of my failures when my mother had suggested it a few days ago. But that was before. Now that Ricky was my boyfriend—I couldn't stop forming those words over and over in my mind, *my boyfriend*—it seemed like the most natural thing in the world.

Ricky kept his eyes straight ahead on the road, his expression locked into a stony poker face. "Am I?"

"I thought you might."

"That's very sweet of you," he said. "But I don't want you to feel too much pressure. I'm happy to take a guest bed or sofa or whatever."

"I don't have a guest bed," I said, staring defiantly at the side of his still resolutely impassive, impossibly beautiful face. "Or a sofa."

"Sounds like you need some furni—*oh*."

The upward twitch at the corners of Ricky's mouth was nearly imperceptible. But the thrum of the engine deepened noticeably as his foot dipped further into the accelerator and the car surged ahead.

He reached his right hand over once again, this time placing it palm up on my leg. I took his hand in mine.

"Let's get home," he said.